Digital ISBN: 978-0-473-66090-1
Print ISBN: 978-0-473-66089-5
               978-0-473-66091-8

The Reluctant Bride

Serena Black

By Serena Black

Leonie's Christmas Miracle
The Gift of Love

For nana,

I couldn't have done any of this without you.

I love you.

Chapter 1

"Why do I have to be stuck with Callie?" Amélie moaned.

They were sitting around playing video games and the girls were once again thrashed by the boys and pouting about it.

"Because she's a handicap no one else wanted *and* its girls against boys," Jarrod said, as Callie poked her tongue out at her brother.

"How about we take turns being on Callie's team?" Gabriel said.

"I'm not *that* bad. I'm just not great with war games. Let's play car racing and I'll beat you all," Callie said, knowing they'd all be clamouring to be on her team. While she might not be good with a gun, she was a great driver.

"Fine," Jarrod moaned, turning to Gabriel. "You have her next since it was your idea."

"Gee, thanks," Callie said. "I'm going to get a drink."

"What's with her?" Jarrod said, after Callie left the room.

"Jeremy Thompson," Amélie said.

"Ah…" A chorus of light bulbs were lit in understanding.

Gabriel couldn't understand why Callie wasted her time mooning over that idiot, Jeremy Thompson. She was very pretty, funny and likeable, and she could do so much better than him. He remembered back to the first day that he had met the Harrison family in particular, Jarrod and Callie…

They had just moved to New Zealand from France and Miranda Harrison, their new neighbour, had invited them over to play.

Gabriel had been extremely nervous, especially since they had no chaperone with them like they would have had in France. It had felt like his parents were sending them into the lion's den by themselves.

Amélie had held his hand almost crushing it as they both knocked on the door.

Miranda had opened it with a beaming smile and ushered the two frightened children inside, where they soon heard screaming and fighting coming from the backyard.

The two St Croix children were silently trembling, never having heard children being so boisterous in their lives especially without an adult scolding them to stop misbehaving.

Even Miranda herself had yelled for her children to come and meet the new neighbours. Both his and Amélie's eyes were wide in horror. Where they came from adults didn't yell for their children. What had they walked into? Gabriel's heart had raced with anxiety.

The introduction was a sight that Gabriel would never forget. A boy his age excitedly came running inside covered in mud splotches on his clothes, mud completely covering his hands and feet with smears on his face and yet the only rebuke from his mother was a resigned, "Oh, Jarrod."

But it was the little girl with mud splotches on her pristine pink dress that had captured his attention. Her strawberry blonde hair, once neatly brushed and put into a ponytail was now mussed and lopsided, not to mention her hands and feet which were also covered in mud.

"Callie, Jarrod, this is Amélie and Gabriel. They've just moved in next door and will be here for dinner. I suggest you two clean up and perhaps play something less muddy," Miranda said.

"Okay, mum," the children said, happily.

It wasn't until Jarrod had turned around that everyone could see that the back of him was totally covered in mud. Callie grinned like a loon.

Gabriel could see that Miranda was trying hard to suppress her laughter as her son walked away as if nothing was wrong. It amazed him that she wasn't in the slightest bit angry with either of her children. His nannies would have been scrubbing him down in the bath along with a long litany of scolding.

Amélie's eyes were wide in shock at the sight as she squeezed her brother's hand tighter, making sure Gabe knew that she was frightened.

They had politely waited in the kitchen where Miranda was placing afternoon tea on the table for them and questioning them about how the move was going.

Jarrod had come back into the kitchen hungry and full of swagger and Callie breezed in looking every inch a little lady. Although they had changed their clothes and cleaned up, there was still the odd dry patch of mud on them, but neither they nor their mother seemed to even notice or care.

That momentous day now seemed like a lifetime ago to Gabe as he looked around the room seeing how much older they now all were. The years seemed to have flown by.

By the time Callie came back into the living room with her drink, the three of them wanted to apologise.

"We're really sorry for teasing you, Cal," Jarrod said.

"Yeah, Cal. You know we all want to be on your team," Amélie said.

"That's such a lie," she laughed. "I'm hopeless and I know it, but its okay because at least I'm only making an idiot of myself in front of you."

"How about if you have Callie on your team, you get a ten point head start?" Gabriel said.

"But it's only up to eleven," Amélie protested.

"Exactly," he laughed.

Callie tried hard to suppress her laughter and look angry at Gabe's teasing but couldn't hold it in.

"You idiot. Why don't you go back to France and harass the girls there? I'm sure they'll appreciate your wit."

Instantly a serious and solemn look crossed Gabriel and Amélie's faces as they traded glances.

"What?" Callie sensed something was wrong.

"Mum and dad told us last night that it's been confirmed that we're moving back to Paris," Gabriel said, looking miserable.

Both Jarrod and Callie were speechless.

"When?" Jarrod whispered, looking like he wanted to cry at the news.

Callie looked at Amélie who was also about to cry.

"A month."

"B-but that's so soon. The school year hasn't finished yet," Callie said, still trying to get over the shock announcement.

"We know, but its summer holidays over there and soon the school year will start and they thought it would be easier for us to make friends if we start on the first day of school," Gabriel said.

Callie got up and ran from the room as Amélie chased after her best friend.

"It'll be okay, Cal," Amélie said, as they lay on her bed staring at the ceiling.

"But you're my best friend. We were going to go to the school ball together, double date, do all those things that we had planned," she wept. "And now, you're going to be living on the other side of the world and forget me."

"I won't, Cal. I'll always be your best friend," Amélie said, with such conviction that Callie believed her. "I don't really want to go either. I love it here."

"Who am I going to share my first kiss and first time details with?"

"We can still talk, Skype, email."

"But it's not the same."

"I know. I don't think dad's that happy either, but mum's pretty excited. She's the only one."

"Then you should stay," she said. "It's three against one."

"Grand-père has finally decided to let dad come back into the family fold and he wants to try and mend the bridge," Amélie said, with a sad shake of her head.

"Then you have to go," she said, furiously wiping the tears from her eyes.

It was common knowledge between the families that the reason the St Croix family had been sent to live in the farthest country from Europe as possible was because of some stupid edict from the family's patriarch, Fabien St Croix to his son, François.

Fabien wanted François' focus to be on business at the expense of his family who he believed should be brought up by nannies who knew best.

François' objection to the edict meant that the St Croix's had in effect been exiled to New Zealand as punishment. To the Harrison family, it seemed overly harsh but François had explained that his father was a tyrant who liked to control everyone and everything.

Gabriel and Amélie were allowed to throw a Bon Voyage party two weeks before they left, which happened to coincide with Bastille Day celebrations, but nothing could stop the tears flowing knowing that the two families were soon going to be living on opposite sides of the world.

Chapter 2

It was a beautiful spring day and Callie was at the park watching over her charge, Suzette happily playing in the sandpit. This was Suzette's favourite activity but they hadn't been able to get out to it lately because of all the rain.

Callie loved being an au pair to Suzette, who was not only adorable but also a well-mannered child even at two years old.

Suzette's parents were both French, and her father Claude Mercier, worked for a big French company who had transferred him to oversee one of their business interests in Mexico.

It was one of the reasons that Callie had been hired, because she spoke very basic French and was willing to live in Mexico. As it turned out, it was only for a year as the company decided to transfer Claude to New York much to Claude's wife, Chantel's ecstatic delight.

With an excitement that Callie had never seen Chantel express since she had begun working with the family, Chantel had left Mexico as fast as possible without a backward glance. All the family's furniture and belongings were left behind because Chantel had deemed them to be not suitable for New York.

Callie had wondered if maybe her time was now up as well.

"Oh no, Callie," Chantel said. "I need you more than ever since I'll have even less time to spend with Suzette because there'll be so much socialising to do."

Considering Callie had never seen Chantel really do any socialising, even with other ex-pat families in Mexico, she could only assume that Chantel just meant shopping. But even then, it didn't change the fact that Chantel wasn't one to spend that much time with her daughter anyway.

Now, here she was in New York, in Central Park no less, enjoying a coffee and watching Suzette play. Her cellphone rang interrupting her peaceful moment.

"Hello Chantel," she said. "Of course, I'll come right back."

Disconnecting the call she went and scooped up Suzette, much to the toddler's displeasure, and then briskly walked back to the apartment wondering what was so important. Chantel was usually out shopping and lunching every day.

Letting herself into the apartment and settling Suzette down for a nap, she then found her employer in tears in the master bedroom.

"Chantel, what is it?" she said, rushing to her employer's side to provide comfort all the while praying that something tragic hadn't happened.

"Oh Callie, the most terrible thing has happened," Chantel sobbed.

Callie's mind immediately jumped to Claude dying.

"No, not Claude," she whispered, tears beginning to well up in her eyes.

Chantel looked at her au pair with a start.

"What? Has something happened to Claude?"

"I don't know," Callie said, confused. "You said something terrible has happened and I just automatically assumed that it was about Claude. Like he had had a heart attack or something."

"I'm sure he probably will upon hearing the news. It's terrible, Callie, just terrible."

Callie rubbed her employer's back trying to soothe her. Not wanting to jump to conclusions again after what had just happened, she waited silently for Chantel to explain.

"One of my closest friends has decided to come over to visit."

"That's great, isn't it?" she said, a degree of cautiousness in her voice since one never knew with Chantel.

"Not when your husband and friend don't get on."

Why did she have to rush back from the park just for this?

"I guess I'll just break the news gently to Claude tonight and hope he'll be okay." Chantel sniffed into her tissue.

"Does she stay here?"

"Oh, gosh no. She only stays at the Waldorf." Chantel looked almost horrified at the thought of her friend staying with her. "The trouble is she always makes me feel so frumpy compared to her. She's got pots of money and is so glamorous, never a hair out of place. All her clothes she wears once and then buys more."

"Chantel, you're one of the most beautiful women that I know. When you're a mother you don't have time to worry about your appearance as much," she said.

Her answer had brightened her employer's face for a minute before Chantel went back to looking gloomy again.

That night when Claude came home, he took the wind out of his wife's sails by announcing that he had to work late the next few nights and then had a conference to attend.

Chantel, who had been on tenterhooks all day trying to work up the nerve to break the news to her husband that Leticia was in town, was so relieved that she didn't even mention Leticia at all, since now Claude wouldn't even be around to know.

Callie noted Chantel's excitement the next morning and assumed everything had gone well with Claude.

The next night when Chantel had gone out to dinner with her friend, Claude had come home late, and saw Callie still up babysitting.

"Where's Chantel?" he said.

"Out for dinner with a friend."

"Listen, I have to do some stuff in my office. Do you mind staying up a bit longer?"

"Sure. Can I get you something?"

"A coffee would be great. Thanks, Callie."

Even though the office door was ajar, Callie still went to knock but as she raised her hand, she heard Claude speaking on the phone.

"Look, she doesn't suspect a thing. I've told her I'm on conference at the end of the week and you'll have me all to yourself. I've already organised a room at the Waldorf under Pierre Bouchier," he said. "We'll have a few days to ourselves with no need to even leave the room. Just make sure that you're wearing your sexiest lingerie, on second thoughts, don't even bother with clothes."

Callie stood there in shock. Claude was having an affair! Claude who always seemed so loving and kind. She never would have picked him as someone who cheated on his wife.

She quickly and quietly took about ten steps back and then took a deep breath before walking nervously towards the office door again. Rapping on it briskly, she waited for Claude to answer.

"Entrez."

"H-here's your coffee," she said, holding it out for him to take, trying hard not to show her hands trembling because of what she had just overheard.

"Are you okay, Callie?" he said, watching her face closely.

"F-fine. I'm just trying to be careful so I don't spill your coffee," she lied.

His eyes raked over her face and she stopped breathing for fear that he knew she had overheard his conversation.

"Okay, thanks. Why don't you get to bed," he said.

Callie was too relieved to even question his sudden change of mind as she hurriedly went to her room. She didn't know what to do about the fact that Claude was clearly cheating on his wife. Was it even her business to be poking her nose into it? The Merciers were her employers, not her friends.

As it happened, she needn't have worried about it at all because the next morning the decision had been made for her.

Chantel had been waiting for her at breakfast with Suzette like any other day.

"Good morning. How was your evening catching up with your friend, last night?" Chantel's pursed lips were Callie's first clue that something was wrong. "What? What is it?"

Anxiety shot through her, hoping that Chantel hadn't gotten bad news of some kind.

"You are to go to your room, pack your bags and leave this house immediately," Chantel said.

"P-pack? W-why?" she said, bewildered by her employer's hostility.

"Why? You have the nerve to ask why?" Chantel shrieked, losing control of her emotions. "How dare you betray the trust and faith we placed in you with your devious, underhanded, disloyal, whorish behaviour."

Callie blanched at being on the receiving end of such a vehement attack.

"I-I haven't betrayed you." As she stammered her protest, her head snapped to the side as a loud stinging slap accompanied it. "Ow!" she shrieked. "What the hell was that for?" Her cheek felt red hot.

"For trying to seduce my husband! Did you think that he wouldn't tell me? Did you really think that you could take my place? Now get your things and get out!"

Callie was stunned and as Chantel continued to scream at her, she finally went back to her room tearfully packing her bags, trying hard to understand what was happening.

Obviously Claude suspected that she overheard his conversation last night and made up a lie to get rid of her and thus making sure that Chantel wouldn't believe a word she said either.

Not knowing whether she was angry or hurt at not even being given a chance to explain, she knew deep down that Chantel wouldn't believe her anyway.

Gabriel St Croix knew that it had been the worst decision ever to come back to France and have his father properly rejoin the family business. But he hadn't had any say in the matter.

Ever since they had returned to Paris to live, their lives hadn't been as carefree and innocent as they once were. His father who had once spent plenty of time with his family had disappeared almost overnight.

His sister had gone from athletic and grounded to a spoilt, petulant, self-absorbed, rich society princess. Only his mother, Marielle had been ecstatic with the move but now she was fighting cancer and his parents had decided to once again relocate back to New Zealand.

The bribery their grandfather Fabien had used on Amélie and himself to keep them in Europe was disgusting, Gabe thought but he was even more appalled that his sister had lapped it up, not seeing anything wrong with their grandfather's machinations.

He, himself had foolishly made a deal with the devil and it was to his own stupidity that he thought that negotiating a move to the London office would give him enough distance from his grandfather, which was now shown to be futile since he always still seemed to be at Fabien's beck and call.

His grandfather also never seemed to let Gabriel forget the disappointment Fabien felt over what he considered his only son and Gabe's own father's traitorous defection.

The St Croix family could afford to hire the world's finest nurses and doctors to privately care for Marielle so that François didn't have to be burdened or bothered with it, something that François had taken exception to when his father had ordered it to be done.

Of course to the world, François' relocation back to New Zealand was the kind of action a man does for love and it was the perfect place to rest and recuperate.

The St Croix family, especially Fabien, was one hundred percent behind the decision but the reality was that Fabien was absolutely livid at what he considered the ultimate betrayal of his son who wasn't putting the St Croix family business first.

How Gabe missed and longed for the simple family life they used to have all those years ago in New Zealand more and more these days, as the burden of being a St Croix and all that entailed, especially from the paparazzi was detailed extensively.

The latest headline to cause an uproar was typically about Amélie. *The Heiress, The Arms Dealer and the Brothel!* The headline banner had been on the front page of all the prominent newspapers around Europe. It was accompanied by a photo of Amélie and suspected arms dealer, Felipe Roderigo looking like the perfect couple.

Although the article only ever alluded to the broader picture, it didn't matter because it was still a smear on the St Croix name linking them with unsavoury characters and prostitutes. It was even alleged that not only had Amélie and Felipe met at the said brothel, but that she liked to work there for some excitement.

Fabien had been so furious that he rounded Amélie up and forced her to explain why she would even be seen in the company of such a person.

She had been tearful, blaming her idiotic friends who had introduced them at a function and insisted that she didn't know who Felipe was and the brothel was a complete fabrication.

Nevertheless, it was front page news everywhere, and Fabien ordered her to stay at the château until the scandal died down.

As only Amélie could do, she pouted, raged and tried to manipulate her grandfather but this time, Fabien refused to be moved. He could no longer afford to have such a reckless granddaughter out in public. It was not only tarnishing the St Croix name but the scandal was affecting their business which to Fabien was the be all and end all.

Now Gabriel had yet another headache on his hands and while this one might not be because of his own family, it was still an unwanted annoyance that had landed in his lap because of his best friend, Luc Grenier.

The one thing that Gabriel had no time for was Chantel's histrionics and it was right at this moment that he wished Luc wasn't his best friend and hadn't rung knowing that Gabe was in New York asking him to help his sister in her hour of need.

Chantel had married Claude Mercier, imagining living a life in the lap of luxury since Claude was far richer than her family.

Sure, they were wealthy but it was nowhere near the level of wealth Chantel had thought she was marrying into as most of it was family money, not Claude's.

It was Gabriel who had everything Chantel wanted in a man except she didn't have the required seduction skills to entice him into her bed and it wasn't from the lack of flirting and constantly trying every time they met.

Gabriel St Croix had a reputation of being as ruthless a businessman as he was a lover and that was why women loved him. He was like an untamed lion, the ultimate bad boy but mega-rich so that they didn't mind that he wasn't romantic and loving and business became before them.

It was worth putting up with him for as long as he wanted because his lovers came away with many expensive pieces of jewellery and other luxury gifts, not to mention the infamy of being seen with him. Now that got you in all the magazines and gossip columns.

It was said that Gabriel's relationship with a woman lasted on average about two months. Only Leticia le Gros had been a year before it was all over and the scandal that had ensued was because she had cheated on Gabriel, causing people to be aghast since she was one of the longest relationships he had ever had.

People had even begun betting on an engagement such was the publicity surrounding the couple at the time. Although an engagement never eventuated, nonetheless, the gossipmongers still had a field day with the couple.

Every event they attended as exes people talked about, from whether they had spoken or simply ignored each other to whether Leticia realising her mistake, was now trying to make Gabriel jealous in an effort to win him back or whether Gabriel was heartbroken and still pining for her or had moved on.

Every partner of his also got more column inches than any celebrity and soon it was indeed a coup to be associated with him, even for only one date or photo opportunity as everyone would know your name and your social stock would skyrocket overnight.

After getting her brother Luc's call saying that Gabriel would stop by and check in on her at this distressing time, Chantel had been ecstatic. Now was her chance to play the maiden in distress so that he could be her knight in shining armour.

"I'm so glad you're here, Gabriel," she said, instantly falling into his arms sobbing and yet still managing to purr his name. "It's been horrendous."

Gabe was feeling uncomfortable at how clingy Chantel was being and, if he didn't know better, believed she was even rubbing herself against him in an attempt to raise some sort of sexual response from him but since she was upset, he simply ignored his instincts.

He led her to the sofa and asked her maid for refreshments.

"Now tell me what's happened, Chantel. Luc said that you weren't making much sense on the phone, but something about Claude cheating on you?"

Chantel wiped her eyes and blew her nose sensing a golden opportunity. Her mind raced at how she was going to spin her story so that Gabriel would not only sympathise with her situation but so she could use it to get closer to him.

She knew from general gossip that Gabriel hadn't had a long-term serious girlfriend since he dumped Leticia some time ago because of her cheating. If she could hook Gabriel then she'd instantly dump Claude without a backward glance.

She also suspected that Callie hadn't tried to seduce Claude, the girl was much too meek for that. That was one of the reasons Chantel had hired her, because Callie would do anything that Chantel asked and had no life.

Chantel suspected that Claude had been having affairs ever since Suzette had been born or probably even while she had been pregnant since they hardly had sex anymore.

When her husband had nervously told her that Callie had tried to seduce him while Chantel had been out, Chantel's first thought was that it had been the other way around and that Claude, more likely had tried to sleep with Callie. Whichever it was didn't matter in the slightest since Chantel wasn't about to give up her cash cow so she pretended to be outraged, believe her husband and thus get rid of the au pair, making it much simpler all round.

Then she had called her brother in a fit of rage hoping that Luc would then offer to find her a new au pair so she didn't have to go through the tedious task of doing it but instead he sent Gabriel to her, which was even better.

She looked at Gabriel and wanted to tear both their clothes off right away. It made her wonder if every woman in his vicinity thought the same thing, after all the man exuded a potent masculine aura that made women highly aroused just looking at him.

His sandy blond hair was styled perfectly, his blue eyes had a tinge of green that only served to make them mesmerising, and his strong facial features showing strength and determination made her weak at the knees. He was *all* man.

He was waiting for her explanation and she licked her lips to not only moisten them but draw his attention to her mouth.

"M-my au pair and Claude were having an affair," she said, bursting into tears once more. "He says she came onto him, practically naked and threw herself at him. He tried to fend her off but..."

The man was weak, Gabriel thought, disgusted.

"I don't know what to do," she sobbed. "I love him but he's betrayed me."

She flung herself into his arms once more before he could do anything to stop her.

"Was it a one time thing?" he said, unsure if it made a difference but perhaps the relationship could be salvaged if it had been and with counselling.

She hid her face in his chest closing her eyes to inhale his scent enjoying being held by him while she thought of a good answer. She needed him to believe that she was so crushed he'd help her get over this misery, but not to the detriment of wrecking her marriage completely in case seducing Gabriel amounted to nothing.

"I-I'm not sure. He said it was just the once but I don't know what to believe," she said. "I've got no family here to help me. You're the only one I've got to depend on, that's on my side."

Gabe gritted his teeth at her words. The last thing he needed was Chantel becoming dependant on him. He wasn't her brother. Maybe he should call Luc and get him to sort his sister out.

"I'll call Luc. Maybe you could go and visit him for a bit."

"No." She almost yelled in horror, that was the last thing she wanted. Taking a breath to calm herself, she said, "I mean, no, I just need some company. I don't want to burden my family."

Now he was becoming stuck between a rock and a hard place. He didn't want to offend his best friend's sister at this horrible time but still, he didn't want to be responsible for her either.

"What happened to the au pair?"

He wanted to ensure that she had at least been sent packing, even if he was fairly certain that she have been.

"I got rid of her as soon as I found out."

"And Claude?"

"He's on a business trip so you see, I'm all alone."

The way she breathed the last part as if she was helpless, made his gut twist in dismay.

Suzette woke from her nap and Gabe was relieved that Chantel had to go and tend to her daughter, giving him some room to breathe. He also took the opportunity to call Luc who swore and yelled down the line.

When Chantel came back into the living room she wasn't holding the baby.

"Where's Suzette?"

He wasn't a baby person but even he would welcome the baby as a buffer.

"Oh, I've got the maid watching her. She'd be too disruptive and we wouldn't be able to talk properly," she breezily said.

He frowned and noted the gleam of desire in her eyes as she then also tried to look distraught.

"I called Luc," he said.

Chantel looked angry by the announcement.

"After all, he's your brother and sent me here to make sure that everything was okay. He was concerned."

"Of course," she said, trying to continue looking distressed. "I just wanted to get my own head around it before I told my family the whole story, that's all."

He had a brief flicker of guilt that he shouldn't have called Luc until later but still, his friend was Chantel's brother and had a right to know.

"I have to get going," he said, standing abruptly.

"Why? Can't you stay for a bit longer?" she said, panic crossing her face. "I really could use a friend."

"I've got meetings," he said. "Besides you'll be fine. Like you said, you need some time to process all that's happened."

Chantel felt almost dumped by his words. It really was true that Gabriel St Croix was the unemotional bastard everyone said, judging by his heartless words, and the fact that he felt no compunction whatsoever in leaving her in her hour of need.

"B-but what about when Claude comes home? How will I cope even being in the same room as him?"

"I thought you said that he was away?" he frowned.

"I-I forgot. See how upset I am. Can't you stay a little longer?"

The way Chantel was acting reminded him so much of past lovers that he had ended it with — the unbecoming, undignified begging and pleading. It didn't even so much as make a mark on the armour surrounding his emotions as he hated melodramatic women especially ones with fake crocodile tears.

"I'm sorry," he said. "But you now have some time to sort out a game plan and I suggest you use it to decide what you want from your marriage. Call Luc, your parents or perhaps a friend could recommend a therapist for you to talk to?"

And with that, the man whose emotions were made out of stone was gone.

Gabriel left Chantel's relieved that he was no longer in her company. He knew he seemed hard-hearted and callous but he had met women like her before and knew Chantel only wanted money. The husband came second in her life…a very distant second.

He wanted a woman with a spine. Someone who didn't care about what other's thought, was happy within herself, could laugh and not be outraged by the silliest things like a stain on her blouse.

She had to have pep or joie de vivre and he had known this since moving back to France where he had only met fluffy air-headed women whose skills of manipulation and persuasion were second to none and who thought that by always agreeing with him, he would find them captivating.

In truth, deep down, he wanted someone who wanted *him* and not the St Croix name or money.

He thought that Leticia had been that woman until he found out her dark secret. He still remembered the moment that he had walked in on her and her hook-up under her disguise as Natalia.

As shocked as she had been, for some reason she thought that claiming she was too young to be tied down to one guy, when she wanted adventure would make him accepting.

Disgusted, he had left without a word, packed up her belongings, changed his locks and wiped her from his life.

She had come begging for him to take her back but he hadn't given her the time of day, in effect pretending she had never existed.

Things had come to a scandalous head when she publicly cornered him at a function. She wouldn't let him just ignore her any longer and began making an awful scene, which to all the gossips and journalists was like striking gold, with every media outlet continually reporting for days on the most delicious, juicy story of the year.

Then someone found an internet video of Leticia. While she was left clearly to be seen, all the men in the video had their faces covered so they couldn't be recognised but it was obvious enough that none of the men in the video were Gabriel.

The media then began vilifying Leticia and her sexual antics because although the men's faces had been blocked out, some of their wives and girlfriends still recognised them causing even more furore. Leticia's social standing was grounded into dust.

Gabe didn't know who had leaked that group sex session onto the internet and he really didn't care until his grandfather had called him into his office and then made him watch the whole thing, disgusting acts and all, and even when he closed his eyes he could still hear every word spoken or uttered.

It was the men that were having sex with Leticia, telling her that she loved what they were doing because Gabriel St Croix obviously couldn't satisfy her and hearing Leticia speak so derisively about him during it, that had enraged him.

"Now I want you to go out and crush them!" his grandfather said, furious. "*No one* attacks the St Croix family and makes us a laughing stock and gets away with it!"

It was his grandfather who had found out the names of all the men involved and gave Gabe personal files on each. To Gabe, it really wasn't worth the effort and he had burnt their files since they were nothing to him.

He didn't care. No matter what anyone thought, women still flocked to be with him, console him and prove that he was not only all man but had the appetite to match.

Chapter 3

A sense of déjà vu washed over Gabe as he stood at the door waiting for it to open. Last time it had been because of Luc. This time, it was because his old neighbour, Jarrod Harrison had mentioned in passing that Callie was now living in London.

The difference was that this time the recipient of his visit was actually someone he was looking forward to seeing again after all these years. He wondered how much she had changed and it didn't take long for the answer to come as the door opened.

"Hello Callie."

She looked completely shocked to see him on her doorstep and instead of welcoming him with open arms and perhaps a smile or even a squeal of delight, she said with dismay, "Oh, it's you, why am I not surprised?"

Gabe almost burst out into laughter but bit the inside of his cheek to stop himself because he saw she looked despondent and wasn't trying to tease him at all.

"Well, I thought I was surprising you but I guess not. How did you know I was coming to visit?"

"I didn't but it really is par for the course, don't you think?" She snorted. "Our parents are happy as pigs in mud renewing their friendship. I'm really sorry to hear about your mum's cancer, by the way," she said. "And for God only knows reason why, but your sister is staying with Jarrod so it only stood to reason that we'd see each other, make it a triple catch up."

His head spun befuddled at her logic. While it sounded logical, it still made no sense. She didn't know he was coming and yet she made it sound almost pre-destined.

"Okay," he drawled. "So now what?"

Callie had no idea. No idea why Gabe had turned up out of the blue. No idea what she was doing with her life. No idea in general.

She sat and shrugged before her shoulders slumped in defeat and Gabe actually felt something tug inside him at seeing Callie like this.

What happened to the delightful young girl she had once been? Then he frowned remembering that it had been years since he had seen her and people change, wasn't he was an example of that? Still it saddened him that the Callie sitting before him seemed to be someone he didn't recognise.

He sat down beside her wondering how he had managed to once more become the guy going to someone else in distress although it wasn't as bad as seeing Chantel because this was Callie, his old neighbour.

"Want to tell me about it?" he said with genuine sincerity that he hadn't offered a woman in a long time.

What was she supposed to say? That thanks to Chantel Mercier, she struggled to find another au pair job and returned to London in the hopes that she might fare better. However, since she really wasn't qualified for much else, it was hard to find employment and she needed to get a job soon otherwise she'd be kicked out of her flat.

She knew that Gabe couldn't be here because of Jarrod or her parents, because she hadn't told them what had happened apart from the fact that her employer no longer needed her services but even then, they didn't know how dire the situation was.

"Why are you here?" she said, not answering his question.

"I was in the neighbourhood?"

It was wishful thinking that she'd believe a terrible lie like that, but to his surprise she burst out laughing.

"What? What's so funny? I could have been in the neighbourhood," he said, trying to look hurt that she didn't believe him.

"Right." She shook her head in amusement. "With what you're wearing, you're either the slum lord or coming to see some of the prostitutes in the house next door."

Gabe looked gobsmacked by her words and she couldn't help but continue giggling.

"Are you so up yourself these days that no one even jokes with you?"

It took him a minute to realise that she was joking…and yet what she said was actually true. Ever since his return to France and the position of his family had been reinstated, no one really made such rude jokes or teased him lest they were fired or their family ruined for saying or doing the wrong thing as that was his grandfather's way.

Callie had bitten her lip worried that she had offended him but the Gabe she knew and remembered would have laughed at her jokes without a second thought, which just showed that she really didn't know the man she had just let into her flat at all.

He looked at her and smiled sensing her relax to his relief.

"Shh, not too loud, the walls might have ears." He leaned closer to conspiratorially whisper. "I guess I can tell you that I'm not only the slum lord but also the pimp for the women next door."

Now this was the Gabe she knew, she thought, bursting out laughing once more at his silliness.

"You're such a moron."

"Me?" His eyes widened. "You're the one accusing me of being an unsavoury character."

"Well, what are you doing here then?"

For the first time in what seemed like forever, he felt relaxed knowing that Callie was treating him like she treated her brother or anyone else. He wasn't being given the special Gabriel St Croix deference and he liked it.

"Wrong door? I *had* meant to knock next door?" he said, waggling his eyebrows.

"Don't let me stop you."

"It's too late. Now that I've accidentally found you, I would rather catch up than…you know."

"Fabulous, because if I'm right, I think they might already have customers unless you booked or were planning on joining them."

He was once again surprised by her smutty jokes and tried to remember the last time anyone or more especially, a woman, had ever said anything like that to him. He couldn't remember and that was almost sad.

"Enough of the jokes," he said in earnest, not feeling quite comfortable going down this road since it had been so long since he had been on it. "I'm here because I…" He trailed off, realising that he actually had no idea why he had landed upon his old neighbour's doorstep at all.

When he was coming to Callie's place he had it all sorted in his mind but now, seeing her and all her jokes had somehow transplanted all his thoughts and he had completely forgotten what had brought him here in the first place.

Callie, seeing Gabe actually look lost, took pity on him and decided to change the topic. She didn't mind him being here, in fact, it was actually comforting.

"Tell me about Amélie and why is she living with Jarrod? He doesn't seem very happy about it," she said.

Gabe heard the undertone of hurt in Callie's voice and remembered her one and only visit to France that hadn't gone well at all. Still, she had asked the question and he answered.

"She's been out of control since mum and dad left to live back in New Zealand. Grand-père overindulged her, basically bribing her to ensure that she would stay in France," he said. "Let's just say that her decision-making became detrimental in some respects, that when she made the front page headlines for something completely unbecoming a St Croix, grand-père in effect put her under house arrest. I managed to persuade him to send her to stay with Jarrod so at least she could have some freedom but I think all its done is unwittingly punished Jarrod."

He looked remorseful for the decision but it was done in the best interests for his sister.

As much as Jarrod was irritated by Amélie's presence on the farm, Callie could understand Gabe's reasoning and imagined Amélie kicking and screaming the entire way.

She also felt awful about not having seen Gabe in years and instead of being excited and happy to be reacquainting their old friendship, she was depressed. He was probably wishing he hadn't come to visit.

Looking at him, he hadn't changed physically except from maturing but she sensed that he was no longer that carefree boy that he had been all those years ago. Now he seemed guarded and had lost his sense of humour and his smile. She had always liked his smile along with his lovely French accent.

Just thinking about it, she once again felt regret that her friendship with Amélie had been lost even though it was through no real fault of her own, but she still wished that she could have managed to salvage something from it, even a yearly Christmas card that rounded up a year's worth of news in one go.

"Callie, is everything all right? You don't seem that happy to see me," he said, concerned. Was it because she and Amélie were no longer friends?

She had two choices: act ecstatic to see him again after all this time or tell him that he should leave because she had something else to do. What, she didn't know, but would make something up. Opening her mouth to say all the right things, nothing came out. Embarrassed, she just stared before somehow her voice made its presence known.

"I…I'm sorry, Gabe. Of course I'm happy to see you…you just caught me off guard that's all. I…need to get going. I've got…friends." She stumbled over her words before realising that she sounded like an idiot and was flushing bright red.

His chuckle did nothing to relax her.

"I'd hope you'd have friends but since you're obviously overwhelmed by being in my presence and keen to get rid of me, how about we catch up another night. How's Friday?" he said, standing up and handing her his card.

"Oh…I…sure. Sounds good. I'll…call you."

He didn't let go of his business card making her look up at him and stare into his vivid blue eyes so she would know that he knew something wasn't quite right.

"Make sure you do, Callie, otherwise I'll come back and won't be leaving until we catch up."

The look on his face was amusement and yet she detected some kind of thinly veiled warning in his words.

"O-of course," she said. "I-I just can't right now."

He searched her face and knew she not only didn't want to talk to him but also looked anxious for him to be gone.

"Callie, are you okay? You're not in some kind of trouble, are you? You can tell me, I'll help you," he said.

She felt like she was going to cry but instead she took a breath and pasted a smile on her face. He could tell that it was fake but said nothing, just waited.

"Don't be silly. I need to go out. We'll catch up Friday," she said, as breezily as possible.

Another intense stare from Gabe almost made her crumble as she held her breath, but he simply nodded and left.

Oh, why did Gabe have to visit? She waited until she couldn't see him anymore, certain he had gone and then sagged against the door in relief.

Gabe walked away from Callie's deep in thought. Never in a million years had he ever thought he'd be walking away from her place so soon. He wasn't that much of a snob that he wanted to leave her dingy little flat as fast as possible. On the contrary, if Callie had genuinely wanted to catch up, he would have happily stayed there all night.

No, it was her hurry to get rid of him that had him perplexed. Was she embarrassed by his sudden appearance, he hoped she wasn't, after all she knew him as a child. He would never have looked down on her, she was his friend.

Part of him wondered if he should hang around and see if she really was going out but deep down he knew that she wasn't. That meant he was going to have to wait until Friday and he hated that he wouldn't be able to help or solve what was wrong with Callie until he talked properly with her.

He respected her privacy enough not to dig into her life but still wondered what was bothering her or maybe it was him, the thought left him feeling depressed.

Planning for Friday's dinner, he felt excited anticipation for the first time in a long time and he wanted Callie to feel relaxed enough to be able to tell him anything.

Callie called to arrange a time and place and Gabe didn't miss the breath she had sucked in when he mentioned his Knightsbridge address.

Quickly he offered to send a car to pick her up, scared that she might baulk if he left her to make her own way. He overrode any protest she had saying that he was worried for her safety. Her laughter at his reasoning relaxed him.

"You think someone's going to mug me…in Knightsbridge?" she joked. "If anything, I'll probably be arrested as the mugger."

He had politely laughed at her self-derision but gnashed his teeth that she could even say something like that about herself.

Lighten up, he chided to himself. Maybe he was reading more into it than that of a silly remark.

When she quietly asked what she should wear, he heard the nervousness in her voice. He had stupidly thought that having her to his house would be more relaxing and now he saw that they should have met somewhere neutral but never mind, the decision had been made and he had told her to just be comfortable so jeans, sweats, he really didn't care as it was only going to be the two of them.

The car had picked her up and now arrived. Before his driver could even get out to open the door, he was there doing it for her.

"Callie, I'm so glad you came," he said, delighted.

"Thanks for inviting me. I've never been to this part of town before. I can't wait to see the inside of your home," she said, awestruck just by the outside.

Gabe took note that Callie was indeed wearing jeans and a jumper and felt better about rushing out to buy a pair himself. He hadn't worn jeans in years, usually preferring trousers and as the thick denim felt stiff on his legs, he remembered why he didn't like them as much but to help put Callie at ease, he'd grin and bear it.

"Wow, this is beautiful. It looks like something out of a magazine," she enthused, standing in the foyer. "Did you do this yourself or was this from the last owner?"

"An interior designer did it for me," he said, unsure why he felt slightly embarrassed since people used professionals all the time.

"Oh, of course, silly me," she said, feeling foolish that she hadn't thought of that.

Gabe felt almost irritated by Callie's remark. Was she some kind of reverse-snob? He had seen people like that and for the second time wondered if inviting her here was such a good idea.

"Come on, I'll give you the tour."

She followed him ooh-ing and aah-ing in a very polite manner the entire way, which did nothing but continue to dampen the mood he was now in.

It wasn't that she was counting dollar signs like some people did when they saw his place, it was more like she was being too polite to say that she didn't like it.

Callie couldn't believe that an interior designer thought that this was beautiful or maybe she was such a hick that just didn't know good taste when she saw it.

The only room she did genuinely like apart from the bathrooms — one of which she was sure that she'd be able to live in, it was that big — was embarrassingly, Gabe's bedroom.

The foyer had been so impressive upon entering the house and then all the other rooms seemed so pretentious and more like a fancy hotel except his bedroom which looked warm, inviting and relaxing.

When they got back to the dining room, he held out a chair for her, and it was on the tip of her tongue to just say, "don't bother, I can do it myself" but Gabe had the strangest look on his face, like he was having second thoughts about having invited her.

She thought of as many plausible excuses that she could use to leave early so that the night wouldn't awkwardly drag on but she sensed that no matter how long she was here, it would feel like that anyway.

Hesitantly, she broke the silence.

"Is there anything you need me to help with?"

"No, Nigel will bring through dinner."

Callie looked around the room. Who was Nigel? She hadn't met or seen anyone called Nigel and as if on cue, a man she could only assume was Nigel, who looked very formally dressed, came into the room holding two plates of food. He set the plates down on the table in front of them before Gabe dismissed him for the rest of the evening.

Her head spun. Gabe had a butler? She had no idea. Then it suddenly dawned on her that she hadn't seen the kitchen, which was where Nigel must have been hiding.

"Is something wrong with the food?" he said.

"N-no, I-I'm just surprised that you have a butler. It's a little…" She flushed, almost blurting out the word *weird*, before realising that it was the wrong word.

"Doesn't everyone?" he mocked.

All she could do was stare at him and blink. Was he for real? she thought before his chuckle gave away his teasing.

"Oh, go back to France." His roar of laughter just made her bristle even more. "It's not my fault I'm not used to this kind of thing."

"Oh, Callie, how I've missed your little comeback, it's been years since I've heard it. I'm glad that you still feel that you can say such rude things to me. If it were anyone else, I'd have their head," he said, amused.

The horrified look on her face at his words, that he would or could do such a thing made him stop laughing.

"You'd do that?" she said in all seriousness, her eyes wide at the thought.

"Depends on if I liked them to begin with."

She began shoving food in her mouth to keep her from saying something offensive.

The man sitting at the table with her was someone she didn't know at all. He might share the same name and similarities of looks but deep down, where it counted, the Gabriel St Croix sitting at the table was nowhere near the same boy who left New Zealand all those years ago.

Gabe was moody again thanks to Callie. He could feel her judgemental thoughts loud and clear as if she had spoken them.

He didn't have to explain himself to her nor did he have to apologise for being who he was. He couldn't change it anymore than she could and she had no right to sit in judgement of him just because he was rich and had the means and power to not have to tolerate horrible or petty people in his life unless necessary.

She put down her knife and fork, the awkwardness making her feel on edge.

"Maybe this was a bad idea," she said. "I mean, we haven't seen each other in years and it's obvious that we don't have much in common at all."

Callie said exactly what he had been thinking and so he should have just gracefully acceded to her wishes and agreed but he couldn't. For some bizarre reason he felt like he needed to spend time with the one woman in the entire world who wasn't fawning over him because of who he was.

Some of the more parasitic people he decided to test just to see how far they would go to have their names linked. At the beginning, it had been amusing until as time went on, he realised that he was turning into his grandfather.

That's why he needed Callie. He needed to remember the best times of his life, be in the presence of someone who never cared about his name or his money, remember when life was so much happier…and simpler.

Callie didn't like the way that Gabe was so quiet or the intense way that he was almost staring at her. Was he trying to decide how to politely throw her out of his house and ensure that they never saw each other again?

"I'm sorry, Callie. For some stupid reason I thought that catching up wouldn't be as awkward as this. Can we start again?"

He surprised himself at not only how honest he was being but the fact that he had apologised. He hadn't felt the need to apologise, at least this sincerely, in years. St Croix's didn't apologise unless they had to, but even then, only if it suited their purpose to do so. Maybe there was still hope for him?

His sincerity made her feel bad for wanting to leave and not even try to make an effort.

"Sure," she said, magnanimous.

Gabe relaxed at her answer.

"So tell me, what's been going on with your life?"

Callie bit the bottom of her lip not comfortable with his question. How did you tell someone like him that you were a complete failure?

"Nothing very exciting. My last job finished a few months ago and I'm looking for another one," she said, trying to act blasé about it.

"What did you do?"

"I was an au pair."

Her answer made him think of Chantel. If he had seen Callie a month ago, he could have recommended her to his best friend's sister. Before he could say something, his cellphone rang. It was Luc.

"Please excuse me," he said, getting up from the table to answer the call.

Callie didn't mind in the least. She didn't want to talk about her situation and was grateful for the interruption.

He had only been gone a few minutes and returned to see that Callie had finished her dinner. Since he wasn't that hungry, he suggested that they sit in the lounge.

"But what about the dishes?" she said, surprised that Gabe looked like he was just going to leave them sitting on the table especially since he had dismissed Nigel for the night.

"Oh, leave them. Nigel can clean up tomorrow," he said.

Seeing the look of horror on Callie's face he knew that it had been the wrong thing to say.

"You can't do that," she admonished. "Look, why don't I just take them into the kitchen."

"No, I'll do it," he sighed. "Why don't you go and sit down."

Gathering up the plates he realised with a clarity that he actually hadn't had to clear the table in years, not since he had left New Zealand that was for sure.

Had he gotten that lazy over the years that even simple menial tasks were beneath him? No, it was the army of servants they had that catered to their every whim so he didn't have to think of anything other than being an important member of the St Croix family or these days, his work.

Going into the kitchen, it was a room he didn't feel comfortable in at all and therefore he rarely came in here because he had Nigel.

He placed the plates in the sink and realised that he couldn't even really rinse them because he had no idea where anything was and a flicker of guilt and shame crossed his mind.

Still he used his logic and found the brush in the cupboard under the sink and rinsed the plates before putting them in the dishwasher.

Satisfied he wasn't a completely lazy idiot he turned and was surprised to find Callie standing in the kitchen, smiling. It was the first real smile he had seen tonight that was the old Callie.

"I wondered why you hadn't shown me the kitchen. I wouldn't have been able to miss your butler," she teased.

"I don't normally show anyone the kitchen and no one ever seems to really care that much," he said, his cheeks rosy.

He hadn't asked for her opinion but she couldn't help but give it anyway.

"I think this is the nicest room in the house."

His eyes widened in surprise. She was obviously teasing him. No one ever thought the kitchen of any house was the nicest room.

"You do?"

"Yes, I do," she said with an emphatic nod of her head. "This is the kind of kitchen I'd love to have one day. It's bright and roomy and at the same time cosy. It reminds me of your old house."

Her answer took him back in time and as he looked around the room, he observed with startling clarity that Callie was right. This room did remind him of their old one in New Zealand. The colours were different but the layout and the big island in the middle were the same. They had many a great time in the kitchen eating and talking back then.

He honestly couldn't remember if the kitchen had always been like this or had it been redecorated? It didn't matter, now that he was aware of the similarities, he was planning on spending more time in here.

"Coffee?" he said.

"Do you know how to make it?" The scowl she received in reply made her laugh. "Okay, yes, that would be lovely."

He made the coffees while she made herself comfy watching him make a few mistakes, cursing and then looking victorious when he had finally managed to succeed. To her surprise he placed the cup in front of her and pulled out a stool for himself. He didn't even ask if she wanted to move to the other room.

"Do you remember the time…" she said, happily reminiscing and from that moment on the conversation, the memories and the laughter flowed.

"Goodness, its two in the morning," he said, seeing the time. He had never talked to a woman this long before in his entire life, even if it was just a trip down memory lane.

That would explain why she was feeling tired, she thought holding in a yawn. She looked at her watch and then at Gabe.

"I'd better get going," she said, sliding off the stool. "It's been fun."

"Let me take you home." He knew that the Tube would be closed.

"No one's going to mug me," she laughed. "I don't even look fabulously wealthy?"

"Who's to say that you don't have a bag full of gems in your handbag?"

"Nope, no gems." She rummaged around her handbag to look. "You didn't leave me alone long enough so I could find your secret jewellery safe. Honestly Gabe, I'll be fine. I'm sure there's plenty of cabs out there just dying to know what a girl like me is doing in a neighbourhood like this."

"No, it's safer for me to drive you unless there's a reason why you don't want me too?"

He searched her face for some tell-tale sign that would provide him with an answer.

"Seriously, I can catch a cab," she said. "There's no need for you to go to all this trouble."

"I thought you said that you're between jobs. Doesn't getting a cab mean spending money that you don't have?"

His logic made her bite her bottom lip and then after a brief moment of thought, she gave in but only because what he had said made sense.

"Fine, you win. Thank you, I'd love a lift."

"There that wasn't so hard, was it?" he grinned, victorious. "Tell me, are you always this independent?"

"I have no idea," she shrugged.

He chuckled and led her to his car — sleek, powerful and a thing of beauty — and as soon as Callie saw it she wanted to drive it.

"Oh, can I drive, *please*."

"Do you even have a licence?" He hoped her answer was no.

"Of course," she chirped, much to his dismay.

"No."

"Oh, come on. It's the dead of night. There's no one even around."

"No."

"Don't tell me that you're one of those insecure chauvinistic males that can't handle a female being a better driver than them?"

"No and still no," he said, trying not to let her goad him. "Now get in or you can walk."

"I never thought you'd be so threatened by a female driver," she said, attempting to persuade him one last time but he wouldn't budge.

"Not going to work but nice try," he said, smiling at her defeated expression.

"So what would it take to let me or any other woman drive your car?"

He pretended to think about the answer and then smiled to himself.

"Marriage."

Her jaw fell open and her eyes almost popped out of her head at his answer.

"Are you serious?"

The grin on his face told her that no, he wasn't but was merely messing with her.

"Oh, why don't you just take your frog's legs and hop back to France," she said, his roar of laughter filling the car.

Chapter 4

Callie's friend, Hazel had just gotten herself a new job at an exclusive gentlemen's club. Callie wasn't surprised since Hazel was every man's fantasy — tall, blonde and beautiful.

It was with Hazel's coercing that Callie came along to see what it was like at her new job in the hopes that perhaps she too could work there.

Hazel's boss, Ross had okayed Callie's visit as long as she stayed well in the background. This was usually how Ross found his future employees, through other employees giving them a glimpse into what kind of work it was. This also reassured the girls that they weren't being employed to do anything sleazy.

They entered through a non-descript back door in an alley which didn't alleviate any of the fears that she had. In fact, it only served to enhance them as Hazel giggled at Callie's face.

"Oh, hon, you look how I did the first time. It's not romantic or classy at the backdoor, is it?"

Still anxious that if the outside was a dump then what would the inside look like, Callie could only nod.

As Hazel entered and Callie hesitantly followed, the loud bang of the door closing made her jump with fright before her eyes widened in amazement. The further along the corridor they went it changed from drab to fab right before her eyes.

Hazel was leading her towards the changing rooms and stopped by an office with a very frustrated looking man sitting inside.

"Ross, this is my friend Callie, whose here to observe the inner workings," she said.

Callie didn't know what to expect but a young, handsome man wasn't it. She had been thinking more along the lines of a fat, balding and angry man like in the movies.

"Come on in, Callie," he said, looking up from his desk.

She looked at Hazel who smiled and nodded.

"I'm just going to get changed. Don't worry, Ross is a good guy," her friend whispered.

Slowly she walked into the office and sat nervously in the chair in front of the desk.

"So Callie, how long have you known Hazel?" he said.

It was a friendly question but Callie could see that he wasn't really in the mood for visitors.

"N-not long. I-I see you're very busy. I-I'll go and leave you to it."

"Sorry." He let out a loud sigh, raking a hand through his hair. "It's just been one of those days. Two of my top girls have called in sick at the last moment and tonight's our busiest night."

"I'm sorry," she said, before getting up to leave him in peace.

"Wait."

She stood there uncomfortably watching him rake his eyes up and down over her body. It was one of those assessing looks and for some reason it didn't revolt her but probably because Hazel worked here and was nearby if she needed to escape.

"Listen, I know you only came to watch and have a look but you'd be doing me a huge favour if you could work tonight," he said, hopeful.

A loud chatter was coming from outside the office and she looked to see who was making the noise, praying it was Hazel.

Three very happy blonde women stuck their heads into the office.

"We're on now, Ross," one said.

"Great. Enjoy all the flirting, girls," he said, as they giggled and left making Callie turn her attention back to him. "So?"

Ross Curtain was the manager of all the serving staff and floor managers at *The Century Club*. He knew what the club's clientele liked in women and looking at the young woman standing in front of him he could see she wasn't their usual type, but there was something about her that just drew him to her.

Possibly it was her vivid blue eyes, that looked like the ocean sparkling on a sunny day or that cute rosebud mouth that beckoned to be kissed, whichever it was, it was enough to ask her to work. She was shorter than his normal girls and her strawberry blonde hair looked like a disaster but she exuded an x-factor that men would like.

"I-I'm not sure. What does the job entail?" she said, her voice barely a whisper that he struggled to hear.

"All you have to do is serve drinks and food, that's it. Can you do that?"

Hazel bounced back into the office before she could answer.

"Hazel, honey, take your friend and doll her up. She's working tonight," Ross said.

"B-but I-I haven't —"

"I'm desperate. Just do your best. I'll get Phoebe to make sure that you only do the easy stuff," he said as Hazel clapped her hands with glee before pulling Callie out of Ross' office and into the changing room.

"Wow, this is a changing room?" She looked around awestruck. "It's huge and flash."

"I know. That's why it's a great place to work. They provide *everything*," Hazel gushed. "I can't believe he's getting you to work tonight, he's never done that before. You must have really bowled him over."

Callie flushed with embarrassment thinking that her friend might have gotten the wrong idea.

"A couple of girls called in sick at the last minute, he said."

"Probably Robyn and Anna." Hazel's face screwed up in disgust. "They're trying to extort more money from him since they're now the two most popular servers."

"Does that happen a lot?" she said, confused.

"Apparently," Hazel said.

Although Hazel hadn't been on the job that long to know all the ins and outs, others had mentioned that every now and then a girl might get a bit of a diva complex and Ross either let them go or they left to fry bigger fish.

"Sometimes it works out, other times they end up with their tails between their legs, and possibly go back to the bottom of the ladder and have to re-earn the right to work the popular nights like Friday and Saturday, and sometimes they're just let go," she said. "All newbies start on day shifts where the tips aren't as much and it also isn't as busy."

Callie felt like she had been poked, prodded and plucked by her friend but by the time Hazel had finished, even she couldn't believe that it was her staring back in the mirror. She waved to herself just to make certain, giggling at her silliness.

"Wow, Cal, you look stunning," Hazel said, full of awe.

"I can't believe that this is me. You've turned me into Cinderella."

"Yeah, a Cinderella that's not in a ball gown but a work uniform," Hazel laughed. "I never knew you had such an incredible figure."

Because she was wearing exactly the same thing as Hazel, it seemed that she looked like a miniature version of her friend.

"How did you get my hair to look so shiny and sleek?" she said, mystified because her hair never behaved for her, it was like an unruly child.

"Product. You know that thing you're too lazy to use," Hazel teased. "Come on, we have to go. I'm late as it is."

"O-okay."

It was one thing to say that you'd work, another to be all dolled up for it and still another to have to actually go out in front of people looking like she knew what she was doing. How was she ever going to manage tonight?

"Ross, want to see?" Hazel smiled, pulling Callie into the office.

Ross, who had just been hoping that Callie would look presentable, had his jaw fall to the ground when a beautiful woman appeared.

He looked around behind her, his eyes wide, wondering if there was another Callie hiding somewhere.

"You're kidding me? *This* is Callie?" he said, astonished, like she hadn't already been in his office moments earlier.

"Yes," Hazel gloated.

"Well, I'll be…damn you're stunning," he said as Callie went bright red.

"Down boy," Hazel giggled. "C'mon Cal, we've got work to do."

Dragging her friend down the corridor, they came out behind the bar. Hazel waved to a woman who looked exactly like everyone else but had a red jacket on for distinction.

"Who's this?" The woman eyed Callie curiously.

"My friend, Callie. She's filling in because Ross said two have called in sick at the last minute. She was only supposed to be observing," Hazel quickly said. "Callie, this is Phoebe, she's the floor manager. She'll help you out, okay?"

Before Callie could even open her mouth, Hazel had disappeared and she had no idea where her friend had gone.

"Hi," she shyly said.

"Do you have any experience?" Phoebe said.

"N-no. R-Ross said that you'd find a place out of the way and give me simple jobs." She was embarrassed at being foisted upon this woman.

Phoebe sighed. At least this girl was being honest, which was something.

"Got it." she said, tapping a finger to her lips. "If anyone needs you to drop drinks to their tables for them, do that. If you're not required then you can just stand behind the bar and observe."

Callie nodded and then Phoebe turned to the barman.

"James, this is Callie. She's new. No experience. We're short-staffed so be nice and show her the ropes and make sure she keeps out of trouble," she said as James saluted.

"Hi, I'm Callie."

"James. So let me guess, the emergency is that Anna *and* Robyn are no shows. Where'd they find you, gorgeous?"

"I-I'm Hazel's friend. She thought that I might like to come and see where she worked and Ross was tearing his hair out, saw me and said to work."

"Sounds like him. He and Phoebe are the good guys…usually," he winked. "Okay, here's what I need you to do…"

He began showing her all the various things and she apologised for being lumbered with her and not having any bar experience, but he seemed to take it all in his stride making her wonder if he was stuck with the newbies often.

"It's going to get a lot busier as the night goes on so we'll try and ease you into it but once we're in full swing, at least try to keep up, okay?"

"Okay, I'll try."

She looked around and the lounge area that they were in was warm and inviting. The lighting wasn't harsh and bright but slightly dimmer to give a warm relaxed atmosphere feeling. The seats were all leather, the dark grey carpet even felt plush under her feet, the décor was very tasteful.

She couldn't see Hazel anywhere and when she asked James about it, he explained the Club's hierarchy. They were the ground floor which everyone — from Club members to the public — were welcomed to come and use.

First floor was for members from two to five years. The third floor was five to ten and the fourth was ten plus. There was also a very special VIP floor.

Anyone higher up the hierarchy could go to any of the lower floors or invite guests onto their floors but lower members had to stick to the appropriate floor unless invited.

Hazel was working the third floor tonight. There had been a shuffling of girls because of Robyn and Anna's absence and that's why Callie was working in the ground floor lounge because she was a newbie and only the very experienced servers worked the upper levels, the most experienced served the VIPs.

Callie was finding *The Century Club* to be a very enjoyable place to work and time was ticking by quite fast when she was being told to take a break. She tried to refuse but James urged her to go.

"Believe me, when you come back the place will be humming and you'll be run off your feet. You might not get another chance so take the break."

She did as she was told and found the break room was more like a giant kitchen and living room from someone's house. There was a huge TV, chefs to make whatever you wanted and a state of the art music system.

A bunch of other girls were already in there chatting away.

"God, I hope he comes in tonight. He makes me wet every time I look at him," one girl gushed.

"Not me. Old Jack's my man," another added to giggles.

"That's because Old Jack likes to think he's gonna get some," the first girl said as everyone laughed.

As they noticed Callie they all smiled, welcoming her. Introductions were made and she explained that she was only temping for the night because a couple of girls were sick.

Everyone instantly rolled their eyes at her explanation because they knew exactly who and why.

"Well that's our good fortune," Bianca, the first girl said. "If those two hadn't called in sick then I'd be stuck on first. Now I'm on second."

Everyone agreed that having the two most experienced and long-time servers away made it better for them all.

"Well, good luck, Callie," they all said, leaving her to sit by herself.

James was right. By the time Callie had returned to the floor feeling refreshed, the lounge had gotten a lot busier but not packed.

"There you are," he said, happy to see Callie return. "Glad you didn't run away. I've got tons of drinks for you to deliver."

Because it was busy, it made Callie feel less nervous as she had no time to think. Doing as James asked, she delivered drinks to table after table and she could swear that she had served the entire floor only to turn around and start again.

The men were friendly and seemed to enjoy seeing someone new but she didn't really stop to make small talk even though they tried to engage her but that was because she was too busy and she politely told them so.

Anyone with eyes could see that she was constantly delivering drinks and then it began that tables would order one drink at a time and every time she turned up with their delivery, a bit more of the conversation ensued.

The only thing Callie concentrated on was getting the deliveries right. She didn't pay any attention to what the other servers were doing nor anything else, and thus a pair of striking brown eyes that continually followed her every move was ignored.

As funny as it sounded, she was actually beginning to enjoy herself as the night wore on. It wasn't hard work as some of the members were quite a good laugh and harmless. No one was drunk or belligerent to her and one of the men even proposed marriage to her surprise but since he was a lovely grandfather, she politely declined.

"I think you've made me busier than I've ever been," James groaned, his smile wide and cheerful.

"Oh please. I thought you said it's always like this," she said.

"It is but thanks to you, they're all ordering one or two drinks at a time *and* they hate having one of the other girls delivering to their tables even if that's how it works. So they're trying really hard to time it so that they get you," he said, amused.

Callie wasn't sure if James was just teasing or serious. She had a couple of trays taken off her recently by other servers, who when they saw her heading in their direction, had asked which table she was delivering to and when she replied one of theirs, they promptly took it for her. It hadn't bothered her in the slightest since she felt like she had walked an entire marathon already.

Phoebe on the other hand just beamed every time Callie looked at the woman.

"Here, take this to table nineteen."

She inwardly groaned. This table was the worst she had served all night. They were young men who seemed to be a little more on the loud and obnoxious side. They had also been drinking quite a lot.

Taking their drinks, she tried to be confident but as soon as they saw her coming their way they began acting up.

"Hey sugar, what time do you get off?"

"Come sit on my lap?"

"How do you feel about serving breakfast in bed?"

She ignored all the unpleasant comments that raucously continued but when a hand stroked her bottom and then slid down her leg, she objected.

"Don't touch me," she hissed, trying to put the drinks down as fast as possible.

"Aw, sugar, we're only having fun," the man guffawed, before his hand started at her knees and went up towards her thighs under her skirt.

"I said, get your hands off me!"

She hit him hard on the head with the now empty tray before dashing out of the lounge not caring about people looking as everyone had stopped and turned to see what was happening.

Callie was in tears as Ross found her in the break room.

"Callie, are you okay?" he said, concerned.

As much as this was a gentleman's club, they had strict rules about harassing the servers.

"I'm sorry, I shouldn't have done that but they thought they could touch me," she sobbed.

"Don't be sorry. We don't tolerate that kind of behaviour here. Flirting and friendliness is fine but *no* touching," he said, making her feel a little better. "The girls aren't allowed to do it either, to the patrons."

She looked at him in surprise, sure that he would be angry at her for causing such a scene.

"Really?"

"Really." His emphatic nod reassured her. "And besides, Phoebe's already thrown them out. They won't be welcome back here any time soon."

She felt a wave of relief flood through her.

"Do you want to go home? Its okay, you've done more than enough tonight."

"Yes, please. Can I say goodbye to James and Phoebe first? They've been wonderful."

"Of course. Just know that if you want to work here full-time, you're always welcome. Make sure you come and see me before you leave, okay?"

"Thanks and I'll think about it."

She went and dried her eyes before going out to see James.

"I'm going now and I just wanted to thank you for all your help in showing me the ropes."

"No problem. I'm sorry you had a bunch of morons hit on you, that's frowned upon."

"That's what Ross said."

"Hey, don't forget your tips," he said, nodding towards the jar she had under the bar.

"Oh, I forgot," she said, feeling silly and as she grabbed it realised that it was stuffed full of money. She had no idea how much money was here since she had been too busy to care. Pulling it out was like having Christmas arrive.

"Here," she said, grabbing a fistful of dollars, holding it out to James. "You deserve this as much as I do."

"Thanks, but I think you should keep it all. You deserve it, you worked your arse off tonight." He beamed at her generosity.

"Are you sure?" she said, giving him a chance to change his mind.

"Yes, but thanks."

James was extraordinarily pleased by Callie's offer. He had been here long enough to know what kind of girls the servers were. The ones who offered him tips from their jars were always the ones who would eventually move on to bigger and better. They were also the ones who didn't seemed to be here to either try and snag a rich man, or try to seduce them, or told to move on because eventually they and their work ethic would become slack and lazy.

Callie then went to see Phoebe to thank her and as they were talking, James came over with a tray and a glass on it.

"Before you go, the man at table three would like you to personally deliver him a drink," he said.

She was confused not only because she was leaving but because she hadn't been near table three all night, the server in that area was overly protective of her territory.

"B-but I'm leaving."

"Believe me, you want to do this last one," he winked and handed her the tray. Phoebe also was smiling and Callie didn't understand at all.

"I haven't served that area all night," she said.

"This man's one of our top VIPs. He's lovely. Now off you go," Phoebe said, and before Callie could even say another word, she was being spun around and gently pushed in the direction of the table.

Her legs were shaking as she looked at the handsome man at the table whose eyes seemed to devour her.

She had never seen him before and prayed that it wasn't going to be a repeat of earlier but felt more reassured because both James and Phoebe seemed quite amused by the order.

Trixie, the server for this section saw Callie coming towards her table and went to head her off. There was no way she was letting a little upstart near not only her tables but easily the hottest and wealthiest men in the room.

"Oh, thanks, I'll take that," Trixie said in a sweetly false tone, grabbing the tray off Callie and then turning her back on her.

Since she had almost reached the table, she couldn't help but wonder why the man had asked for her.

Trixie turned on her most flirtatious smile as she delivered the drink but irritation crossed her face at seeing Callie still standing there.

"You can go now," she hissed.

"Actually I specifically asked for her to bring me the drink," the man said, standing, obviously having seen and heard Trixie.

"Oh," Trixie gasped, her eyes fluttering. "And here I was under the impression that you liked the way I've been serving you all evening."

The man simply ignored Trixie's flirting and came closer to Callie making Trixie stomp off in a huff.

"W-why did you want me to bring you a drink?"

Not only was this man's French accent dreamy, his whole self was dreamy. She looked like a deer caught in headlights and had to crane her neck since he was taller than her.

"To make sure that you were okay after those idiots earlier."

His voice caressed her and she briefly closed her eyes.

"I-I'm fine, thank you. I-I was just leaving."

His smile at her answer seemed to dazzle her.

"Please, since you're not working, will you join me for a drink?" he said.

She hesitated because it was against the rules but this man made her want to break them.

"I'm sorry. I need to change and go."

"Can I drop you somewhere then?"

"N-no, I'm fine but thank you for asking," she said, remembering what Phoebe said about this man being a VIP and therefore she didn't want to offend him.

He may have only gotten three hours sleep but Gabe woke up feeling more energised than he had in a long time and knew that last night's dinner with Callie was the reason.

Thinking over what a great time he had laughing and reminiscing about the good old days had worked wonders on him.

Admittedly, at the start she had seemed so on edge and reluctant to even talk about herself which was a problem he had never encountered with any other female that he knew. It wasn't until they were sitting in the kitchen that she truly relaxed and the night flew past.

Thanks to Callie and much to Nigel's astonishment, he was now sitting eating breakfast in the kitchen. When Nigel had politely inquired about the dinner dishes, Gabe couldn't help but cheerfully tell his butler that he had rinsed and put them in the dishwasher.

It was the first time in Gabe's memory that Nigel not only looked gobsmacked but had also tripped over his feet at his employer's answer. Nigel's reaction made Gabe have a silly smile on his face but Nigel being the very proper kind of butler recovered with a simple, "very good, Sir."

The way his morning had started, it could only be a great day, he thought happily to himself. He had a little work to do but then he was meeting up with Luc later tonight at the Club. The two men together was always good fun and hopefully he might even find himself someone to warm his bed.

Gabe was immediately put on high alert and suspicious when his grandfather called him in such a jovial mood. It was so very unlike Fabien that Gabe knew when his grandfather acted like this, he was either up to something, had settled some sort of score, or even better, had made a truckload more money.

Since this time Fabien wasn't discussing money, or gloating of his success, he had to be up to something because he politely summoned — not decreed — his grandson to Paris for dinner on Friday night. Gabe not only suspected it was some kind of trap, he could smell it.

He'd put his loyal assistant, Stefan onto the case on Monday but for now he was finally heading to the Club to meet Luc who hadn't minded one bit that he was late.

Gabe knew his friend would be flirting with all the servers, he always did, but it was Luc's surprise announcement that he would be waiting for Gabe in the ground floor lounge and not the VIP room as usual that had his attention. They never went into that lounge — ever.

Seeing the crush that already was forming in the lounge, he gritted his teeth. That's why they never met down here. Too many people, and most of them wannabe's or idiots just trying to make themselves look notable.

He greeted Rosie and then went into the throng to find his friend. A slight hush fell over the room as people recognised him come in but he ignored them all as he marched straight over to Luc and sat down opposite him.

Now he was going to have to wait forever for a much needed drink to relax but just as he thought it, one was placed on the table in front of him.

Bless Rosie's little heart, he thought gratefully, mentally reminding himself to give her a big tip on the way out. She must have ordered it for him. Normally when VIPs entered, Rosie would advise the floor of their arrival so their preferred drink was waiting as soon as they exited the elevator.

"Why the hell are you sitting in this circus?" he said, irritable.

Normally upon entering *The Century Club* and checking in, Luc would immediately go up to the very top floor for VIP members only but tonight as he flirted with Rosie at the front desk, he was told the latest round of gossip, unsurprised to hear Robyn and Anna were sick. Those two were the kind of women that men like him could see coming a mile away — they were talking money magnets, the more the better. But he also suspected in Anna's case that she was trying to wrangle more money because she was developing an unhealthy drug addiction. He had noticed the glassy look in her eyes the last time he was here.

As he turned to the elevator, movement caught his eye in the ground floor lounge and as he turned to look closer, he grinned. Ignoring the elevator, he instead walked into the lounge and found himself a very comfy chair at an angle that saw the entire room.

"There's a very sexy new server in here. I've been watching her all evening," Luc said, a devilish glint in his eye.

Gabe twisted in his seat to scan the room but couldn't see anyone worth a second glance.

"Really?" he said, sceptical.

"She's not here at the moment. Some idiots hit on her and she gave him a hard smack on the head with her tray," Luc said. "I'm waiting for her to come back. Until then, tell me what's new?"

Gabe told him about his grandfather's very polite and jovial invitation to dinner in Paris on Friday and even Luc had raised his eyebrows with suspicion.

"What does the old man want?"

"Hell if I know." He raked a hand though his hair. "I'm going to get Stefan to start snooping on Monday, but I bet it'll be something that I won't like, it always is."

Gabe noted that Luc was now only half-listening and that something or rather *someone* had taken his friend's attention.

"There she is. Pity you didn't arrive now, I could've got her to bring your drink."

Once again Gabe twisted in his seat and was almost stunned to pick out exactly whom Luc was referring to in an instant among the crowd. The woman, although he couldn't see her face, was like sunshine. He saw all the men's reactions as she walked by or approached their table. They were all drooling.

He had to admit from what little he could see, her figure although petite was curvy and her bottom pert as he watched her walking.

Getting a sore neck from watching he turned back to see Luc grinning.

"Told you. I saw her first."

Gabe's jaw clenched. After starting out so well, his day really was turning into crap.

"Fine," he sighed, resigned to Luc's good luck.

His phone vibrated and taking the call he then wished he hadn't as it was Amélie still moaning about her life on the farm. When he hung up he closed his eyes for a minute and could swear that he was now hearing Callie's voice. Now he knew he was going mad.

Standing up from the table to stretch and tell Luc he was calling it a night, he froze in shock at seeing the woman that his best friend was flirting with.

"Callie?" he rasped in stunned surprise.

A head leant to look around Luc and her eyes widened in shock.

"Gabe?"

As he got a better view of her, he was speechless. The Callie that he had seen last night and the time before looked nothing like the siren standing in front of him right now.

"You two know each other?" Luc's shocked reaction and seeing the way that Callie and Gabe were staring at each other was his answer.

"I thought you said you were unemployed? Why are you working in a place like this?" Gabe said, outraged.

"I *am* unemployed," she hissed, furious at him for embarrassing her. "*My friend* works here and brought me along for a look. They were short-staffed and so they asked me to help them out by delivering drinks." She pointed her finger at him. "What are *you* doing here?"

"I'm a member."

"Why am I not surprised," she said, rolling her eyes.

"Callie, this isn't the place for you."

"Excuse me?" she said, bristling. "I've had a lovely evening working here, thank you. You don't get to tell me where I can and can't work, Gabe."

"Wasn't it you who got hit on earlier tonight? You know Jarrod wouldn't be happy," he said, childishly bringing her brother into the conversation.

"Oh, why don't you just go back to France! *And*, stay out of my life!" she snapped, then stomped away leaving him to explain to Luc what had just happened.

"That's *Callie*?" Luc said, stunned. "The same Callie that used to be your neighbour?"

"Yes," he said, grumpy.

"Wow, somehow I pictured her with pigtails, glasses and braces wearing denim overalls," Luc chuckled. "If my neighbour looked like that, I wouldn't have wanted to move either."

"She didn't look like that back then or even…before," he said, not wanting to think about how beautiful she had become in under twenty-four hours since he had last seen her.

Luc looked at his best friend thoughtfully, knowing he had never seen Gabe act so out of sorts and a secretive smile crossed his lips.

"So you don't mind if I date her then? Since you know her, we'll have something in common."

Gabe was still staring in the direction that Callie had departed and shrugged.

"Whatever, but don't you dare do your love 'em and leave 'em broken hearted crap on her. This is Callie, she deserves more than your playboy ways," he said, almost snarling.

"Understood. No playboy ways."

Gabe's attitude made Luc chuckle as he pondered on what he should do. Finding out that the sexy waitress was Callie from Gabe's childhood was a nice surprise. Hearing the way she talked to him was an even better one. The girl either had no clue as to who Gabe really was or she simply didn't care which made her the only woman in the world who thought that, that wasn't related to him.

Gabe had been grumpy at the sight of his old childhood neighbour especially when she refused to do his bidding. While Luc could put it down to the fact that no one — especially a mere woman — had ever told Gabe no or scolded him, he had seen Gabe's reaction. Gabe hadn't been the least bit fazed by Callie's reaction so it had to be something else.

Yes, he was going to woo Callie and see which way the wind blew for Gabe and if Luc was lucky, maybe Callie could be the one to make his best friend settle down.

Callie was in the changing room pacing and furious with Gabe and his stupid accusations like she had lied to him. What were the odds of seeing him last night unemployed and then seeing him tonight with temporary employment?

Finally she stopped pacing and looked at herself in the mirror. It sounded silly even to herself but even she thought that she looked different to when she stood in this very same spot only hours earlier marvelling at how Hazel had transformed her from drab to fab.

She seemed more confident and she liked this new her. Maybe she should take Ross up on his offer to work here full-time. Having men flirt with her was good for her ego and what made it better was that it was harmless.

The tips were fantastic, she had to admit, not that she had actually counted yet, but she knew they were all sizeable notes.

Changing, she then went to say goodbye to Ross.

"Thank you for everything."

He looked up at her with a tired look on his face.

"No, thank you."

He smiled coming around from behind his desk and held out a piece of paper to her.

"What's this?" she said, warily taking it from him then teased, "Not your number?"

"No, it's your night's wages," he laughed.

"B-but I thought that the tips —"

"Are a bonus for a great job well done."

She looked at the cheque in her hand and gasped as her eyes widened at the number written on it.

"This can't be right. I didn't do much."

"Believe me, from what I've heard, you did more than anyone else did all night. You had everyone eating out of the palm of your hand."

Everyone except one, she thought miserably as she went home. Why did she have to run into Gabe? If only she had just met his hunky friend alone but now the gloss had been taken off tonight thanks to Gabe and his insufferable big brother attitude.

And how did Gabe know about tonight's incident? He couldn't have been at the Club because he would have voiced his objections and given her an earful a lot earlier. And, fancy threatening to tell Jarrod, she continued to fume, like her brother would care. She wasn't doing anything wrong as Gabe well knew but she was sure that he'd twist it in such a way that Jarrod could only come up with the wrong conclusion.

Lately it seemed that every French person she knew had it in for her. Well, the lesson had finally been learnt…stay away from the French. She'd be a lot happier that way.

It was easier said than done.

She had hardly made it out the club's door when Jarrod called. Bloody Gabe and his big mouth. Seriously, was he that childish that he had to call Jarrod — who had his own problems with Amélie, Gabe's own sister she might add — to tell her brother that his little sister was working at a place unfit for someone as nice and wholesome as her.

Nice and wholesome? Jeez, that made her seem like some innocent who knew nothing about the world.

Now she had just finished getting an earful from her brother about her unsavoury delinquent lifestyle. After explaining Gabe's obvious *misunderstanding*, Jarrod had calmed down a lot but she knew that the next time she saw Mr Pain-in-her-arse, she was going to be giving him a strongly worded piece of her mind.

To think, she had only become reacquainted with the aggravating man a week ago after years of silence. If she had known just how much of a pain he was going to be, she would never have caught up with him again. Even better, she'd have slammed the door in his face with delightful satisfaction.

Having Gabe come barrelling back into her life like a tornado was not what she wanted or needed.

Working herself up into a fine rage, she stomped her way to the Tube trying to calm down, but all the way, all she did was fume.

Chapter 5

Gabe was once again meeting Luc at *The Century Club*, but this time for lunch. He needed to discuss his grandfather and Luc knew Fabien well enough to understand Gabe's aggravation and suspicions.

They arrived at the same time and as they went in and saw Rosie, Gabe couldn't help but wonder if Callie was working at the Club or not. He had talked to Jarrod and made it sound like it was more of a Club with special favours knowing that Jarrod would then get on Callie's case about it. As he glanced into the ground floor lounge, Luc who hadn't missed what his friend was doing threw back his head in laughter.

"You're checking to see if she's here," Luc said to Gabe's irritation.

"No, I wasn't. I was just seeing how busy it was," he said, turning to Rosie. "Rosie, can you let me know if Callie Harrison ever becomes an employee here."

Seeing Luc's smirk made him even more annoyed.

Rosie looked at her VIP guest with a slightly puzzled look on her face. Gabriel St Croix was one of the nicer VIPs along with his friend, Luc Grenier.

"Sure. I don't know the name," she said.

"She worked here on Saturday night as a temp," Luc grinned.

"Oh, she's the girl that everyone's talking about," realisation dawned on Rosie's face. "I know Ross and Phoebe and even James hope she joins us," she said, unaware of Gabe's concern.

Gabe's jaw tightened at the praise for Callie. Luc just continued to chuckle to himself.

"That's her. Come on, Gabe, let's go eat, I'm starving. Thanks, Rosie."

Gabe let Luc lead him over to the elevator but was dying to wipe that silly grin off his friend's face.

"Oh, would you just stop it," he snapped, as they entered the elevator, but Luc kept that face the entire silent ride up to the VIP lounge.

As soon as the doors opened, Robyn and Anna were both there to greet them, a surprise since they never did day shifts but maybe they were being punished by Ross.

"Gentlemen, it's lovely to see you. I'm sorry that we weren't here the other night, I heard that you ended up down on the ground floor," Robyn said, trying to sound sympathetic but her hint of a smirk showed that she thought they hadn't stayed up in the VIP room because the two women hadn't been there. Anna too, had the same smug look on her face.

"Believe me, the view on the ground floor on Friday night was sexy. Kept me entertained for hours," Luc said, crushing their arrogant smugness.

The smiles promptly vanished because the women knew exactly who Luc was referring to. Gossip about the temporary girl had spread fast and Ross had also gloated to them when they decided to return to work.

"Oh, and Anna," Luc said, taking his drink as Anna looked at him in anticipation. "You need to ditch the drugs, honey. They're making your skin look sallow and malnourished."

Anna's jaw dropped and she looked like she was ready to cry at Luc's comment. Gabe had to admit to himself that it was true though, Anna used to be beautiful but lately, she was looking very haggard.

"Yes, I agree. Do something about it or we'll be advising Ross to move you *downstairs*."

It was one of the dreaded things about working in a place where everyone understood the hierarchy. Moving *down* was the kiss of death that then led to oblivion.

Now Anna was in tears and Robyn who was supposed to be her friend, moved slightly away from her. She didn't want to be moved *downstairs* just because of Anna's drug problem and knew that being associated so closely with her, whatever happened to Anna, she too could be tarred with the same brush.

Ross had vehemently refused to give them any more money even though they were the Club's top servers. Now that Anna's drug problem had come to light, Robyn was going to have to distance herself and make sure that Ross knew that she was still at the top of her game, that her diva attitude was just an aberration.

"Good call," Luc said as they sat down knowing that Robyn was following them closely.

"I thought so. Especially when their faces fell at the mention of Friday." They ordered lunch and got down to business.

"So what's happened with Fabien?" Luc said. "Has Stefan found anything out?"

"No." Gabe rubbed his chin. "That's the weird thing. Stefan usually manages to find out *something*, but he's gotten nowhere so the answer is either that grand-père is holding something so close to his chest that no one else knows, which is like him, or that its private St Croix family business."

"Its personal family business. Just think, Fabien was happy that day he *invited* you to dinner on Friday. You know Fabien, he never invites, he always orders even if it's for a special occasion. No, that wily old man definitely has something up his sleeve."

Luc was right. His grandfather *never* invited anyone, he always ordered people to be at an event. And the worst thing was, he suspected that he was the only one invited which meant it had to be personal St Croix family business. A sliver of dread snaked up his spine causing him to shiver.

They talked about other things like how Chantel was managing with the new au pair and her marriage hitting a bit of a speed bump.

"According to Chantel, Claude has been seriously putting in overtime to make it up to her. Showering her with gifts and romance. She thinks that baby number two might even be on the way, they're having that much sex," Luc said.

"Thanks, now there's an image I don't need."

"That's what I thought when she overshared with me so I figured as my best friend, you can share too," Luc chuckled.

"Did I tell you that Callie is, was, an au pair?"

"No."

"Well, I only found out but if I had known earlier I would have recommended her to Chantel."

"She qualified?"

"Not sure." He frowned. "I would have checked into it all first, of course."

"Speaking of Callie, do you have her number? I'd like to call her, see if she'd like to catch up for a coffee or something," Luc said, nonchalant but could see Gabe tense before shrugging.

"Sure. Just remember what I said."

Gabe's tone may have sounded casual and light but Luc could feel the strength of his best friend's warning like an icy polar blast.

"I will," he grinned.

Gabe's week went from bad to worse and yet, here he was going to Paris because his grandfather commanded it in the most polite and jovial way.

The fact that Stefan hadn't been able to find out any kind of information on what tonight was about had Gabe on edge.

Knowing his grandfather so well, the happy mood Fabien was in meant that Gabe was about to become miserable…extremely miserable.

He was also irritated by Luc wanting to date Callie. Yes, Luc was his best friend but his reputation wasn't one of serious boyfriend, it was more of a playboy nature and Callie was too nice for someone like Luc. Girls like Callie were just babies in their world and he didn't want Callie to get hurt.

That was another thing that annoyed him, since when did he care about a woman's feelings? He and Luc were cut from the same cloth and used women liked disposable tissues. Maybe that's why he was worried about Callie, because he knew her like he had known no other woman in his life.

Before he could even decide whether he wanted to tell Luc to leave Callie alone or not, the plane had landed and he had to get his mind focussed on dinner.

He felt the same awe every time the car went through the wrought iron gates to the château. It was a beautiful piece of architecture which made it a pity that his memories of the place weren't ever happy. The small house on the other side of the world that could have easily fit into the garage of this place, was where the happiest times of his life occurred, not in this palace that was fit for a king.

As always, every servant bowed and scraped as he walked past until he reached the inner sanctum of his grandfather's wing. He was announced and strolled in looking every inch the confident St Croix grandson but in reality, he could feel his nerves jangling.

Fabien happily greeted his grandson with the perfunctory kiss on both cheeks.

"Gabriel, welcome. How was your flight?"

"Fine, grand-père. Now tell me, what's got you in such a good mood?"

If his grandfather could act happy so could he, but always with cautious wariness so his guard would constantly be up and he could hopefully see the trap coming.

"Dinner with my favourite grandson, of course."

Now Gabe knew without a doubt that his grandfather was definitely up to something. Not only did Fabien rule the family with an iron fist but he was trying to butter up Gabe with the 'favourite grandson' tag.

Marcel, his cousin and the only other boy in the family, was usually used as competition against him if Fabien was trying to get Gabe to do something that he didn't want to do. It was always blackmail — pure and simple. To Fabien, Marcel wasn't considered a true St Croix but, when he needed to keep Gabe in line, Marcel was.

Marcel was also an idiot. He was a wastrel who lived only for himself and didn't even work. Oh, he had the high paying job with the fancy title but that's all it was. He hadn't actually worked to earn either. He had gotten them from his father who was a wealthy businessman.

Gabe's aunt and Marcel's mother, Hélène had spoilt her only child rotten from the moment he was born and thus Marcel felt entitled just by existing.

Now Gabe and his grandfather sat having a lovely dinner with Fabien being very chatty and seemingly interested in how Gabe was actually doing when Gabe knew that Fabien had people keeping tabs on him. Fabien had done it to everyone in his family, all their lives.

"So, Gabriel, you'll be thirty soon. Any big plans for your birthday?"

The seemingly innocent and cheerfully posed question had him tightening the grip on his knife.

"Not yet. Haven't really thought about it to be honest. Its ages away," he said, giving a dismissive shrug.

"Did you know that all the St Croix men married by the time they were thirty?"

"No, I didn't," he said, not missing a beat but his heart had started accelerating because he now knew exactly where this was all going.

"Yes, generations of St Croix men all married by thirty. Not just married to any woman either. They married only the crème of Society. Do you know why?" Fabien dangled the bait knowing that Gabe would ask the question.

"No, why?"

"Because if they don't, they give up their claim to the St Croix fortune and are disinherited. It has been the rule since the beginning. Our family didn't get to where we are today by just good luck. We are related to royalty and as such, we live by a different set of rules than others. This is one of them."

"Fine, I'll consider it."

That's when Fabien's demeanour changed to the one Gabe had known all his life as his grandfather's fist banged down loudly on the table.

"Non! You will not *consider* it. You will be marrying!" the older man roared. "I have a list of all potential and *acceptable* brides for you. You will select one and court her and then on your birthday, you will marry her."

"No. I'll consider it but I will not be bullied into marrying some brainless air-head for the sake of the family fortune," he said, furious at the edict.

"Stop being so stubborn and ridiculous! You need to do your duty just as others before you have done. If you don't, everything goes to Marcel and you will be left penniless and out on your ear. Don't expect me to keep you on in your job and don't think that you'd be getting another one because I won't let that happen. Pick a girl and marry her!"

Gabe laughed at his grandfather trying to goad him into doing what he wanted.

"Oui, give it all to Marcel. The family fortune will be gone just like that." He snapped his fingers. "*All* the St Croix legacy will vanish. Even this fancy palace will be sold because Marcel is a selfish wastrel who only cares about himself. So good luck with that."

Gabe knew that his grandfather knew he was right, which was why Fabien was demanding he marry because he would never leave the family fortune to Marcel.

Fabien's face was going deep red at his grandson's rebelliousness.

"I see that you have no sense of family duty. Very well, you make your choice, you can live with the consequences."

Now Gabe was worried, his grandfather usually raged but this quietness was new and that meant that he was even more dangerous.

"Look, I said I'd consider the list." It was an olive branch. "But honestly grand-père, I need to find a wife to make me happy. I'm not living in a loveless marriage."

Fabien looked at his grandson, disgusted that his sense of duty to the business and family wasn't first and foremost. Had he loved Vivienne when he married her? Of course not, but he had done his duty. Had François loved Marielle? Probably not but now look at them, they were comfortable together and probably loved each other in their own way.

Softening his tone because he needed Gabriel to marry and knew that he was cornered, he said, "Just marry any one of them. Wait a respectable amount of time when you've had your heirs and then find yourself a mistress."

Gabe looked at his grandfather in shock.

"If I'm going to do all that, I might as well just divorce the woman."

"Non!" Anger crossed Fabien's face again. "St Croix's *do not* divorce *ever*! *Do you understand?*"

Oh, he understood all right. St Croix's did their duty and then did whatever the hell they wanted not caring about anyone but themselves.

"Just give me the list and I'll think about it."

It was a truce of sorts but for Gabe, it was his future and he had a lot to think about. He also wasn't about to let his grandfather bully him into marriage, that was for sure. He needed to talk to his father and see the list before any decision would be made.

Fabien wanted Gabriel's assurance that he would do as asked before he departed but his stubborn, mule-headed grandson wasn't about to do that. He should never have allowed Gabriel to work and live in England. He should have made him stay here in Paris and therefore could have managed his life better but at the time he had needed Gabriel to stay in Europe more, so he had given in.

His daughter, Hélène had been beside herself with excitement when she realised that Gabe was coming up to thirty without any prospect of a bride and had gloated about Marcel being Fabien's heir.

Fabien couldn't be annoyed with Hélène and her greed because that's how they were raised, but he'd rather give it all away before he let Marcel inherit and ruin a dynastic legacy. What generations of St Croix men didn't know until the death of their father was that there was no rule to say that the men had to marry by thirty. It was more that one of the St Croix ancestors had found a way to keep his children in line and to settle down.

Turning it into a marriage that suited the family was also another great reason and thus each generation after were told the same story to coerce them into making great marriage matches and to ensure the family lineage. Each man that had married did their duty to the family and now it was Gabriel's turn whether he liked it or not.

It was only during the flight back to London that Gabe felt safe enough to open the piece of paper to look at the names of the women his grandfather considered his match.

Looking at it in dismay, he immediately struck off the top five since he knew that there was no way they would be a marriage made in heaven but more like a marriage made in hell and he would at least like to have a wife he could get along with civilly.

The next five names he also struck off as he knew the women, had even slept with them and knew that they wouldn't be any more faithful to him as he would be to them. No, he needed a wife that would be faithful since he certainly would be faithful to them.

That left the last five. Some of the names he didn't know and others were… he heaved a sigh and felt a headache coming on. He'd get Stefan to discreetly investigate the last five women and then he could make a more informed decision.

The first thing he did upon his arrival back in London was phone Luc. He didn't really want to rehash all this but he needed his friend to rant and rave too.

Hearing his friend's explanation for being unable to catch up until tomorrow, Gabe threw his phone at the ground smashing it in fury.

Luc was out on a date with Callie.

Callie had been surprised to receive a phone call from Luc Grenier, Gabe's friend. At first she had thought it was Gabe from that dreamy French accent, but then realised her mistake and stupidly wondered how she could ever have gotten them mixed up in the first place, especially when Luc was charming and not snarling and growling at her like Gabe.

Luc had rung to ask if Callie would like to have coffee with him. She had politely declined but then he had used Gabe as his bait telling her that Gabe had told him so many hilarious and wonderful stories about his time in New Zealand that he too wanted to become friends with her since Gabe held her in such high regard.

It was such a snow job that she would have been stupid not to have recognised it a mile away but Luc's French accent really was dreamy. Then he totally got her attention when he mentioned that Gabe was currently in France and had said that they should get together.

Now that had taken her aback. Gabe had told Luc that she and Luc should get together? Why? Did Gabe really think that they could all be happy friends? Not after what happened at the Club and definitely not because she was still unemployed. She didn't even have the amount of money that they would keep in their wallet.

Still, she agreed somewhat reluctantly and was unsure whether it was a good idea or not but once she had said yes, the delight she had heard in Luc's voice was quite an ego boost.

Then she had asked where to meet him and he had said not to worry that he'd send a car for her. Was this what all wealthy men did? Just send cars for their dates? It just wasn't normal to her.

Resigned to the fact that she was now going for coffee with a man that she had briefly met once, in a car that he was sending, to a place she had no idea about, she could only hope and pray that what she wore was suitable.

She was already nervous and on tenterhooks about the whole meeting including what she was wearing, but seeing where the driver had stopped to drop her off, she almost flatly refused to get out and demand that he take her back home.

It was meant to be coffee! she wanted to scream as clearly Luc's version of coffee was very different to hers.

He was waiting outside one of the city's most expensive restaurants and she could only be grateful that she was wearing her best dress and not jeans since she would have been even more mortified than she already felt.

"You look beautiful," he said, kissing both of her cheeks and smelling the faint fragrance of lavender on her. He couldn't help but note that Callie was nervous.

He then mentally kicked himself for picking such an expensive restaurant. He was just so used to women always wearing designer clothes and wanting to be seen at the most expensive restaurants that he had in turn just lazily done his usual date night.

"T-thank you."

Seeing Luc standing there looking very handsome in a pin-striped suit and every inch a French model had her feeling even more anxious.

"I-I thought we were only having coffee," she blurted out, not wanting to go into the restaurant and be laughed at.

Quickly he looked around and breathed a sigh of relief when he saw a café across the road.

"But of course, you didn't think we were going in there, did you?" he teased, motioning to the restaurant they were both standing outside and the flush of her cheeks at her mistake bowled him over.

"So where are we going?" she said.

"Over there." He pointed across the road. "It was easier for the driver to drop you on this side, that's why he stopped here."

The way he explained it so easily, Callie felt like such an idiot and so relieved at the same time. She had honestly thought that Luc had wanted to take her to dinner in that expensive place but now that she knew he meant what he had said, she relaxed.

Luc marvelled at how easily he could lie, even though he had years of practise. He knew if he had even tried to take Callie into the restaurant she would have just run off. Now seeing her relax, he sensed that keeping his word would mean more to her than a fancy dinner. That alone was quite a novelty.

"Sorry, I didn't mean to overreact but I'm not dressed for a restaurant like that and you did say coffee, not dinner," she said, unable to look at him for that's how foolish she was feeling.

"Ma belle, I would not care if you were wearing a sack but I know that you women get all nervous and funny if you don't look the right part," he smoothly said. "Besides I think getting to know each other over a coffee is more relaxing, oui?"

The blinding smile that she gave him almost knocked him off his feet and he knew that Callie was definitely a one in a million kind of woman. It was the most genuine smile he had ever seen.

Like Gabe, he had grown up wealthy and being best friends with someone like Gabriel St Croix just made you even more of a magnet to all kinds of women, especially those who liked rich men.

Now basking in the glow of a smile like Callie's, Luc knew that a man wouldn't care less if he were the poorest man on earth if a woman smiled at him like that. No wonder Gabe had been protective of Callie, she was definitely special and only a fool wouldn't try to have someone like her as his wife.

Wife? Whoa, where did that come from? He may be enamoured with her but he definitely wasn't looking for a wife. He had far too many oats to sow before he was ready to settle down. As taken as he was with Callie, she didn't have that je ne sais quoi that completely captivated him.

"Oui," she said with a firm nod as they walked across the road and went into the very quiet café.

After spending two hours in her company constantly laughing, Luc was enjoying himself immensely. He was also mentally revising his earlier thought about Callie not being his kind of woman. She really was a delight.

The stories she told of Gabe when he was younger were hilarious and she had just finished another one when his phone rang and it was his best friend.

It was as if Callie sensed it was Gabe calling even though Luc never said his name and they spoke in rapid French. The conversation had been very short but she knew because of the way he looked at her. It was with the eyes of victory and she almost shivered at the thought that she was some kind of trophy because she wasn't.

Gabe was her friend and Luc, well Luc was lovely but she sensed that the man was a playboy. From the moment they sat down and the waitress arrived, he couldn't help but check her out and then discreetly continued to do so like Callie wouldn't notice.

He had only stopped in the last half hour because the waitress had left for the day but not before advising them of that fact with eyes that devoured him and offering her number to him by writing it on the back of the receipt.

The shock on Callie's face would have been comical if anyone had seen it as she couldn't believe her eyes. Sure, she and Luc weren't an item but if they were, it was…she didn't know what it was because she was speechless.

"Does that happen to you a lot?" she said, finally finding her voice.

"Oui." He grinned.

"Well, sucks to be your girlfriend then."

"Callie, you're like an innocent little butterfly. How do you think that the women become my girlfriends?" he laughed.

"The usual way," she mocked. "You see someone, you ask them out, you then begin dating."

"Yes, but then you see someone else and they intrigue you so isn't it only fair to see if they are the right person? After all, you wouldn't want to miss meeting your possible *soul mate*," he said, using the words most women loved to think of in their romantic future.

She looked at him as if he had grown two heads. Was this really what he did? She felt better that she wasn't his girlfriend.

"I see. So what you're saying is that you'll just keep going through women until you either run out or somehow, by a holy miracle, find your soul mate. You're not going to even bother making sure that you can weather the good and bad times together. You just want sex."

Luc looked at Callie who sounded almost angry at the way he viewed women but he could understand it.

"You forget, most of the women that I've been with know the rules. They want to be associated with me for my money, my friendship with Gabe, and the five minutes of fame that it gives them. Not to mention the perks of jewellery and clothes that I gift them along with the hot sex of course. You can't be that naïve, sweet Callie, that you too wouldn't do that?" he said, amused by her indignant nature.

"Of course not!" she said. "I'm not for sale at any price unless it's for love. I don't need jewels or fame. I want a husband that loves me and I love him."

"Ah, and here I was thinking that there's no more innocent people in the world. You've proven me wrong, sweet Callie. Whose to say that you don't meet a man and fall in love, marry and have kids before you realise that he's cheating on you, has done so ever since you met and declared your undying love?"

She hated him. Right now, she really hated Luc. Tears were threatening to make their presence felt and she wasn't about to give him the satisfaction of seeing her cry.

"You're probably right but at least I'm willing to try, to believe in love. Not like you, you're just a user and I can't wait for the day that you get your heart broken. Then you'll know what it feels like."

She ran out the door and he just watched and sighed. He had been a bastard to her but ever since Gabe had called, he knew deep down that she wasn't even close to being the one for him and he wanted to make sure that she knew it too.

Staring at his phone, he took the piece of paper that the busty blonde waitress had given him and called it.

Callie had gone home and cried her eyes out wondering what she had done to make Luc be such a jerk. She thought that they were having a nice time getting to know each other until Gabe called. That had to be it. Gabe had gone all big brother on Luc and that had to be why he had blatantly flirted with the waitress in front of her.

Gabe.

The continual thorn in her side who knew no boundaries nor cared even if he did. Oh, she was going to have words with him. Then she shook her head and changed her mind. No, she wasn't going to have words with him because she was never going to talk to him again.

Yes, better plan. No talking or seeing Gabriel St Croix again.

Chapter 6

Gabe was catching up with Luc at *The Century Club* and felt like a complete zombie. Ever since he had gotten back from France, work seemed to be busier than normal.

He also hadn't heard a peep from his grandfather making him suspicious that Fabien knew Stefan was doing some checking and thus his grandfather was leaving him alone…for now.

To be honest, he had also been avoiding Luc and sensed that his best friend had likewise been doing the same, but now it seemed that they were ready to discuss whatever it was that was the cause of the avoidance…Callie.

Never had any woman ever come between them — and many had tried — and they had always managed to laugh it off but Callie was different. Callie was…Callie.

Moodily, he exited the elevator to find Robyn handing him his drink. He wasn't in the mood for niceties since he needed to clear the air with Luc and therefore didn't even acknowledge her with pleasantries. He just found a seat far away from anyone so that he and Luc would have some privacy.

Luc arrived a few minutes later and much like Gabe had done, gotten his drink and marched straight over to his friend and sat down.

"So, how's Fabien?" Luc said as he sat but honestly, he felt a little hurt that Gabe hadn't called him to catch up apart from that one time when he got back. Did him going out for one coffee with Callie stick in his friend's craw that much?

Gabe's face turned into an almost scowl. Yes, he wanted to talk about his grandfather but not right now. Now he needed answers.

"Are you seeing Callie?"

"No. What on earth made you think that?" Luc said, stunned by the ferocity of the attack.

"So you did just sleep with her and dump her, breaking her heart after I explicitly told you not to," he growled.

"What the hell are you talking about? Is that what she said? Well she's lying," Luc said. "We had coffee, nothing more, full stop. I haven't seen her since."

The tension in Gabe left as he relaxed back into his chair knowing that his friend wouldn't lie but that didn't explain why Callie wasn't talking to him, was avoiding him like the plague.

"Then why the hell won't she answer my calls or return them?"

Guilt flickered across Luc's face and Gabe felt rage boiling again inside him.

"What the hell did you do?"

"It wasn't what I did, per se, it's more that we had a little honest heart to heart and I may have told her that she was much too delicate and that someone like me would chew her up and spit her out."

"What? She likes you and you went and crushed her?" he snapped, getting ready to rise from his chair and thump his best friend.

"Of course not. Would you just sit there and hear me out."

Although Gabe did as he was asked, his hands gripped the chair so tightly that his knuckles were white.

Seeing that Gabe was close to erupting, Luc quickly began to explain what had happened. As Luc talked, Gabe began to relax understanding just what his friend had done and now he understood that Callie might be slightly bruised by Luc's honesty, but it still didn't quite explain why Callie wasn't talking to him unless it was because Luc was his best friend.

Now that they had cleared the air and both men had calmed down somewhat, Gabe explained to his best friend what exactly Fabien had wanted.

"Are you kidding? Please tell me you're kidding." Luc stared incredulously at his friend, completely gobsmacked.

The serious look on Gabe's face only proved that he wasn't kidding.

"At least tell me that you told him where to shove it?"

"No, I left with a sort of compromise, but not before he threatened to fire me and make sure that I never worked ever again so would either have to beg him for money or kowtow to his demands, dancing to his tune for the rest of my life, like that is ever going to happen."

"Do you think that it's true what he's asking you to do?"

"Well I did talk to my father, and dad said that he was given the same ultimatum but it was different because he was already half in love with mum so it was no hardship. He told me to do whatever I wanted because he'd stand by and support me. I think he still feels guilty about returning to France all those years ago. I didn't have the heart to tell him I've got my own money and would be fine."

"Wow, so who was on the list?" Luc said, eager, yet scared to know. He screwed up his face after Gabe told him the first five names. "Forget it, tell Fabien to go jump."

Gabe smiled at his friend's remark knowing he thought the same thing about those women. Then he advised the next five names he had already discounted.

"Talk about ho-hum." Luc gave a little mock yawn. "Is he trying to get you to slit your own wrists and make your life an absolute misery or something?"

"Exactly what I thought," Gabe said. "The last five names had potential but only because I don't know them and so I asked Stefan to do some very discreet but very in-depth digging for me."

"Wouldn't Fabien already have done all that? You know the wily old bastard would know all their secrets."

"Yes, but I still think grand-père's checking up on me because he hasn't turfed me out on my backside like he threatened so I'm using Stefan's snooping to buy me some time until I can figure out what to do."

He told his friend the last five names and Luc was quick to strike one off the list.

"Well you can cross her off. I understand that her father has some huge debts and up to now has managed to keep them quiet. He won't be able to much longer from what I understand. I wonder why Fabien would still put her on your list?"

"Because they're still an important family, can trace relatives back to royalty like ours. If I chose her, you can bet your bottom dollar that Fabien would wipe their debts so no one knew. Then he'd have them dancing to his tune like puppets and they wouldn't even see it coming because they'd be too excited by the dollar signs. Yet, another reason why I would never choose her," he said. "Resentment."

"How about just eloping with the next girl you see. No scratch that, the next *hot and sexy* woman you see," Luc said, a twinkle in his eye.

For the first time in weeks he laughed and knew telling Luc was a good idea. Luc really was the best friend anyone could ask for.

Luc was helping Gabe on the sly to suss out all the women left on the list. They had narrowed it down to three — Emme, Zazabee and Holly. To be honest, Zazabee was borderline because of her name alone. Neither man could imagine having a wife or child with the name but as it stood, she had some noteworthy credentials.

They were at the Club discussing Luc's latest spying mission on Zazabee.

"You can definitely cross her off," Luc said, emphatic and not beating around the bush as he came and sat down by his friend.

"Oh?" Gabe's eyebrows arched with curiosity.

"Yes. Let's just say that if her name wasn't bad enough then her non-stop baby voice would drive you insane in the first five minutes, not to mention the fact that all she talks about is sex, quite crudely I might add." Luc screwed up his face before taking a gulp of drink looking like he wanted to down the whole thing but decided against it.

"Why Lucien, are you blushing?" he teased. "I didn't think that anything could surprise you anymore."

His friend shot him a look that only made Gabe chuckle.

"I don't think half the things that woman said was fit for anyone's ears. She even made *me* feel prudish."

"Thank God, it was you and not me then," Gabe said, roaring with laughter.

"You owe me big time for that alone."

"Duly noted. Okay, so porn star Zazabee is out. That leaves only Emme and Holly. Any thoughts?"

"After what I've just been through…no," Luc shivered.

Gabe wanted to laugh some more but he saw something over Luc's shoulder that caught his eye and a scowl immediately crossed his face instead.

"I thought we were over this," he muttered and stood.

Luc, unsure what was happening, looked in the direction that Gabe was striding and immediately felt very sorry for the woman his best friend was about to confront.

Callie had taken Ross up on his offer of work to his delight and had been working at *The Century Club* for three glorious weeks. After last time, she didn't want to work nights unless James and Phoebe were with her to which Ross instantly agreed making her feel better.

She started off on the ground floor with James, who was ecstatic to see her again. Trixie had been a little miffed by her appearance and simply ignored her but Callie didn't care, she was here to work not make friends.

Ross was no dummy and ever since the night that Callie had worked, he had heard customers talking about her and knew that having Callie onboard would make a lot of the members very happy indeed. Since word had gotten around about the new server, he had been inundated with polite yet curious enquiries as to when the woman would be working again and on which floor.

Such interest in a new girl was unheard of and it was even worse for Ross when he had to tell everyone that the woman had only been temporary. That had then brought in a lot of offers from men saying that they were willing to pay her wages if that's what it took to get her back and these were men who hadn't even seen her.

Ross called it the Callie effect as members explained that Callie was like a bright ray of sunshine whose cheery smile and personality made everyone she came into contact with feel like they were important. She treated everyone the same and wasn't trying to make more tips, she was a genuine people person.

Thanks to Callie's sudden employment, more men were happily having lunch or meetings at the Club knowing that she'd be working and yet she seemed to take it all in her stride and couldn't see what the fuss was about.

Because of the unprecedented interest in her, they had tried giving her a section but once that was filled, members actually put themselves on some kind of unspoken gentleman's waiting list to the floor manager's amusement and when someone vacated a table then someone else would replace them.

Although they knew it wasn't Callie's fault, the other servers were a little disgruntled with their clients moving tables so to stop any kind of revolt, Ross decided that Callie should be like she had been on that first night — a floater — and that way she got to talk to everyone which kept everyone happy.

Callie especially enjoyed the changes as she enjoyed talking to all the different men. Some of them were funny and lovely, others bordered on crude and she tried hard to not have to spend that long with them because she didn't want a repeat of that first night.

She actually preferred the day shifts because she found the men a bit friendlier, a lot more sober and generally less obnoxious. She hadn't realised until one of the other servers pointed it out that whichever floor Callie happened to be working on was always the busiest and thus the other servers were happy because that meant they also got better tips for the day.

Today she was on the VIP floor for the first time and had to admit it was quite a lot different than the other floors. Everything on the VIP floor was ornate and plush. Even the glasses they used were of the finest quality crystal. The uniform she wore although very similar to her usual one, had a vest and the blouses were a lovely burgundy red instead of white.

While she had expected it to be busy, what she hadn't expected was to know a lot of the gentlemen who entered. She had met them on the lower floors she worked and not realised that they were VIPs and the surprise on her face showed every single time she saw someone she recognised.

To Callie, she seemed to be repeating herself over and over saying, "I didn't realise that you were a VIP."

Every man beamed and seemed to fall under her spell a little more especially since she remained the same friendly and effervescent person she normally was after finding out the truth.

Throughout the day she had been asked out on many a date which she would politely laugh and decline, treating each offer as something the men couldn't possibly be serious about.

After having a break, she came back onto the floor and it was almost as if a runaway train was barrelling down the track at full speed and heading straight towards her. She was frozen to the spot unable to move or look away.

Gabe was striding towards her in with an unmistakable look of seriousness and it was directed right at her judging by his face that not only looked like thunder but his eyes glittered with anger.

Grabbing her by the arm, he pulled her to one side.

"What the hell are you doing working here?" he growled. "I thought we discussed this."

Callie blinked, her mind slowly recovering from her stunned surprise to answer.

"You don't own me," she hissed, keeping her voice low so no one could overhear. "I need a job. Unlike you, I actually need money and have to work to get it. Besides, I like this place. Everyone's friendly and the tips and pay are fantastic."

Before he could respond, someone interrupted with a clearing of their throat.

"Is everything all right here, Callie? St Croix isn't bothering you, is he?"

Callie heard the apprehension in the man's voice as she turned to see Peter Lehman standing there and beyond him all eyes were also glued in their direction. Gabe gave a low growl.

"No, I'm fine but thank you so much for you concern, Peter." She sweetly smiled at the man, who flushed at the compliment, before shooting Gabe a look that he could only assume was some kind of warning before leaving them alone.

"Oh my God, half the men, if not all of them are in love with you," he said as Peter walked off and seeing all the concern around the room on the men's faces for Callie's well-being. "They're ready to beat me to a pulp and make themselves feel like superheroes coming to the rescue of the damsel in distress."

"Don't be stupid," she chided. "They're just customers who happen to be friendly, unlike you."

Irritation shot through him that she had a stack of admirers ready to take on a St Croix even if they were scared witless, but Callie clearly inspired all these men to be heroic for her.

"Now, if you're finished your big brother act, I have work to do," she snapped, annoyed by his high-handedness that he thought that he could just come in here and run roughshod over her.

As she walked off, she smiled at the entire room making sure that all the men knew she appreciated their lovely gesture but when it came to Gabriel St Croix, she could hold her own.

Gabe stood there fuming as Little Miss Sunshine entranced the whole room with her smile and the sway of her hips. No wonder they were willing to take a beating for her. If she smiled at him like that, he would probably be acting the same silly way.

What grated on him even more was the first table she went to and every table after that, everyone was offering their concerns to her and he knew it because of all the quick glances directed his way. He wanted to snort at their stupidity — like he would hurt Callie — although right now he was quite irritated with her.

Callie continued on with her job pretending Gabe didn't exist and made sure to visit Luc before Gabe returned to his seat after he had left to take a phone call.

"Would you like another drink?" she said, seeing his glass was empty.

"Enjoy poking an angry bear, do you?" he said, amused.

"Not particularly but that bear's a bit overprotective when it's not even warranted."

"Oh, I think it's warranted. You have the entire room eating out of your hand."

"That's what Gabe said, but you and he seem to be the only ones who think that. Oops, here he comes. Drink?"

"No, thanks. I want to make sure I'm dead sober to watch the next instalment of the Callie and Gabe Show. It's bound to be riveting."

Callie quickly scampered away before Gabe could have more words with her.

"Just what were you two so chummy about?" he snapped.

"Calm down. I was just asking if she liked to play with fire, that's all."

"And?"

"It seems that she does. Although I think she likens it to it as a small match rather than a blazing inferno."

"Just what I thought, she has no idea what danger she's putting herself in by working here."

Luc observed Gabe. His best friend's body was a tight ball of tension about to explode.

"She's as safe as all the others, as you well know," he said. "She was right about you being overprotective though."

"*Please*...I am not," Gabe snorted. "I'm doing exactly what Jarrod would do if he were here."

Luc didn't reply, not because he didn't know Jarrod, but more because if he said anything else it would probably be the straw that broke Gabe's composure and his friend would snap leading to fisticuffs, he was sure.

Callie had gotten under Gabe's skin with that remark about him having money and her having to work like normal people for it. It wasn't his fault he was born into a family who were wealthier than a lot of countries.

Callie should be counting her blessings that she hadn't been born into his family but hers, which was loving and supportive and were there for each other — not being manipulated into doing things and told how to live their lives — that to him counted for more than money ever could.

If money was her problem then that he could help with. Going around to her dingy flat and banging loudly on the door, before she could say anything he launched into his verbal tirade.

"Callie, I know you think you need to —"

He stopped as suddenly as he began when he realised that the woman standing in front of him at the door wasn't Callie at all.

"Who are you?" he said, stunned at seeing a very scantily clad woman that wasn't Callie.

"Henrietta," she purred, batting her eyelashes while thrusting her bountiful breasts towards him. "Who are you? On second thoughts, I don't care. Come on in."

Her invitation only had one meaning and Gabe ignored it.

"Where's Callie?"

"Who?"

"The woman who lives here — young, pretty."

He raked a hand through his hair in frustration. Callie had better not have a flatmate that used her room to prostitute herself.

Henrietta had now undone two buttons on her top as she tried to look even more enticingly sexy for this man. Now he was a man that exuded money and she knew men loved her breasts.

"I'm young and pretty and live here. You can even call me Callie if you like. Why don't you come inside and we'll talk about where this woman you're looking for could have gone," she said, using her best sultry voice and come-hither eyes.

He didn't bother to respond but just rudely turned and walked away. Henrietta simply shrugged and shut the door feeling a little disappointed that the man didn't take her up on her offer. Hell, she would have done him for free.

Gabe was frustrated and driving aimlessly trying to work out where Callie could have gone. An almost furious thought crossed his mind that one of the club's VIP members had put Callie up in an apartment and then came another hideous thought about Callie being their mistress.

If that was the case, there would be hell to pay because Callie deserved better than to be some rich man's kept mistress. He'd find which man was showering her with money and make him wish he had never done it and give her up.

First he needed to find out where she was living and short of bullying Ross at the Club for the information, he would have to either get Callie to tell him or put a PI onto it.

Calming down slightly, he decided that he should first give Callie the chance to tell him. Calling Rosie at the front desk, he asked if Callie was working. Unfortunately she wasn't until tomorrow and so he had to cool his heels until then.

Knowing that there was now not much he could do until he talked to her, he went home.

She sensed his presence before she'd even seen him and could also feel her defensive shield rising without a word even being spoken.

It was Ruby who alerted her to the fact that Gabe was not only on the same floor as her but was also requesting her presence. Dutifully she walked over to him feeling like she had lead in her shoes.

Gabe noted that Callie wasn't happy to see him or to have to come and dance attendance on him and it made him feel better that maybe this time she'd be docile enough to talk to him and tell him what he needed to know.

"Hello, Callie," he cheerfully said.

"Gabe," she said, terse. "What do you want?"

So much for docile, he grimaced.

"I went to see you at your flat but you weren't there." He put his cards on the table.

A flicker of guilt crossed her face because she knew actually where he went and she quickly shooed those thoughts away because Gabe wasn't her family, he was just a nuisance.

"Oh? Why?" She tried to sound as nonchalant as possible.

"Because I thought about what you said and I wanted to help." He sounded so sincere that her annoying twinge of guilt flickered again. "So where did you move too?"

"I found a new flat in a better neighbourhood thanks to my job." He seemed to relax at her words, happy that she had just moved by herself. "Oh, and I heard that Amélie's left Jarrod's to live with your parents."

"Really? I hadn't heard," he frowned, wondering what his grandfather thought about that and instantly knew the answer to his own question...he'd be beyond furious.

"No, I talked to Jarrod last night. It's just happened. Amy was miserable he said and so it was decided that she should live with your parents until your grandfather lets her come back."

He was deep in thought and knew he'd have to talk to Jarrod about what happened. He knew his parents didn't know that his sister wasn't supposed to see them let alone live with them because Fabien had cut them off.

No, he was only surprised that his grandfather hadn't had a complete melt-down over it. He had always thought that it had been a stupid edict trying to ban a child from seeing their parents but Fabien didn't care about that, his word was law and defying him was worse than poking a wounded, angry bear caught in a hunter's trap with a bush fire raging all around it.

Unable to help but wonder what his sister was thinking, he could only think that Amélie just didn't care anymore and needed the love and comfort only parents could provide to a child.

Callie was still awkwardly standing there waiting for Gabe to say something. He looked at her as if remembering where he was.

"Right. Well I'm glad that you've moved to a safer neighbourhood and thanks for letting me know about Amélie," he said. "I'd better get going."

She couldn't put her finger on what had changed and she was almost disappointed that he wasn't going all 'big brother' on her but he seemed distracted and once again she felt a little flicker of guilt.

"Gabe," she said as he turned to look at her. "Thanks for checking up on me."

He nodded and left, leaving Callie wondering what was wrong.

An hour later Gabe talked to his parents and then Amélie. Brother and sister had a quiet and serious conversation so that their parents wouldn't be alarmed.

"Are you okay?" he said, concerned.

"Oui, of course," she said, biting her lip. "Although I'm so tense and nervous, it's like I'm waiting for lightning to strike me."

He understood her cryptic answer knowing that Fabien would come down hard on her.

"Then why did you leave Jarrod's? You know grand-père's going to have a fit and disown you now."

"You know, Gabe that for the first time in years, I actually feel like myself. I feel free. Not a society poodle that gets paraded around," she sighed. "Jarrod said some stuff that made me realise that I don't like the Amélie that I was, that I can't keep living my life for what grand-père wants. I want to live my own life — the good and the bad."

"What exactly did Jarrod say?" he said, an underlying hint of anger because he knew that if he didn't like the answer then he was about to come down on Jarrod like a ton of bricks, friend or not.

Amélie laughed hearing Gabe's tone knowing that he was being protective of her and as nice as it was, it wasn't needed.

"Calm down. I was the one throwing a tantrum at poor Jarrod and he had to tell me a few home truths which at the time I hated, but after we talked it actually helped."

She saw her brother exhale and realised how much of a burden she had been to him with her frivolous superficial lifestyle.

"I'm really sorry, Gabe."

"What for?"

"For being another unwanted stress in your life. If I had just stayed the same person when we moved back to France instead of becoming a selfish, self-absorbed, spoilt princess then you'd have less stress," she said, tears falling down her face.

Gabe was stunned. For the first time in years, his sister actually was acting her age and yet looking at her through the computer she looked years younger and he wanted to reach out and hug her so badly, to protect her from hurting.

"It's okay. That's what big brothers are for. You haven't been a burden…a pain, perhaps?" he teased, to get her to smile and she did.

"What about grand-père?" she quietly said, ensuring that he knew she was truly afraid of the consequences and he felt like they were children again knocking on the Harrison family's front door, holding each other's hands tightly while shaking in their shoes.

"Amy, do what makes *you* happy. Don't worry about grand-père. Do you even want to come back here?"

"Not yet. I'm enjoying spending time with mum and dad. We've had some really good heart to hearts and I feel like this was how we were meant to be, what would have happened if we never left all those years ago."

"That's great. When you're ready to come back, let me know."

He disconnected the call and leaned back in his chair thinking. Fabien was surely hitting the roof at Amélie's disobedience but after talking to his sister, he felt like she truly was being the person she was meant to be. Like the sister he had grown up with and that made him happy because she was genuinely happy, he could see it and hear it in her voice, plus the fact that she didn't go ballistic at him calling her Amy, yet another sign that she really had changed.

To ensure her happiness that meant protecting her in any way he could.

If that meant entering into a loveless marriage, so be it.

Chapter 7

Fabien St Croix was becoming more than upset and closer to extremely furious with his family, in particular his grandchildren.

First his own weakling of a son, François defied him years ago and now, more recently, his most favoured grandchildren, Amélie and Gabriel were showing the same rebellious streak like their father.

If only his daughter, Hélène had been a boy. Yes, Hélène had the same ruthless streak and haughty greed that a St Croix needed but if you looked at the way her son, Marcel had turned out even with all those genes, well, what was the lesser of the two evils.

He thought he had managed to keep them under control until Amélie had splashed the family name over the front pages of every news outlet in the world bringing unwelcome gossip and scandal to their front door.

Hélène had rung to crow about Amélie's fall from grace and although he had been angry at his granddaughter, he had taken it out on his daughter, punishing her by cutting off her allowance until she came begging to him to reinstate it.

He knew Hélène's family lived off her allowance since her husband spent all his money on gambling and his lover, and her son had a similar nature but also included drugs into his repertoire.

Sending Amélie away was the only thing left to do to keep her out of trouble and let the scandal die down but in generously agreeing to allow her to live in New Zealand on a farm, she wasn't to have any contact with her parents. Now he just found out that she not only broke that rule but was living with them.

Furious with his granddaughter, he cut off her allowance and couldn't wait to watch her come crawling meekly back begging for money when she realised that it had run out. That thought warmed him only slightly.

His other headache was Gabriel. He had thought that advising Gabriel that he had to marry to inherit the family fortune had pulled him into line and by all accounts he had received, Gabriel was taking the matter seriously so why was he now chasing around after Calliope Harrison? A woman who from what he had learned had turned him down constantly but maybe that was the lure. The woman was smarter than all the others by making Gabriel chase her.

Prudently, he had Callie, as she called herself, investigated and found out nothing notable except that she was working as a waitress at *The Century Club* and that she had been accused of having a fling with Claude Mercier.

Even he could see that it wasn't true by all accounts because Claude was having an affair with Leticia le Gros, Gabriel's ex-girlfriend. Thank God, he had managed to end that relationship before the St Croix name was dragged through the scandal sheets with more of her vulgar antics.

There was definitely no way he was ever going to be welcoming a waitress into the family. St Croix's married beneath them but only because no one was on their social level but to marry a waitress was too far.

The lowest any of the St Croix men had deigned to marry, was the daughter of a lowly Lord and that was only allowed because the family had a strong lineage to royalty and were considered cousins to the current royal family.

Fabien also knew that he was never going to allow his other useless wastrel of a grandson, Marcel to inherit the family fortune as it would disappear in under ten years with that drug-addled idiot at the helm.

No, he was going to have to turn the screws harder on Gabriel since his own son wasn't the man he had been raised to be. This would achieve the desired result that he wanted.

After all, protecting the St Croix name and business interests was paramount.

Nothing else mattered.

If Gabe thought that he was over being surprised and speechless, he was wrong…completely wrong when his grandfather walked into his office unannounced.

"Grand-père, what are you doing here?" he said, instantly on guard.

"Surprising you, of course."

"Why?"

"Because its time you told me which woman will be the future Mrs Gabriel St Croix."

"And this couldn't have waited until next Friday when I came over?"

"No. I've been hearing disturbing things and so I thought I'd come and see you."

"Disturbing things? What disturbing things?" he said, feigning innocence.

"Amélie has broken my rule and is now living with your parents."

Gabe didn't even pretend any kind of shock or ignorance.

"Is that so bad? After all, they are our parents."

"My own son has betrayed me to live in some dingy backward country instead of working by my side," he raged. "*And,* I only allowed Amélie to go live on a farm in that godforsaken country because *you* asked. Stupidly I agreed on the proviso that she never contacted her parents. Now she's living with them!"

Gabe didn't even flinch at his grandfather's rage.

"They went to see her and wanted her to live with them," he said, knowing that as a reason it wouldn't cut any kind of sympathy or kindness from his grandfather because the old man had no feelings at all.

"How did they even know she was there?"

"I don't know. Maybe Jarrod told his parents and they told mum and dad. After all, they are best friends."

"Well, I've cut off all her money so soon she'll be wishing she hadn't defied me."

Gabe's jaw clenched at the vindictive nature of his grandfather. It didn't surprise him since Fabien based everything on money and he suddenly wondered why he even put up with it.

"Anyway, enough about her. Tell me, whom have you decided to marry?"

"No one. I've looked into all your candidates and none have appealed whatsoever."

The satisfaction knowing that his answer would send his grandfather off the deep end was almost too much to hope for. He didn't have to wait long for the result.

Fabien's cheeks went bright red as rage rose up inside him. He had hoped that his subtle warning about Amélie would push Gabriel in the direction he wanted but clearly the boy had the same rebellious streak as the rest of his family.

"Are you sure?" Fabien's tone was forceful, designed to intimidate his grandson into complying to his wishes. "I'm not above giving everything to Marcel and throwing you out on your backside penniless," he said, but there was something in his eyes...fear.

It was then with startling clarity that Gabe realised that his grandfather was afraid, truly afraid that he would have to make good on his threat and it filled him with the right amount of courage and bravado that he needed to answer.

"Oui, grand-père. I won't be marrying anyone on your list."

It was Gabe's firm decisive tone that had Fabien shaking with rage.

"Fine. You've made your bed. You're fired. You won't get another penny from me. Clean out your stuff. Oh, and don't think that anyone, anywhere will employ you. They'll suffer my wrath if they do. You'll soon be begging me to take you back but unless you marry one of those women on the list, don't bother."

"Oui, grand-père. By the way, you might want to get Marcel to rehab as soon as possible. Can't have the future of the St Croix empire being a drug addict now, can we…he'd probably just give it all away for another hit."

It was the only retort he felt brave enough to give, to let his grandfather know that he wasn't about to be pushed into a corner, not when he knew that Marcel was nowhere near ready to run the empire that they owned.

It would take a lot more than just a sober Marcel to take over the reins. His cousin knew nothing of the complexities of SCE, let alone how to manage them all at the same time.

For the first time in his life, Gabe felt almost free from the heavy burden and shackles that came with being a St Croix. That then gave way to being scared for his future. He had been secure for so long, he wasn't sure what he was going to do.

The only good thing was that when he had been issued with the marriage ultimatum, he had begun saving as much as possible in the event of such a declaration from his grandfather.

To most, it would be more money than they'd ever seen but for Gabe, it truly was a pittance to what he was used to.

He was also going to have to think about his future since it was no longer mapped out for him. If Fabien made good on his promise, which was a certainty because his grandfather was vindictive enough, he would have to find a whole new career. And since he had never had a choice about what that would be, he found that although the possibilities were infinite, he had no idea where to start.

It was a problem that was going to have to wait because his secretary entered his office with a box looking dazed and confused.

"I was told to bring you this."

"Thanks, Sue. You obviously haven't heard that I've been fired."

"B-but you're —" The shock of disbelief on Sue's face was expected as she looked about to cry.

"Fired." He felt awful since Sue had been his and Stefan's assistant since he had come to London. "Sue, can you ask Stefan to come in here please."

The woman went to do his bidding still in a fog of bewilderment as he began packing his things up.

"Mr St Croix, what can I do for you?" Stefan said, walking into Gabe's office.

"Stefan, I think we've now officially moved past that stage and onto a precariously equal footing now that my grandfather has fired me, effective immediately. I just wanted to say that you've been nothing but a brilliant and loyal assistant to me and I'm sure that whoever your next boss is, you'll be just as fantastic and helpful to them as you have been to me. I could never have done so well without you," he said, matter of fact.

"Are, are you sure? M-maybe I should call Mr St Croix and make sure that there hasn't been a misunderstanding," Stefan said, shell-shocked by the news.

"I know it's hard to believe, but its true, hence the box and my packing. I wish you nothing but every success in the future."

Stefan Molyneaux genuinely liked his boss and knew that one day Gabriel would be the head of all the St Croix empire thus making him very loyal when he was first asked to be Gabriel's assistant knowing that he too would become one of the most powerful men in the organisation. All he had to do to be in such a lauded position was to report Gabriel's comings and goings to his grandfather.

At first it didn't bother him at all but the more he got to know Gabriel and Fabien's demanding edicts, the more he sided with Gabriel and kept his reporting to the bare minimum.

Shock at finding out that Fabien had fired his own grandson just proved to Stefan that he had been doing the right thing and trepidation filled him.

"I'll probably be next," he said under his breath.

"Why? I'm sure that Fabien wouldn't be that vindictive to fire my assistant and secretary just because he's mad at me." He wasn't as confident of that fact because his grandfather would do just that on a whim.

Stefan knew it was now time to come clean.

"When I was hired, it was under strict instructions that I also had to report back to your grandfather," he said, frightened of Gabriel's reaction.

Gabe's face was stunned at the news. He had suspected such a thing but Stefan had proven his loyalty so many times that he thought he was being a little paranoid or that it was perhaps Sue that was the spy. Now to find out that he had been right all along, it was a painful blow.

"*But* as I got to know you and seeing your...tenuous relationship with your grandfather, I began to refuse to impart any knowledge I had unless it was superficial, like meetings or clients who rang. All that other stuff I've done for you, I haven't told your grandfather," he said. "I suspect he knew that I wasn't being completely honest and has another one or more spies on his payroll. My loyalty is, was, to you."

"Thank you for your honesty and if grandfather does fire you, I'll help you find another job although my word probably won't carry much weight."

Stefan left and as he finished his packing, Gabe looked around his office one last time.

The end of an era.

The end of his prison sentence.

Once he stepped out the door and into the fresh air, he was free to do whatever he wanted.

He had barely made it home when Luc rung.

"Tell me it's not true," his best friend said, before he had even managed a hello.

"What's not true?" he said, knowing full well what Luc meant.

It was true gossip of this magnitude spread like wildfire but for Luc to have heard it so quickly, something just niggled at him.

"Fabien fired you," Luc said, exasperated.

"How do you know?" He hated the deep down churning sensation in his stomach, knowing the answer…his grandfather.

The hesitation on the other end of the phone was his answer. Gabe felt like Luc had stabbed him in the heart. The pain was immense, unlike anything he had ever felt before.

"I never imagined that you of all people were spying on me *for him*," he said, so quietly that the hurt was undeniable. "You were the one person I thought I could trust. More fool me."

"It's not like that. *You're my best friend.*"

"And yet you were still willing to be one of Fabien's lackeys. I *trusted* you, told you things…private things and you told my grandfather so he could use it against me."

"Not everything, I promise. And I am your best friend, Gabe."

Luc's pleading fell on deaf ears as Gabe hung up not wanting to even listen to the litany of excuses he was sure to have.

This was the moment that he realised that he was all alone. He had been betrayed by the one person he thought he could trust. Now he knew that the only people in his life that he could trust, that ever had his back and loyalty were the Harrison family.

And for the first time in his life, he wished his grandfather were dead.

The scandal broke with a muted piece stating that Gabriel St Croix had decided to resign his position at SCE to seek other challenges with his grandfather, Fabien's blessing.

St Croix searches for new challenge! The headline banner read with Fabien's accompanying statement. "*When Gabriel told me he felt like he needed a new challenge and wanted to take time out for a while, I thought it was a great idea. Every young man needs to find his own path. Of course he has my full blessing.*"

This sent everyone into a frenzy about what it meant and what had exactly happened to make him resign. Shares in some SCE companies reacted wildly for the day but then everything calmed since Fabien was still at the helm ruling with his iron fist.

As always, everyone in the know remained tight-lipped for fear that anything leaked to the Press would result in Fabien's ire and their lives would be a misery because of it.

Gabe screwed up the article and threw it across the room. His grandfather made it seem like this was all Gabe's idea. He wasn't surprised since protecting the St Croix name was paramount to his grandfather.

Depressed and not knowing what to do for the first time in forever, he lazed in bed until he got bored. Then he visited Nigel in the kitchen and drove the butler mad with his inane chatter.

Luc called constantly and as much as he missed his friend, he couldn't bring himself to talk or see him. Luc had even tried to turn up at the house but Nigel turned him away.

The only people he had told the truth to were his family, who were proud of his decision to stand up for himself.

Marcel, on the other hand thought it was wonderful news. He hated his grandfather and cousins with a passion and his mother had been so ecstatic by the news, telling her son that he would now be heir to the St Croix throne. There was no better reason to go out and celebrate, ensuring that everyone knew that he was the new heir.

He may have laughed gleefully at the headlines that his cousin, Amélie had made about being at a brothel with an arms dealer which had her sent to Coventry. However, the next day, his own headlines were even worse since photos had been taken of him high and surrounded by naked prostitutes — male and female — writhing all over him.

His mother had screamed and thrown things at him. His grandfather had people pick him up and admit him to a very exclusive rehab centre where he was isolated from talking to anyone.

Still this didn't stop everyone who was there that night selling their stories about what Marcel had liked, said and done. It was fodder for every news outlet for weeks.

Chapter 8

As soon as Callie saw Luc at the Club, she was on her guard for Gabe's arrival, only he never appeared. Luc had come alone a few times now so she went to over to talk to him.

"Hi Luc, where's Gabe? Away on business?" she said, looking around to make sure that he wasn't in the vicinity because he'd never let her forget that she cared enough to ask after him.

He looked at her with a sadness that she couldn't quite understand and she automatically reached out and sat down beside him.

"What's happened?" she said. "H-has something happened to Gabe?"

She felt her anxiety rise. Gabe might be an annoying pain in the butt but she still knew him and cared.

"No, nothing has happened to Gabe unless you think that his grandfather firing him and cutting of all access to the family money and then to top it off, learning that his best friend has been spying on him for years, reporting things about his life to his grandfather as something happening to him, then yes, something has happened to him," he said, with self-derision and loathing.

"Why? Why would you do that? *How* could you do that to him if you're supposed to be best friends?"

"Made a deal with the devil, didn't I," he shrugged. "At the time, my family had made some bad business decisions and one wrong turn could have sunk us so when Fabien very generously offered to wipe all the family debts for the odd bit of insider knowledge on Gabe's life, well, who was I to say no. Stupid really but I didn't want to ask Gabe for help because I wanted and valued his friendship more. Now look where that's got me."

Callie's head spun. Gabe's best friend had betrayed him and although she did understand to a certain degree, how could Luc have done that to someone like Gabe?

"Oh God," she said. "Is he all right?"

"I don't know. He won't talk or see me. Do you blame him?"

"Why didn't you tell him years ago?" She had to know why Gabe's best friend couldn't have been honest.

"Because I'm a coward, Callie — pure and simple. I haven't really told his grandfather anything over the past eight or so years and definitely nothing that Fabien wouldn't already know. I'm not stupid enough to think that I'm the only one spying for Fabien, there are probably plenty more people out there doing it."

Anxious and desperately needing to see Gabe, Callie left Luc and work in a hurry not caring what Gabe thought about her turning up out of the blue.

When she got to his place she banged loudly on his door and waited impatiently for it to open before banging on it some more. She was tempted to yell out as well but felt that perhaps for this neighbourhood it would have the police turning up in quick smart time.

Eventually the door opened and she had been about to launch into her spiel when she noticed that the dour man opening the door wasn't Gabe at all.

"Is Gabe home?"

"No, Mr St Croix is not home."

"Nigel, right?"

"Do I know you?" he said in a haughty manner.

"No, you don't," she snapped, annoyed at his British pomposity. "But I need to see Gabe, see if he's okay. Gabe! Gabe!" she yelled, trying to look around the butler.

"Miss, please leave or I'll call the police."

Her shoulders slumped dejected, knowing that she was never going to get past Gabe's butler.

"Fine. Just tell him that Callie stopped by."

She turned and begun walking away when Nigel's incredulous voice stopped her.

"*You're Callie?*"

Turning back to look at the butler, she nodded.

"Yes."

She wasn't surprised Nigel hadn't recognised her since they had never truly met. That one very brief time he served her dinner wasn't that memorable to either of them. To Nigel, Callie had been just another dinner guest in a long line of Gabriel's revolving door and to Callie, she hadn't even really taken note of Nigel at all since she had been so nervous about catching up with Gabe.

"You're the one who introduce Mr St Croix to the kitchen." His tone became warm and friendly and with what Callie wanted to believe was a hint of a smile. "Come inside," he said, standing aside to allow her entry.

"Are you sure? I don't want to disturb him."

"I think that you'd be the perfect guest."

Callie smiled and marvelled at the complete one-eighty change in Nigel's demeanour towards her now that he realised who she was. It was like they were almost co-conspirators against Gabe.

When the scandal broke, Gabe had come home and interrogated his butler to see if he too were spying on Gabe for his grandfather. Nigel's vehement denials that he was loyal to Gabe since he paid his wages and quite well enough that there was no need to supplement his income, plus spying went against his own moral ethics that abhorred that type of thing.

Gabe reassured by Nigel's answer kept him on in his employ after firmly stating that the butler was to tell anyone except his parents, Amélie, Jarrod or Callie Harrison that he was not home and he hadn't been seen. Anyone with half a brain would know it wasn't the truth but he needed time alone to think.

As predicted Luc and his grandfather rang and Luc had even turned up looking for Gabe to apologise but Gabe was still too raw from his friend's betrayal to even wish to speak to him.

Luc was persistent though, he texted Gabe non-stop and finally gave up after getting the hint by Gabe's silence. Still Luc persisted and a letter turned up. Gabe couldn't help but read Luc's regrets and sincerest apologies including the real reason he had spied on him for Fabien.

If Luc was standing in front of him, he would have wrung his friend's neck for his stupidity. Not only should Luc have told him but Luc knew after years of Gabe telling him about Fabien, what Fabien was like.

If Luc had been honest with him, then he would have forgiven him and definitely wouldn't have thought that Luc had been trading on their friendship.

Gabe let out a loud sigh at the mess this had all become. None of this would have come to light if he hadn't stood up to his grandfather. He would have continued to blissfully carry on with his life completely unaware that people he knew and trusted were lying to his face and that's what really hurt.

This was all about his grandfather controlling and manipulating everyone especially his own family. Well now that the truth was out — no more.

He wasn't about to do anything that his grandfather asked, no matter what, unless *he* wanted to do it.

With his new firm resolve he stood only to have Callie come flying into the room with a look of distress and panic.

"Oh, thank God you're okay," she panted, trying to regain her breath before hitting him hard on the upper arm.

"Ow! What's that for?" he said, rubbing his arm.

"That's for being a moron. My God, the way Luc was so miserable and then Nigel being so...Nigel." She didn't know Nigel and so that was the best description she could think of. "Jeez, I thought you were a broken mess or depressed, or something and now I find there's nothing even wrong with you," she scolded to his amusement at her heroine routine.

"Well, I'm glad you still like me enough to be worried even with my supposedly overbearing personality," he mocked.

She shot him an irritated look as she stood with her arms folded, annoyed for worrying about nothing.

"So you saw Luc. Let me guess, he spun you his sob story to send you fleeing to me to beg on his behalf to forgive him?"

The puzzled look on her face was his answer and it actually made him feel better that Callie had come of her own accord and that Luc hadn't sent her on his behalf.

"Whoa." She threw her hands up in the air. "I don't know what exactly is going on but I saw Luc at the Club and he really was miserable, like he had lost his best friend," she said. "He did confess that he had ruined your friendship by betraying your trust and loyalty to your grandfather because of his family's debts. I got a quick rundown from him that your grandfather fired you and cut off all access to the family fortune."

Gabe rubbed his chin noting that Luc had told Callie the truth or was it the truth that his friend wanted Gabe to believe.

"So you know some of the story. Did you also know that my supposedly loyal trustworthy assistant, Stefan was also spying on me for grand-père?" he said, bitter and she saw pain of betrayal in his eyes. "No, I didn't think so. So why are you here then, Callie? Ready to offer me all your wages? Teach me how to be poor? Or maybe like other people I thought I could trust in my life, you're also here to report back to my grandfather."

Tears instantly pooled in her eyes at his harsh accusations and guilt flooded through him for lashing out at her.

"I don't know why I thought that you might need a friend. I guess St Croix's really are arrogant, superior bastards. You wonder why people spy on you? Because you do nothing to earn their trust and loyalty apart from just being," she said, furious.

He flinched as if she had taken a knife and stabbed him, her words wounding him more than Luc or Stefan's betrayal ever could.

She wiped her eyes and turned to leave.

"Callie, wait. I'm sorry," he said, contrite and sincere.

She didn't move, upset that Gabe could be so cruel when she had done nothing to deserve it. Then she felt his hands on her shoulders as he gently turned her around and pulled her to him.

Holding Callie close he silently called himself all kinds of names and knew he had hurt her with his insane accusations.

"I'm sorry." His voice barely a whisper as he stroked her hair. "I didn't mean to lash out at you. I know that you and Jarrod are the only two people in the world that I *can* trust."

"Then why were you so mean?" she sobbed.

"Because I'm angry. Angry that I didn't even suspect that Luc and my assistant, Stefan were both my grandfather's spies. I expect people to use me, my name, for their own purpose but Luc was my best friend. I've told him things I'd never tell anyone else except maybe Jarrod and to find out that he was telling my grandfather…it's such a betrayal."

She could hear the pain in his voice as she looked up through her wet eyelashes and stroked his face.

That simple action almost undid him. All the anger, disappointment and even hurt he had been wallowing in seemed to evaporate at Callie's touch. Part of his mind rationalised that any woman giving him comfort would have provided him with the same reaction but he knew that it wasn't true. Callie's touch somehow affected him in a way that it was like a soothing balm on his soul, probably because she was the longest platonic relationship with a woman outside of his family that he had ever had.

He reached up and held her hand to his cheek and was able to see her mouth and eyes widen in surprise at the simple action.

"W-what are you doing?" she said, embarrassed that he had taken her simple gesture and made it more intimate.

"Enjoying the feel of a woman's hand against my cheek," he said, a hint of jest.

"W-why?"

Reluctantly he lowered both their hands sensing her discomfort and he felt like he needed to explain so he led her to the couch to sit down.

"I didn't mean to frighten you."

"You didn't," she hastily said.

"Do you know that you're the only non-related female in my life that I can trust, utterly and completely? Never once have you traded on knowing me or my family. *And*, you're not afraid to speak your mind to me whether I like what you say or not."

"Why are you telling me this? I mean, it's easy to give you a piece of my mind because I've known you since we were kids," she said, confused.

"Because I've just realised that *you'd* be the perfect wife for me."

He said it so casually and with such ease that they could have been dating for years and this was just the next step in their relationship.

Callie's heart beat furiously as she just stared at him in bewilderment before she managed to comprehend what he had just said.

"I…ah…you…wow," she said, speechless. "I'm not sure what you're trying to say."

It sounded like a silly thing to say even to her own ears because it was kind of obvious and yet she felt like she needed clarification.

Gabe may have understood her reaction but he actually wanted to laugh because a million girls would have just automatically answered 'yes' but not his Callie. His suggestion was completely out of the blue but what he had said was true, she would be perfect as his wife. He would never have to worry about her loyalty to him or marrying him only for his money.

Now that Gabe had given her a moment to think about what he had just said, she still didn't understand.

"I know that being fired and finding out that your best friend was spying on you has hit you hard, but have you hit your head or are possibly having a mental breakdown?" she said, concerned.

"Of course not." He gave her a placating smile.

"Maybe you need to talk to someone…a therapist, perhaps?"

All he did was look at her and she squirmed under his gaze. He seemed as normal as he could be…for Gabe.

"Let me explain," he said.

She sat and waited silently praying that he really wasn't having some kind of breakdown because she had no idea how to handle that kind of situation.

"After the first time I saw you in the Club, my grandfather decided that he wanted to make sure that I would follow in the family tradition," he said. "That is, that for generations, St Croix men — or more particularly, the heir — married by the time they were thirty if they wanted to be the beneficiary of all that being a St Croix entitled."

His poor little Callie seemed almost like a baby, her face showing stunned disbelief at his announcement as he continued pacing back and forth as he talked.

"Anyway, grand-père even drew up a list of fifteen women he found imminently suitable to honour the St Croix name."

"I'm one of them?"

She whispered the question in awe that he felt a stabbing guilt for what he was about to say.

"No, you weren't."

Her crestfallen face was devastating, not because she would have truly thought that she made the list but he knew it was that tiny speck of possibility that she could of. If he had made the list, she probably would be the only woman on it.

"The list was ridiculous. The first five names were immediately crossed off. There was no way I'd ever consider them. The next five I also ruled out for various reasons leaving me the last five which were discreetly looked into before deciding that none of them would suit *me*."

"I don't understand."

"If, when, I married or marry, it's for life. I don't want to be divorcing but nor do I want to marry a woman and then live separate lives only being seen together for the sake of public appearances but in private…" Callie nodded, understanding. "I want what your parents and mine have, a loving relationship," he said.

Her heart might have gone out to him but…

"It still doesn't explain why you would want to marry…me. You just said that I'm not acceptable to your grandfather. We don't love each other Gabe, that's important to me too."

"I know, but when I finally, for the first time in my entire life, truly stood up to grand-père, this is what happened. He was beyond furious and even threatened to leave everything to my spoilt wastrel of a cousin, Marcel," he said. "A decision grand-père still might make out of spite and then regret it forever after, but I refuse to bow down to him so as long as I'm single, he'll use every trick in the book to bend me to his will. If I marry first, he'll have to wear it."

"But me?"

The bewildered way she said it tugged at him. She really was like a newborn lamb, so vulnerable…innocent.

He raked a hand threw his hair trying to keep focussed but there was a niggling feeling deep in his gut that this was something he shouldn't be doing.

"Like I said I believe marriage should be for life but since I also need to marry quickly to keep my grandfather off my back and since I know and trust you, if you wish to divorce, I'll make sure that our pre-nuptial agreement would be extremely fair."

Her brain was a muddle. What Gabe was telling her was almost some kind of backhanded compliment. That he was willing to marry her without love because he trusted her and even though he wasn't planning to divorce, he would allow her to do it.

"I-I —" She didn't know what to say. This was never how she expected to be proposed to nor did she ever think that she could marry someone she didn't love, but Gabe was a friend and he needed help. "Can't you find someone else?"

He came and sat down beside her but didn't dare touch her. He needed her to make the decision in a rational manner.

"No one that wouldn't try and tell me all the things I want to hear but I wouldn't know them as well as you to know their true character or motives."

"B-but you don't know me…mine," she said. "I-I could have a-a…" She was trying to think of some kind of shady past but it was hard to think of something quickly on the spot. "I could be after all your money or find another man and have an affair."

She wanted to try and make him see how ludicrous this all sounded.

An amused then angry look crossed his face before he calmed and relaxed.

"If…*if* we marry there will be no affairs. You can have other men once we divorce and not a moment before. If you think that you can cuckold me by living the high life and having someone on the side then I'd toss you out on your arse without a penny," he said, frightening her.

If he was acting like this and it was only a discussion, how was he going to act if they were really married? Why did she care? Was she even entertaining the idea? She wasn't going to marry Gabe, she was just trying to help him see sense and decided to try another tack to help him.

"Another reason you don't want or shouldn't marry me is that fact that I don't fit into your social world," she said, ignoring his little outburst. "I didn't when I was sixteen and I wouldn't now. *And* to be honest with you, I couldn't deal with all the catty, bitchy, snobby women looking down their haughty noses at me because I'm *way* under your level of class and sophistication."

He opened his mouth to say something but she barrelled on so he couldn't get a word in.

"Not to mention the fact that because I married *you,* they'd all be nice and delightful to my face and then nasty behind my back. I don't need that. I'm a very simple person. I don't need much and don't really care for being seen or noted in magazines or on TV. To sum up, it's a very lovely offer but I politely decline."

Gabe didn't know what to think. No one, correction, no *woman* would have ever turned him down and especially not an offer of marriage and in his mind that made Callie the best choice even more. He just needed to make her see it.

Her observations about the Parisian elite especially were true. Callie was like a delicate fragile flower and those women — like his Tante Hélène — were the kind that would crush her but he didn't spend much time in Paris or France these days, in part to keep his distance from his grandfather.

Ignoring all her concerns and deciding that he could always hire someone to help with her styling and etiquette, he ploughed on.

"*Please* think about it," he said. "If we marry, I promise that I will take care of you financially for the rest of your life."

Callie shook her head sadly. She had never seen Gabe almost beg, it was indeed a very rare sight but not enough to sway her. Also it seemed sad to her that all he was offering was financial security. It might be some woman's dream but for her, it wasn't enough.

However it was a lot to take in and so she stood.

"I'd better go. I only came to make sure that you were all right. You look fine so I'll get going."

Panic shot through him knowing that if he let her walk out the door then she would have too much time to decline is offer.

"Will you promise me that you'll at least think *seriously* about it?"

"Sure." His look of relief really meant it was a bigger deal than even she thought. "But please, don't pin your hopes on me. I suggest you also think of other women that could help you."

He nodded but couldn't think of anyone who would suit his purpose better than her.

"Oh, and please try to at least understand Luc's position. He really does feel guilty and looks completely miserable without you as his friend."

Once she had left, Gabe spent hours thinking and wondering about how he was going to get Callie to marry him and knew for once that money wouldn't help. She was his perfect choice. What he needed was someone to talk to and in these circumstances the first person he would normally turn to was Luc but his best friend's betrayal still hurt deeply.

Nigel came into the room to ask if Callie was staying for dinner but seeing that Gabe was alone, he instead said, "Is there anything you need, Sir?"

"Instructions on how to woo a woman without money," he said under his breath.

That night the Callie situation played havoc with his mind. Would it really be so bad to persuade Callie into marrying him knowing he didn't love her? After all, he would ensure that she had everything her heart desired…but that one thing.

Maybe she could learn to live without that kind of romantic love, surely a marriage based on friendship would stand the test of time better since everyone knew that passion always faded over time but friendship, well friendships got stronger. And besides, he had magnanimously offered to divorce her.

Chapter 9

The next morning Gabe decided it was time to stop moping and live up to the St Croix name and do something with his life. He wasn't about to let his grandfather win and was determined to get another job no matter his grandfather's malicious intent to block every opportunity.

Luc would give him a job but in spite of everything, he didn't want Fabien to take his wrath out even more on his friend.

Another surprise was yet another letter from Luc.

Dear Gabe,

I know you still believe that I'm not your friend and to prove that I am and hopefully as a first step to regaining your trust I'm writing to advise that Fabien is beyond angry at what he perceives as your rebellion.

The fact that he can't find you is another reason that I got the most unpleasant visit from the man. A visit, I might add, that has left me completely deaf thanks to all his roaring. It took all my willpower not to provoke him even more by asking...what the *hell did he expect? But I already knew the answer, he wanted you to cower and grovel to him.*

I told him in all honesty that I haven't seen or heard a peep from you after I had admitted spying on his behalf. Well as you can imagine, I was now in the firing line but that's okay because I finally had the gumption to stand up to Fabien, something I should have done years ago.

I also advised your grandfather that our friendship was now over and if by some miracle you ever did forgive me then I was not going to spy on you for him ever again. I fear I may end up in the poor house after his vitriolic threats that are still ringing in my ears, but it is worth it to be free of his tyrannical ways.

Anyway, that's the latest news. Fabien still can't understand why you just didn't marry one of those women on his list and life would be all roses again and continue on. I did try my best to tell him that money doesn't motivate you like it does him and I got a hard whack from his cane for my efforts.

If you ever need anything, you know where to find me.

Luc.

Gabe put the letter down and was once again in deep thought. Of course he knew that his grandfather would be apoplectic that Gabe hadn't come grovelling to him. But now his eyes were finally wide open because he knew that if he did this one thing for his grandfather, then his entire life would continue to be controlled, if not by his grandfather but also by his wife who Fabien would have scared, paid or blackmailed into doing his bidding, just like he had done with Luc and Stefan.

He didn't know whether the need to control and manipulate people came from generations of St Croix men or it was just his grandfather but it had to stop.

His father had taken a stand but at that time he was the only adult male heir so Fabien couldn't completely cut him off. Since his cousin, Marcel could also technically inherit, Fabien thought that he had a way to make Gabe kowtow to his demands and bring him to heel.

Luc's letter just made one thing even more abundantly clear, he needed to marry quickly before he resurrected himself and for that, he definitely needed Callie.

There was no other way.

He turned up on her doorstep after dark with a bouquet of flowers. Although she shouldn't have been surprised by Gabe's appearance, she was. It reminded her so much of that first time months ago when he had done it *sans* flowers though.

The flowers were lovely but she had firmed her resolve not to let her guard down.

"Callie, I'll get right to the point," he said, entering her new private domain and liking what he saw. The place was not only more modern and cleaner but the furniture and accessories seemed to suit her better too.

"Please do," she said, sensing a feeling of dread. It was better that he just told her upfront what he wanted even though she knew deep down what it was.

"I need you to marry me. In fact, I'm truly begging."

The look on his face and the urgency in his voice told her that he really was serious this time.

"Y-you said I could think about it…it's only been a couple of days!"

"I know and I'm sorry about pressuring you but time is now of the essence. I need to be married and go on a honeymoon before I resurrect myself in society. It would also put the final spoke in grand-père's plan for me. There's nothing he can then hold over my head or manipulate me into doing," he said, hanging in head in shame. "Admittedly once everyone finds out that I'm married, we'll be hounded by paparazzi constantly and your every move will be noted, your dress sense picked apart but I'll hire you a bodyguard, a whole security team if that's what you need. You'll have to give up your job because it'll be impossible to work there and I'll be honest, women will be very jealous that you managed to marry me when they couldn't so they'll be complete bitches and tear you apart but whatever you decide to do as my wife, I'll support you, I promise."

"Are you daft?" It was the first thing that she managed to get to come out of her mouth after his lengthy spiel.

"No."

"You've just explained how extremely and utterly truly horrible and miserable my life will become if I marry you, and you think I'm going to say yes? Are you sure you're not daft? Insanity runs in your family?"

Her incredulous tone made him choke out an uncomfortable laugh because Callie was right. His description of married life to him would turn any woman off. Only those attention-seeking, gold-digging women would lap it all up. Anyone else with half a brain would be frightened and daunted by the prospect and rightfully so, that they would just say no, but he couldn't give Callie that option. He needed her too much.

"No insanity…just pure desperation."

"I know you want to be married for life but I don't think that I can live like that, so how long would you expect to be married?"

She wondered why she was even asking the question and giving him any kind of hope that she was about to agree.

"A year?" Hope flared in his chest like a skyrocket exploding.

Three hundred and sixty five days didn't seem so long.

"A-and we wouldn't be having…*you know*." She flushed with embarrassment to even say the word.

"Conjugal relations?" he teased, her cheeks turning an even brighter shade of red. "No. I think I can wait a year."

Her posture relaxed at his answer. He didn't know it but Callie had talked to Jarrod about Gabe's crazy idea. She hadn't done it to laugh at Gabe but more because she actually pitied him for needing to do this and felt that her brother would also reiterate just how crazy Gabe was, but after talking to Jarrod about everything that had happened, it stunned Callie to hear her brother say that she should do it.

"What? Why?" she said, speechless.

"Because what he's saying is true. His grandfather is a complete bastard. Look at what he's done to them and that's just the parts we know of. Okay, so Amy brought some of it on herself," he said. "But honestly, Callie, any woman could say anything or agree to anything and then once the ring is on, make his life a living hell. *You* wouldn't do that and I have to say it speaks volumes that he thinks so highly of you."

"But I'm a nobody. Everyone's going to tear me apart like wild wolves with a rag doll. I don't have a thick skin."

"Then put a time limit on it so you can see light at the end of the tunnel. Think long and hard about what you're willing to do, to get at the end, for your troubles."

"You mean money?" she said, not thinking that Jarrod was that mercenary.

"If that's what you want. Maybe you want to live in Alaska, have him build you a house up there, I don't know but I think you should seriously consider it, Cal. Not because I agree but its Gabe. He's the guy we grew up with, my best friend and I don't doubt that he wouldn't have asked if it wasn't *that* important. Look at what he did for me, no questions," Jarrod said, and Callie knew her brother was right.

"But buying you a farm is completely different to marrying the man, living together, pretending to be in love."

"I know. Just think about it."

Callie realised that seemed to be the catch phrase with all the men in her life at the moment — just think about it.

"What about Amy? She thinks I'm a hick. Imagine her or their parents gaining *me* as a daughter-in-law even for a brief time. They'll be so embarrassed."

"They're here, you're there. You won't even have to see them."

"Thanks, Jare. I'll think about it."

And she did. For the past few days it consumed her every thought and all she felt was scared and frightened. She wasn't adventurous enough to jump in with both feet. She was too scared to even dip a toe in and now, Gabe was in front of her needing not only an answer, but the right answer.

"Callie?" he said, knowing she had drifted off in her mind to somewhere else.

"Isn't there someway I can see if I like being seen with you?" she said, hope in her voice.

"I'm sorry, I can't." He shook his head with regret. "If you say no then I need to find someone else pronto. Time really is of the essence. I'm not just saying it to pressure you."

"We can't tell anyone. I don't need my parents knowing I got married and they didn't even come to the wedding."

"Callie, it would be *impossible* for everyone not to know. It'll be all over the news," he said with a hollow laugh.

"Oh."

She sat down deflated and he sat beside her, gently clasping her hands in his.

"I'll tell you what, I'll draw up a pre-nup and give it to your attorney to read. They can advise you and then you can decide but it'll have to be done in the next couple of days."

"I don't have an attorney," she whispered, feeling like the room was closing in on her.

"Okay then I'll find you a very reputable one. One that would tell you the truth and advise you properly."

He could see her buckling under the stress of just this conversation. How would she do as his wife? Guilt once more assailed him and yet he selfishly and desperately needed Callie to agree.

"I want trust funds for all my children so that they can study and become doctors, dentists, electricians if that's what they want or to buy a house. I want to be able to send them to private or public schools without the worrying about money," she blurted out.

Kind-hearted Callie, he thought to himself. She didn't ask for herself, just other people and in this case, her future children.

"Done," he said, and for a moment saw her as the most loving and wonderful mother to a whole bunch of children and it made him melancholy.

"Okay, give me until I see a lawyer and then I'll make my decision," she said.

Now that Gabe knew she would seriously consider his offer, hope once more flared through him. Maybe he had just found light at the end of his tunnel.

All this worry and indecisiveness was making Callie sick and turning up to the prestigious offices of Lord Gloucester who was to be her solicitor didn't make her feel any more comfortable or better. In fact, the way she was being fawned over by his receptionist and then secretary just made everything worse.

"Miss Harrison." Lord Gloucester welcomed her with a hearty handshake. "We are delighted to make your acquaintance."

"Thank you," she said, but knew that the only reason he was probably so happy was because of Gabe's name and money.

As soon as refreshments were served, they got down to business.

"Now, I have read this pre-nuptial agreement very thoroughly and as far as I can see there is absolutely nothing detrimental in your favour. If anything, it's not only overly generous but everything is actually *in* your favour." Lord Gloucester beamed. "If only all my clients should be so fortunate."

Callie smiled at his chuckled offhand remark because it was expected.

"What does it say exactly?"

The man opposite her looked astonished by her simple request. He was the expert and if he said everything was up to snuff then that should be enough for her to simply take him at his word.

Knowing that the mere slip of a woman sitting opposite him could shortly become one of the most influential and wealthiest women in the world one day, he took no offence at the question, after all, should she divorce her future husband, this woman would be extraordinarily wealthy and need future legal assistance.

"Simply that you must stay married for a minimum of one year from the date of marriage before divorce papers can be served. Any kind of infidelity from either party during this time until the divorce is final will render the pre-nuptial void. Should Mr St Croix be the adulterer then you will have the right to sue for half of his estate. However, should you be the adulterer, then you shall receive nothing other than any gifts given during this time. There's provision for Trusts to be set up for your future children but once again, only if you have adhered to stipulations of the pre-nuptial agreement. It states your monthly allowance, how much you will receive upon the divorce et cetera, et cetera."

Callie was grateful that Gabe had kept his word but now she had to make the final decision. Signing the pre-nuptial was agreeing to marry him. To live that life that he had pictured for her. The one that wasn't at all appealing. The one that was downright terrifying.

"D-do you mind giving me a moment to myself?" she said, trying hard to rein in her anxiety.

"Of course not, my dear." Lord Gloucester didn't look perturbed in the slightest by her question. "Take all the time you need. I've got something else I need to check on, so have my secretary come find me when you're ready."

He left the room and Callie bent over with her head tucked between her knees trying to breath. Her head ached with a dull throbbing and she closed her eyes trying hard to envision being married to Gabe.

Nothing seemed to come to her mind. All she felt was fear and dread while being completely overwhelmed and knew deep down that she couldn't do it. Tears slid down her cheeks because she'd be letting him down. She wasn't strong enough to handle the stares, whispers, gossip, paparazzi and all the other horrible things that came with being a St Croix. She learnt that horrible lesson through Amélie and her haughty friends when she was sixteen.

Taking some deep breaths, she stood to go and find Lord Gloucester's secretary. Outside there seemed to be a loud commotion happening and before she could even take a step, the door to the office swung open and a handsome older gentleman appeared looking extremely angry.

Lord Gloucester came rushing into the room looking somewhat angry that his private office was being invaded by a non-client.

"Sir, this is my private office. You cannot just come barging in."

The unwelcome visitor turned and gave Lord Gloucester a cold, hard glare and Callie could see the poor man almost quaking in his shiny Italian handmade leather shoes.

"I can do whatever I like. Now, shut the door on *your way out*. I need to talk to this little upstart *alone*!"

Lord Gloucester's eyes darted to his client and Callie looked just as afraid as the solicitor but he meekly obeyed leaving her alone with the man.

"W-who —"

"Sit down!" he barked and she promptly did as she was told.

The older man was handsome, he looked in his seventies perhaps, but possibly was older, she couldn't quite tell. What she did know was that while he wasn't a pleasant man, he wore very nice clothes. Perhaps if he smiled more, he wouldn't scare people so much.

"I know what you're doing and I won't allow it." There was no mistaking the ferocity of his tone. "Does Gabriel really think that I'm that stupid? That by marrying a nobody that I still won't cut him off without a cent, not to mention cut him completely out of my will?" he ranted, before looking pointedly at her. "How much to get rid of you?"

She blinked once and then twice. Completely speechless.

"Are you deaf?" he snapped. "I said, how much to get rid of you?"

"W-who are you?" she said, her voice trembling and sounding more like a mouse than a lioness.

"Are you honestly trying to have me believe that you do not know who I am? I wasn't born yesterday and your acting skills aren't that great either. Now stop wasting my time and give me a number. Believe me, you're not going to get more trying to play innocent. I will not let my grandson throw his life away on a *nobody*."

It suddenly became very clear that this horrible, odious man standing in front of her was in fact Gabe's grandfather. Blood instantly drained from her face at finally meeting the very devil himself.

All the stories she had ever heard over the years, she had to admit she thought that they had been exaggerated. Now seeing and meeting the man standing in front of her, in the flesh, she knew that none of it was exaggerated at all. The stories were unfortunately all true.

"A billion dollars." She blurted out the most outrageous number she could think of.

Fabien's eyes glittered with anger that terrified her and yet in some regards, looked almost pleased by her answer.

"A million dollars, that's my final offer."

"Then why even ask?" Her knees were knocking together at her own provocation towards the older man.

"Its more than you could ever hope to make in a lifetime. Stop being impudent and accept my offer."

"Or what?" Surprise was written all over her face that she was talking back when she was petrified.

"I'll ruin you. Do you think I'd ever let someone like *you* marry my grandson? He's a St Croix. Someone completely out of your league."

"So you'd ruin any chance of your own grandson's happiness for some stupid, outdated, male chauvinistic view?"

He became so red with rage that Callie thought his head would explode, but before he could begin to utter another caustic reply, she quickly went and opened the door.

"Lord Gloucester, please can you come back in. Mr St Croix was just leaving."

Lord Gloucester looked stressed and relieved when the door opened.

"O-of course, Miss Harrison," he said. "M-Monsieur St Croix, it's nice to see you."

Fabien St Croix stormed out of the office in a rage. If his grandson thought to marry this dreadful woman then he had another thing coming. He was going to enjoy publicly destroying her and teaching Gabriel a lesson in the process.

She might have declared war but he would be the victor, he always was. All he had to do was time it right to get the maximum effect and Gabriel would finally come crawling back on his hands and knees to beg forgiveness, not daring to put a foot out of line ever again.

The door clicked quietly and the two people in the room breathed a sigh of relief. Callie's heart was beating furiously from the encounter and Lord Gloucester mopped his brow with his handkerchief.

"Well, that wasn't pleasant," she said under her breath, as if she still wasn't quaking in her shoes.

Lord Gloucester looked at his client in amazement before choking out a laugh.

"I'm afraid that you seemed to have faced the beast much better than I could ever have, Miss Harrison. Having never met Fabien St Croix before, I now in all good honour insist on making sure that marriage to his grandson is truly what you want."

Callie looked at Lord Gloucester and realised that the moment Gabe's grandfather came barging into their meeting, the solicitor had now stopped treating her like a client with money and was showing elderly concern, which made her like him so much more.

"Thank you, Lord Gloucester for your concern. Admittedly this was my first encounter with the man and I can assure you that unless it's my duty, I'll be avoiding the likes of him as much as possible. My future husband is my main concern," she said with such conviction that she surprised even herself.

The way this day was turning out, she should have expected that any decision would have been made in the moment and yet, what Lord

Gloucester said next was another surprise.

"Miss Harrison, I may be an old stuffy and snobbish member of British Society and can admit that having you in my office today on official St Croix business is not only a feather in my cap but I, too saw the dollar signs and the chance to be aligned with such a powerful name," he said. "However, now having met the infamous Fabien St Croix for the first time, my natural inclination has now become concern for you. As your solicitor there is nothing wrong with this pre-nuptial agreement as I have already stated. In fact, if you were marrying anyone else, I'd say sign it with an eagerness unbecoming my station."

His confession earned her respect and appreciation.

"Now that I know the truth about this document and can safely assume that Fabien St Croix definitely wasn't here to give his felicitations, I am concerned that you are being asked to enter into a marriage of misery."

His kindness made her want to cry and as she went to respond, he held up his hand to halt her.

"Yes, I know many marriages are based on worse things and Lord only knows that we, British have been doing miserable marriages for alliances and dowries for centuries and so I feel I have a moral duty to warn you that marriage to Gabriel St Croix will not be easy in the slightest, but should you tie the matrimonial knot, just know that you are welcome to come and visit me whether to hide out or for any advice — free of charge," he said, giving her a sincere smile. "And I will stand by you with whatever you need."

She burst into tears at the older man's lovely eloquent speech and since she didn't have her own parents here, it was just the reassurance that she needed.

Lord Gloucester came around his desk and held out a pristine white handkerchief to her which she gratefully accepted.

"Thank you so much for your kind words. I've been feeling so lost lately especially as my own parents live on the other side of the world." She resisted adding that they also knew nothing about what was happening.

He sat down in the chair next to hers and held her hand gently.

"You're not being pressured into marrying him, are you?"

"Oh no, although it is very complicated."

"I can only imagine," he said. "Do you need more time to decide?"

"No. I think that Gabe's grandfather actually helped me to make up my mind. Where's the pen?"

The look on Lord Gloucester's confused face made Callie want to smile. The poor dear man had no idea that until Fabien St Croix's appearance, she had been about to decline Gabe's very generous offer but after meeting the man and almost seeing Gabe's life flash before her eyes, she couldn't in good conscience let him down. After all what was a year in her life if he would spend the rest of his miserable until the day Fabien died?

No, if she could help her old childhood friend then she would. She would learn to grin and bear all the nasty comments directed at her and then disappear once it was all over. Jarrod's suggestion of Alaska wasn't such a bad one after all.

She wasn't about to let that horrid old man win. Shoulders drawn back, she stood and signed the document with Lord Gloucester saying that he would make sure it was delivered post-haste to Gabe's solicitors.

"Thank you again for your kindness. You might regret offering me a place of sanctuary when I turn up every day," she said.

"It would be the highlight of my day," he smiled. "Good luck."

Gabe couldn't believe it. Callie had signed the pre-nuptial agreement. He had to admit that right up until the moment that he had heard from his solicitors, he had paced furiously, feeling so tightly wound and anxious that she would decline him.

Clearly his very generous settlement swayed her mind but that didn't matter. Now all he had to do was marry her before his grandfather got wind of it.

Since he had left Callie's flat the other night, he had made a decision on where to get married without his grandfather knowing until it was too late.

There really was only one place he could think that would make everyone happy, especially Callie and he could only hope she'd agree.

It was the dead of night and they were both on a private plane. She had never travelled in such luxury. He was used to it. The stewardess offered champagne before leaving them alone.

"Callie, I know this isn't the most romantic of reasons to marry and I truly do appreciate what you're doing and giving up for me so I thought it would be at least nice if I actually proposed properly," he said, kneeling down on one knee. "Callie Harrison, my childhood friend, will you marry me?"

He asked with such a bright smile that stupidly she began to cry. This was her first marriage proposal and it wasn't the least bit romantic but she appreciated his gesture.

"Sure, why not?" she glibly said, wiping the tears from her face as he reached into his pocket and pulled out a small velvet box. Opening it, she gasped as the sparkle from the sapphire was brilliant even in the dim light.

"I thought you might like sapphires to match your eyes," he grinned, as she offered a trembling hand to him so he could slide the ring on her finger.

"It's beautiful," she whispered in awe, unable to take her eyes off it.

"Why are you crying? Do you want to change your mind?" He was trying hard to sound as normal as possible but until she said 'I do' he was going to be a nervous wreck, scared that she'd back out at any moment.

"No. I'm crying because…I'm just being silly, that's all," she said, continuing to stare at the ring, the only real piece of jewellery she owned of any kind of value apart from her watch which wasn't even close to being in the same vicinity of value. "Where are we going?"

Since she couldn't get out of the plane, he decided that the truth would be best.

"I thought about what you said and I hope you're not mad but I thought that we should marry in New Zealand, in front of our families."

That prompted another round of tears. What would her parents say to her marrying Gabe because he needed a wife to get away from his grandfather?

"I can't, I can't lie to them…any of them. They'd be devastated to know that this is a sham."

Gabe hadn't thought about it like that. He knew his family would understand the marriage of convenience and would be glad it was to Callie but Callie's family? What if they protested and changed her mind? God, he was an idiot. He had been too busy thinking that every girl wanted her parents to be there on her wedding day — whether it was for convenience or not — and that it was as far away from Fabien as possible, not thinking his gesture would upset her.

"Actually, my parents sort of know the truth. So does Amélie," he said, sheepish. "Not the whole truth but the part about grandfather's demand for me to marry and the fact that he's cut me off."

"Well, Jarrod sort of knows too," she said to Gabe's shock as her cheeks went pink. "After that first time you broached the idea, I needed someone to run it by and tell me that you were just as insane as I thought. Unfortunately Jarrod was more of a fence-sitter and could totally see your point of view."

"Wow." Gabe shook his head in disbelief. "So the only people who don't know anything are your parents? What do you want to do then? Tell them the truth?" He offered to do the right thing but was sick to his stomach of the consequences.

"I think that it's only fair that we tell everyone the real truth."

His worst nightmare coming was true but at least if everyone close to them knew the reality, maybe it would in fact be better, he prayed silently to himself.

It was a long flight and Gabe thought it would be better and more relaxing if he left her to her own thoughts. Goodness knows that he too could use the time to come to terms with what was about to happen.

"Gabe?" she said, her voice quiet. He looked at her and waited. "What happens if I'm a really terrible and embarrassing wife?"

"Oh Callie," he sighed, and gave her hand a squeeze. "I'll be there by your side and nothing you could do would ever embarrass me. We can learn how to be a married couple together."

"Promise?"

Her eyes shone with so much hope and trust. He didn't want to let her down. That one word now made him feel like Atlas and he could only hope that he was strong enough to support the burden for her…for them both.

"Promise."

His answer relaxed her but she still worried about what her parents would make of her marriage of convenience.

Chapter 10

It was a surprise homecoming that had everyone in tears. Squeals of delight with hugs and kisses and more hugs and kisses going around and around.

"Why didn't you tell us you were coming?" Miranda Harrison chided, ecstatic that Callie was home.

"Then it wouldn't have been a surprise," she laughed.

It was so nice to be in the bosom of her family again. She could feel the love and it overwhelmed her. It took a few more minutes before anyone even noticed the ring on her finger.

"What is that?" Miranda shrieked, delighted. "John, John, do you see the ring on her finger?"

"Yes dear, but I didn't realise that you had a serious boyfriend?" he said, perplexed as Callie bit her bottom lip.

Now was the time for the truth but it was hard to get the words out. Confessing was much harder than she had imagined.

It was Gabe who stepped in and cleared his throat before answering for Callie.

"Actually that's why we're here. Miranda, John, I'm not sure if mum and dad have told you the latest news that Fabien has cut me off without a cent unless I marry by the time I'm thirty which is only a few months away," he said, and to his relief they nodded. "Well, Callie agreed to be my wife. We know that it's a bit of a shock but it's only for a year and then we'll divorce."

"Son, are you sure about this?" his father said, concerned as he put a hand on Gabe's shoulder.

"Callie? You're willing to marry Gabe in a marriage of convenience?" her father said, more concerned for his daughter.

"Yes." She nodded. "It's the right thing to do."

She saw the anxiousness on her parents' faces and felt a pang of guilt that this wasn't what they wanted for their only daughter.

"And you're not being coerced?" John said, not to be rude but to be sure.

"No, of course not,' she said, emphatic, much to Gabe's relief.

"Ma chérie, you don't have to do this. We can find another way." The voice who had spoken up surprised everyone in the room. Tears pooled in Marielle's eyes. "I know Fabien. He won't like this and I want you to be sure. Gabe will protect you as much as possible but Fabien is…well Fabien. I won't have you being hurt and manipulated by the St Croix family."

François was proud of his wife for looking out for Callie and Callie too, was stunned by Marielle's touching concern.

"Thank you for your support. I'm glad that you all know the truth because I'd have hated to deceive you all. Even though this might be a marriage of convenience, Gabe wanted us to marry in front of our families…I do too," she said, moisture in her eyes as everyone else seemed to feel the same way.

"We're family…" John said, finally breaking the moment of silence. "And family sticks together. Welcome to the family, son."

Congratulations and delight went around as if the engagement was real and then they called Jarrod who promised to be on a later flight.

Amélie had come home and squealed her delight at seeing Gabe again in the flesh and was then awkward around Callie. This was the first time that they had seen each other in years and she was still embarrassed and feeling guilty over the way she had treated her friend.

Everyone discreetly left the room to leave the two women to talk in private.

"Hi Callie, how are you?" Amélie said.

"I'm good, thanks. You?" she said, with the same stiff politeness.

"Great."

The silence between them was thick and uncomfortable but Amélie knew she had to make the first move.

"Callie, I…I want to apologise for my atrocious behaviour all those years ago when you came to France for my sixteenth birthday. I didn't mean to be such a bitch to you." Amélie looked and sounded contrite but then confessed, "Okay, at the time I did. But I swear I've changed and I want us to be friends again if that's possible."

Seeing that Amélie's apology was sincere, Callie decided to offer an olive branch remembering that Gabe had recently lost his best friend too, and if she could forgive Amélie then maybe Gabe could try and forgive Luc.

"I guess we should try to get along if we're going to be sisters-in-law," she said.

"Pardonne?" Amélie's eyes widened in confusion and surprise.

"Gabe and I are getting married…for convenience," she quickly said, hoping that Amélie wouldn't react too harshly at the news and was stunned to see her old friend's face light up with delight.

"Seriously? That's fantastic."

"Really? You're not upset because I'm not rich and part of your social circle?" she said, unable to quite believe that Amélie's reaction was genuine.

Guilt flickered across Amélie's face until it became a wide smile again.

"No, I think it's fantastic and Gabe couldn't have picked a better wife."

"It's a marriage of convenience."

"Doesn't matter." Amélie waved her hand dismissively. "Now we really can be sisters like we wanted all those years ago."

Callie couldn't quite believe the change that had come over Amélie. She was like the Amélie she had grown up with and yet Callie was wary of this change in her old friend's attitude. Had the haughty, bitchy Amélie gone for good or was she just hiding for now?

Amélie gave her a tight hug and then led her into the kitchen.

"Congratulations," she squealed, hugging her brother.

"Did Callie tell you that…"

"It's a marriage of convenience? Yes, but it doesn't matter because now we'll really be sisters and you couldn't have picked a better person to marry."

Everyone in the room looked speechlessly at Amélie.

"What?" she said, indignant before waving her hand dismissively. "Yes, I know, I was an utter and complete bitch before but now I know Callie is, was, the only true friend that I've ever had and I'm not going to give up on winning back her friendship and trust. Besides, you all know that Gabe couldn't have picked a better person for a marriage of convenience."

"And you were worried that our families wouldn't be happy for us," he teased as Callie gave him a hard nudge in the ribs. "Ow, I'm going to be a battered husband. I might have to rethink this marriage."

It was a wonderful dinner and the level of noise and laughter only got louder when Jarrod finally turned up.

By the time dinner had finished and everyone was relaxed about their family reunion and bringing Jarrod up to speed on Gabe and Callie's engagement, it was François who turned the conversation serious.

"So when will you have the wedding?" he said.

"As soon as possible. No fuss. Just our family and the celebrant. I don't want to give grand-père too much time to try and stop it."

"You'll have to go on a honeymoon," Marielle said.

The happy couple looked horrified by the idea.

"No, this can be our honeymoon as well, catching up with family that we haven't seen for ages," Gabe said to Callie's relief.

"At least spend a couple of nights in a hotel then, for appearances sake," John said.

Everyone murmured their agreement and soon Callie was being pulled to one side to discuss dresses and flowers. By the time she went to bed, she was exhausted. A low-key wedding was still turning into a big to-do thanks to Amélie and their mothers.

"We'll have to go dress shopping," Amélie squealed.

"And get makeovers," Miranda said.

"No, no, no," Callie said, horrified. "It's supposed to be low-key."

"That doesn't mean that you can't look beautiful on your wedding day," Marielle said as the other women agreed.

"It's a marriage of convenience," she said. "We don't need all of that kind of fluff…please."

"If you want Fabien to buy it then you will have to look like a totally in love bride," Marielle said.

Callie bit her lip. Her future mother-in-law was right but after meeting Fabien, she knew that he'd never accept their marriage, genuine or not.

"But I really don't want that much fuss. Seriously, even if this wasn't a marriage of convenience, I'm just not that kind of girl," she said, hoping that the other women wouldn't go overboard.

Once upon a time she had been totally that kind of girl but now she wasn't as worried about her appearance as she was when she was younger. However, it had taken seeing herself after Hazel had dolled her up that night to realise just how far Callie had let herself go, so now she did put a little more effort into her appearance but still, she wasn't comfortable being completely made over.

François and John had managed to find a celebrant to marry their children at short notice and it was decided that tomorrow would be their wedding day.

Even though everyone knew it was a marriage of convenience, it still didn't stop an electric atmosphere permeate the houses of both families. Gabe decided to stay with his family to spend time with them and they were to be married in John and Miranda's garden where they had spent so many happy years.

The morning of her wedding, Callie was a mixture of nerves and excitement as if this was the real thing. She couldn't help it because wedding of convenience or not, she would soon be Mrs Gabriel St Croix.

A light rap on her door opened to her mother's beaming smile at seeing her only daughter awake.

"How are you feeling?"

"Like this is a real wedding," she said, nerves fluttering in her stomach.

"It is real, honey. You still have time to change your mind if you want. No one will be angry."

"Thanks, mum but what's a year in my life? I've haven't told anyone, especially Gabe this, but I've met Fabien, mum. The man is truly a horrible tyrant and none of the stories were exaggerated. I could honestly see Gabe's life flashing before my eyes. He should be able to live his life his way and not have to dance to his grandfather's tune, because it really would be soul destroying."

"When did you meet Fabien?" Miranda was wide-eyed at the news.

Callie explained what had happened in Lord Gloucester's office before begging her mother to promise not to say anything.

"Please don't say anything, mum. Gabe would be furious with his grandfather but it helped steel my resolve to help Gabe. I don't want Gabe to get upset over it. I wasn't hurt although my knees were definitely knocking. Fabien is very frightening and intimidating."

It was only now that Miranda truly and completely understood Callie's reasoning for marrying Gabriel. It wasn't as if she was concerned for her daughter because she trusted Gabe like a son to look after Callie, but she had to admit to a little anxiety that perhaps Callie's motives hadn't been as altruistic as they had been led to believe. Relief and pride flooded through her that her daughter really had grown into a beautiful woman, inside and out.

Miranda tucked some hair behind her daughter's ear as she and Callie continued to have a loving heart to heart with Callie confessing everything that had happened ever since she had been fired from her au pair job, which now seemed like a lifetime ago.

They were still sitting on her bed when another light rap on the door sounded.

"Morning, honey. Listen, Amy and Marielle will be over in a couple of hours and I'm making your favourite pancakes. I thought we could have a nice family brunch," her father said.

"Great idea. I'll just get up," she said. "Mum, thanks for not being mad at me." Giving her mother a tight hug she felt safe and happy…loved.

"Of course I'm not, darling. I just wished that you felt you could have told me, that's all."

Callie got changed and came downstairs to catch up with her family.

"You're sure about this, sis? You don't have to do this if you don't want to," Jarrod said, as everyone looked at her.

No matter how many times Callie said yes, she was sure, her family still made her feel reassured and loved that her happiness was paramount to them and she had missed it after living so far away.

"Now why don't you boys go next door and you can catch up with each other and send the girls over. We have so much to do," Miranda said, breaking up their family reunion

The Harrison men took the hint.

"We'll be back to get dressed around four, okay, hon?" John said.

"Perfect."

While Callie was upstairs killing time by painting her nails, she heard laughter and squeals from downstairs and knew that Amélie and Marielle had arrived, hearing their excited chatter the entire way to her room.

"Happy wedding day!" they chimed in unison making her smile.

"We have a present for you," Marielle declared as Amélie held up a garment bag and unzipped it before pulling out a beautiful white silk dress. Callie's eyes popped out of her head.

"We know you don't want a fuss but darling, it's your wedding day and we wanted you to feel like a princess," her mother said.

"B-but h-how?" She stared at the most gorgeous dress she had ever seen in her life.

"It's one of my designer dresses that I've never worn," Amélie said, hoping that Callie would not only like it, but not mind that Amélie had brought it for herself even if she had never worn it like so many other items of clothing in her wardrobe.

"Its beautiful," she breathed in awe, fingering the soft silk.

"I'm so glad that you like it. I'd love for you to wear it as your wedding dress," Amélie said, hesitant but with hope in her voice.

"Would it even fit?" She was too scared to dream that such a dress could fit her since she and Amélie weren't exactly the same shape.

"Well, let's try," Marielle said, and before she could even blink, Callie was undressed and then redressed in the beautiful silk dress by a top French designer.

She needn't have worried because the dress fitted her like a glove with the only exception that the hem was slightly too long because Callie was shorter and therefore it pooled at her feet. Since this was meant to be her wedding dress, it wouldn't matter much about the hem because no one would really notice.

"You look beautiful, utterly gorgeous." Her mother beamed, dabbing her eyes.

"Oui, magnifique," Marielle said.

"I can't picture a better or more beautiful bride for my brother," Amélie added, tears also in her eyes and Callie knew then that her best friend was truly back and genuinely happy for her.

"Then you should be my bridesmaid," she said to Amélie's elated squeal and hug.

The four women in the room were once again crying with joy and excitement.

The second surprise of the day was that Amélie was doing her hair and make-up.

"B-but you've already given me a dress," Callie said.

"I've been taking a hairdressing course so I can do mum and Miranda's hair whenever they like but also because I've decided that I want to start a charity or something to help women with cancer, to pamper them or help them style themselves so they can feel better about themselves," Amélie said, leaving Callie speechless.

Never in a million years would she have predicted someone like Amélie being a hairdresser, even doing the course and yet she was so proud of her friend. This truly was a new Amélie.

"What a wonderful idea," she said, as Amélie beamed at Callie's support.

Looking at herself in the mirror, Callie looked and felt like a princess. Marielle had lent her some very real diamonds and a tiara making her nervous that she would lose them but Marielle just laughed.

"Darling, no one's going to rob you and its only family."

A knock at the door this time signalled that it was her father. He poked his head around the door to see four gorgeous women in the room but his fatherly pride and love was ready to burst at seeing his beautiful daughter.

"Ready, darling?" he said, his voice suspiciously choked up as the three women exited the room to give father and daughter a moment alone. "My word, you look absolutely stunning, Callie."

She blushed and he held out his elbow for her.

"Last chance to do a runner. I can get the car, you change and I'll fly you to Mexico," he teased, making her laugh and relax.

Callie didn't realise how much tension she had been holding in until then.

"I'm actually excited and in some weird way, it really feels like my real wedding day."

"Well, that's because it is your wedding day, no matter the reason, we *all* just want you to be happy."

"I will be, dad. Gabe will take care of me."

"Good." He gave a firm nod of his head. "I'd hate to have to box his ears in."

She gave another laugh and let her father lead her to the altar.

Gabe was wearing a simple suit and had Jarrod standing up for him as his best man. They had a great catch-up last night and this morning even with Jarrod's big brother warning not to hurt his sister to which Gabe promised that he would try his damnedest not to. He would never forget the sacrifice Callie was making for him.

They were standing outside in the garden and even though there was literally only family and the celebrant, he still had nerves and wanted to laugh at how ridiculous he felt. He was finally getting married, not in a church with hundreds of guests but in a backyard garden with family and this seemed so much more overwhelming.

It may not be to the woman he loved and a marriage of convenience but he was still nervous as hell. Would he have been worse if he had been in love with his bride or would he only be able to relax once the celebrant declared they were married because then his grandfather couldn't do a thing about it.

"You okay?" Jarrod said, seeing Gabe's nervousness as his friend fidgeted.

"I can't believe how nervous I feel and it's not even for keeps."

Before Jarrod could say something in return, Amélie appeared and the music began as she walked down the imaginary aisle before someone changed the music again for the bride.

Since the dress was a little too long, Callie had to hold it up with one hand as she also held a tiny bouquet of flowers.

Out of all the scenarios he had envisaged, seeing Callie looking like a real bride in a drop-dead sexy dress wasn't one of them. Fidgeting with his hands as she approached, he gave her what he hoped was a happy smile but was still afraid that it might look more nervous.

As she went to stand beside him, he leant down and whispered, "You look gorgeous."

She blushed at his words and then the whole ceremony went past in a complete blur until he held her hand and slid a matching sapphire and diamond wedding band next to her engagement ring.

Looking up at him under hooded eyelids, she saw his Adam's apple bob and then his strong jawline before seeing the smile on his face. It warmed and reassured her that she really had done the right thing.

"You may kiss your bride."

Gabe wasn't quite listening as he was frozen at the look that Callie was giving him. So much trust and faith in her eyes and he prayed that he wouldn't let her down.

A subtle nudge from Jarrod brought him back to reality and as he recalled the celebrant's words, he realised that they had never talked about the kiss.

This would be the first time he had ever kissed Callie and he quickly decided that a quick chaste kiss would do especially since everyone knew that they weren't in love so they wouldn't be expecting something passionate.

Callie's eyes automatically closed as she saw Gabe's face come closer and realised with a start that he was about to kiss her. Her mind screamed no! very loudly and she wanted to run away. They hadn't discussed any kind of kiss nor how they would handle it in public. Before she could put her thoughts into any kind of order she felt the lightest caress across her lips but it could have easily been the breeze and then heard cheering and clapping.

Had Gabe even kissed her? Oh God, what if he had and she didn't even realise? Scared, she slowly opened her eyes to see him grinning at her and then pulling her towards him for a big bear hug.

"It's all over," he whispered and she felt all the tension drain from her body. "Thank you."

He let her go and the rest of the family surrounded them showering them with hugs, kisses and congratulations.

It wasn't until much later that she realised that she didn't even really remember much of what had happened. She could have agreed to only wear purple for the rest of her life for all she knew. She could only hope that they really had done the right thing.

"Tu ressembles à un ange," he quietly said, looking at his bride.

They were now alone in their hotel room and Callie's keen sense of hearing had heard him.

"Pardon, what did you say?" she said, hoping it wasn't cursing at being shackled to her because it was too late for regrets now.

"I said, you look like an angel. And along with the tiara, you could have passed for royalty."

"Oh, this was one of Amy's dresses that she's never worn." His words made her blush furiously. "And it was your mother's tiara that she had kindly lent for the occasion." She hoped that he hadn't gotten the notion that she had purposely gone out and brought something special for the day.

Gabe looked at his *wife* and couldn't even begin to picture his sister in the same dress looking as angelic as Callie.

"Well, it suits you. Do you want the bathroom first to freshen up and change?" he said, changing the subject.

"That would be nice. Do you mind if I have a bath?"

They were both being so polite with each other but not in an awkward way.

"Take your time, I'm going to watch some TV and unwind from a long day." He almost laughed wondering if any bride or groom in the world right now was having a wedding night like his.

Coming out of the bathroom, Callie felt refreshed and snug in a hotel robe. Although the room was empty, she could feel a draught and saw the door to the balcony open. Gabe was leaning on the balcony railing with his arms holding a bottle of beer, looking out into the night.

"Gabe?"

He turned his head towards her but didn't move otherwise so she stepped outside to him.

"All finished? Feeling better?"

Callie was wearing a luxurious fluffy robe, her skin looking fresh and pink.

"Are you okay? No regrets?" she said, concerned and worried that he was indeed regretting their hasty marriage. She felt the urge to hug him tightly but stopped herself.

"Just enjoying the quiet, it's been a long day," he said. "I really do appreciate your sacrifice for me and I hope that you don't have any regrets either."

Instantly her heart went out to him. She looked down her at her feet for a moment before lifting her head to look at him.

"I don't and you don't have to keep thanking me. I was only doing what was right."

She could see the burden he was carrying and had hoped that by marrying him, it would be lightened but clearly it weighed as heavily as ever.

"I'm going to bed."

"Goodnight Callie, sweet dreams."

She gave him one last lingering look like she wanted to say something more but instead went back inside.

It amazed her as she pulled back the covers and picked a pillow that she wasn't afraid to sleep in the same bed as Gabe. This might not be how she had envisioned her wedding night but she was honestly too tired to even think about it or care. Crawling beneath the covers she was asleep as soon as her head hit the pillow.

Gabe spent a little longer outside contemplating his life. It surprised him today that it had been so easy to say such meaningful vows in front of their families to someone he didn't love like a life-partner but a sister. Now he had a wife to provide for and take care of, even if it was only for a year.

He watched her sleep a while, amazed that she hadn't kicked up a fuss about sharing a bed although the way she slept so soundly perhaps she had been too tired to worry about it. Rubbing his face with his hands, God he was tired. Easing himself into the bed beside her, he closed his eyes and prayed that he had done the right thing.

Chapter 11

Callie woke and stretched, feeling like she had slept all cramped up and yet as she turned her head, she realised that she was in a king-sized bed, because Gabe was miles away from her still asleep.

She felt rested and noted the time was after nine and therefore she must have needed the sleep to wake so late but now that she was awake, she remembered that the two sets of siblings were supposed to spend their day together before Jarrod went back to the farm.

Sliding out of bed, she tried not to make too much noise as she bustled around. The sun was up and it looked to be another sunny day so she found denim shorts and a very light summer top.

Her stomach growled making her aware that she was hungry but should she go downstairs to eat at one of the hotel restaurants or should she order room service?

She couldn't even order breakfast for Gabe because she had no idea of his preferences and that caused her brow to deeply furrow.

How embarrassing was that? She was now a wife without any clue to any of her husband's preferences regarding food or anything else. It pulled her up short that big yawning gaps in their marriage had appeared on day one of their new life like giant sinkholes appearing out of the blue.

As she dithered about what to do for breakfast, Gabe loudly yawned, rousing from his sleep and noted that Callie was no longer in bed.

"Good morning, did you sleep well?" he said, stretching and yawning some more.

"Breakfast!" she blurted out, flustered.

"Did you order some? Should I get up before it arrives?" he said, unsure what had her so panicked.

"Sorry," she flushed. "I was just realising that we don't know anything about each other like eating habits, favourite colours or even music. We're married and we don't know each other."

Gabe heard the panic rising in Callie's voice and sat up and rubbed his face to focus.

"Okay, calm down, one thing at a time. Have you had breakfast or ordered any?"

"No," she said. "I didn't know what to do…eat downstairs or order room service. Then I didn't know what you'd want and —"

"Callie, it's okay. Breathe," he said. "We're supposed to be spending the day with Amy and Jarrod so why don't you order breakfast, make mine coffee with…" He quickly scanned the menu. "A big breakfast and I'll get up while you do that."

His instructions seemed to calm her down as she did his bidding. It was the kind of morning that she would have loved to linger and eat but since they were supposed to be meeting their siblings shortly, they managed to eat quickly and leave the hotel.

It was yet another round of delighted hugs and kisses when they turned up to their family homes to pick up their siblings. Amélie had heard of a place down in the Waikato called The Home of the Magic Gnome and it was where they all decided to go on a road trip. All four happily set off with a constant chatter about anything and everything.

"You know what I can't understand?" Jarrod turned off the radio so he could hear his sister. "How come everyone is so happy Gabe and I married? It's not even real."

"It's real, Cal. We have an official piece of paper that says it," her new husband said, facetious.

"Yeah, Cal, it's real," Amélie said. "And why can't we be happy that the Harrison and St Croix families are finally united by marriage?"

"Because it's a year and then we'll be divorced."

"But marriage is marriage and I know that all our parents think of all of us as their children, now it's more official. Besides, you'll forever be known as *the first* Mrs Gabriel St Croix. *Now* that's a title not to be sneezed at," Amélie teased as Callie loudly groaned.

"Do you really want to know the truth, Cal? The absolute truth as to why both sets of parents are so happy and overjoyed that you two married, for real or convenience?" Jarrod's serious tone now had everyone's complete and undivided attention judging by the acutely curious looks on all of their faces.

"Why?" She was scared that Jarrod's answer would be something she didn't want to hear, like Gabe and Callie were meant to be together forever.

"Because until this…" He paused for emphasis. "*None* of us were even likely to marry. *None* of us even have serious partners and so even though it's not quite the way anyone imagined it, to see their son and daughter marry, is a dream come true for them," Jarrod said, as everyone remained silent. "Think about it, every parent's dream is to make sure that their children are happy, settled, all that stuff so to have a wedding and especially one that unites our families is like the Holy Grail to them."

The car remained silent as everyone thought on Jarrod's words. There was a certain ring of truth to them since who knew when any of them would have actually got married.

"Jeez, who knew that smelling all that cow manure and country living would make you such a deep thinker, Jare," Callie teased, lightening the mood to make everyone laugh.

"It's true, Jare," Gabe grinned. "You've never been known for your philosophical ramblings. Obviously farming's making you more intelligent."

"Well, if that's true, then why are we all driving to the middle of nowhere to see a bunch of supposedly magical gnomes?" he said, and the atmosphere in the car turned back to bantering and laughter.

The Home of the Magic Gnome was truly was an impressive place. A bright yellow castle out in the middle of nowhere. A castle filled with various mythological and fairy things and to Callie it really was wondrous as she stepped over the threshold and saw row upon row of shelves filled with purportedly magic gnomes.

How would she be able to choose one with all this choice?

She browsed the mail board filled with letters from all over the world advising that the magic gnomes had indeed worked and how.

To Callie it was a testament that this had to be true. There was no way that people would write all these letters if it wasn't.

They all took their time browsing and laughing as they showed each other the various little figurines. Jarrod saw a little gnome sitting on a tractor, there wasn't another like it and so he grabbed it.

That was one of the things Callie liked about this place, all the so-called magic gnomes were practically one-off and thus she reasoned was why they worked because each one was meant for a particular customer.

She tried hard to think about what she wanted in her life to happen. Right now she needed courage to face the world, especially Gabe's grandfather now that she was Mrs Gabriel St Croix.

Also she needed the strength to withstand the barrage of nasty and snide comments that people would enviably make about her, but then she decided that it was only for a year so maybe she should concentrate on her life after that. Perhaps meeting the man of her dreams, marrying for love and having a family.

As she continued to browse, a little gnome seemed to jump out at her. It was writing a book and Callie immediately thought of Amélie as she wrote her new future. She then saw a gnome family happily living in a farmhouse and got that for Jarrod.

It seemed strange that she could instantly find gnomes for the others but not herself. Maybe she was just being too picky but she quickly shook her head.

Everyone was going to be surprised to find out that she had also bought them a gnome. Then she hesitated, biting her lip in worry. Would the gnomes still work their magic if you had more than one? Perhaps it would only partially work but even though she was buying the gnomes for them for sentimental reasons, she still hoped their magic would work.

It wasn't until she turned to go into the next aisle that she saw the perfect figurine for Gabe — he had always talked about finding someone he could love and trust, that wasn't after his money — well, the little boy gnome was holding someone's heart in his hands but was looking around for the owner.

If she hadn't been thinking about Gabe, she could have mistaken it for a serial killer gnome, she giggled to herself but instead she knew that this was perfect. He was this gnome, looking for the owner of the mysterious heart.

Looking at her watch, she was surprised to find that they had been in the store for well over two hours and yet it felt like no time had passed at all.

Feeling a little down because she couldn't seem to find a gnome for herself, Callie knew she was in a muddle about what she wanted. Going around the store again, she noted that she hadn't seen any of the others since they had split up earlier. It wasn't that the place was overly large but she still felt like they had disappeared.

Continuing to wander and growing despondent that maybe there was just no specific gnome for her indecisive mind, and that she would be going home empty-handed, she finally came across the perfect gnome for her. It was a pretty little gnome standing with her husband and children outside a mushroom home.

Callie could have sworn that she had seen each and every gnome the place had on offer and yet, she had missed this one. The little figurine seemed to sum up exactly what she wanted as her future and so she picked it up off the shelf to buy.

Gabe had to admit that he thought that Amélie's idea to come to this place was childish until he stepped over the threshold and almost felt a tingling sensation in his body. He knew it wasn't real but he felt it would be nice to have fun and believe in it while he was here. Goodness knows, he could use a little magic in his life right now, as well.

Since they had all agreed not to show their purchases until later that evening, he felt comfortable browsing and quickly lost sight of the others.

He wasn't sure what any of them were planning on buying but he immediately felt his focus drawn down onto a bottom shelf to see two gnome friends sitting on a bench laughing. It reminded him of Luc and although he still felt betrayed, he decided it could be a peace offering.

Then he saw a girl gnome dancing with happiness and he thought of his sister as she seemed to have a new lease on life. He picked that figurine up as well hoping that Amélie wouldn't think it odd that he had brought her a magic gnome when she was buying her own.

For himself, he found a gnome that seemed to have broken out of prison. The little gnome was wearing prison stripes and the ball and chain had been taken off, leaving him jumping for joy. It was exactly how he felt. A fresh start.

As he continued to browse, it was almost as if the sunlight had shone specifically on this one particular figurine making it sparkle. Getting closer, he realised it must have just been a trick of the light as he stood there simply staring at it for ages.

It was a knight down on one knee looking up at his princess with love. He knew that's what Callie would like — a man who could not only defend her but could openly declare his love — a knight in shining armour.

For Jarrod, he could only wish happiness and decided on a set of scales that had an equal balance with money on one side and a little baby gnome on the other side smiling happily, which to Gabe represented the gnome being happy with his well-balanced life.

The return trip home seemed to fly by as they excitedly chattered about the different gnomes they had seen. Amélie had been laughing at one where the boy gnome seemed to fall at the girl gnome's feet. It reminded Gabe of the gnome he had brought for Callie, and yet he hadn't seen the one that his sister was describing.

Both Gabe and Jarrod had seen the gnome sailing away on a luxury yacht and Callie had laughed at a girl gnome holding lots of purchases in one hand and a fistful of dollars in the other.

They decided to show each other their purchases after dinner. Their parents had happily grumbled about being excluded, but the four children seemed to sense that this was a special moment for all of them.

They each carried their bag into the room and sat on the floor in a circle.

"Can I just say before we start that Amy and I are so grateful that the Harrison family came into our lives. It seems that you are always helping us, coming to our rescue and have been nothing but wonderful, loyal, honest and loving since that first day we knocked on your door," Gabe said, his voice choked with emotion that had everyone especially the girls in tears. "I don't know when we'll all be together again like this but I just want you to know how honoured we are to be best friends."

They all stood to hug each other tightly and it reminded Callie of all those years ago when Gabe and Amy had to return to France, only this time she and Gabe would be the ones leaving and as husband and wife.

"Okay, who wants to go first?" Jarrod said, looking at everyone.

"I will," Callie said, "but first I have to say that I brought you all one too…but only because they really did seem to jump out at me and I couldn't resist."

"I did too," Amélie echoed.

"Me too."

"And me."

They all looked at each other in astonishment.

"So we all brought each other and ourselves gnomes?" Callie said, in disbelief.

"So we all have *four* magic gnomes…is that allowed?" Jarrod chuckled.

"I can't wait to see what you all think that I need," Amélie giggled.

"Why don't we all open our own to show and then surprise each other since we don't know what those are?" Gabe said to everyone's excited agreement.

The first round of show and tell had everyone laughing at each other's choice of gnome for themselves.

Then Callie enjoyed telling Amélie that she had picked the little writing gnome because she could now write her own future and that had her friend in tears. She felt nervous explaining to Gabe in front of their siblings just why she had chosen the gnome for him but he simply nodded his head in thanks.

Receiving her gnome from Gabe in return made Callie tremble slightly as he had picked such a lovely and thoughtful figurine. She only just managed to blink back the tears that were rapidly threatening.

Jarrod went to pack his figurines away back at the Harrison home and Callie had also gone to have a private word with her brother before they went to the airport.

"Are you going to be okay?" he said, full of big brotherly concern.

"I hope so. I'm a little scared but I keep telling myself it's just a year and then I can slink off into obscurity," she said, trying to sound confident.

"You call me for *anything*, okay?" he said, hugging her tightly as she cried.

"I will."

"Marriage of convenience or not, you make sure that Gabe treats you well."

"He will."

"Be happy."

"You too."

She thought that she was all cried out but it seemed that saying goodbye to her brother at the airport was just as hard and the car ride back to the hotel was silent.

Gabe was grateful for the silence as he thought about today and the little gnome that Callie had brought for him. It was similar in a way to the one he had brought for her and it made him wonder if they could both find that special someone. He wasn't certain that for him such a love could exist but for now that would have to wait as first he had to find a job.

"When are we moving back home?" she said, when they reached the hotel.

"Ah…" He wasn't quite sure which home she was referring to. "We go back to London in another week."

"I meant to mum and dad's or your parents'," she said, a little disappointed that their time in New Zealand would soon be over.

"We're not. We're staying here for the duration," he said to her shock.

"B-but why? We're here to see our families, spend time with them."

"We decided that in order for this to look proper we needed to stay at the hotel, for honeymoon privacy." He raked a hand through his hair. Seeing her crestfallen face he quickly added, "But why don't we spend the last couple of nights at our parents."

She seemed to brighten fleetingly before asking, "Whose 'we'?" Because she knew that it wasn't her that he was referring to.

"Our dads and Jarrod and me," he said, sheepish.

She wanted to argue that it wasn't their decision to make for her but decided against it because they were probably right. If Gabe's grandfather had spies in New Zealand — which was highly likely — they would need to look like a couple in love that wanted privacy.

"Okay."

He seemed relieved at her easy acceptance and then felt a little disappointed by it. Realising that he was only being silly, he pushed the feeling aside.

This morning Callie got the leisurely breakfast that she had wanted yesterday and Gabe happily joined her. They both were quietly reading the newspaper when Gabe put his down and broke the silence.

"Have you any thoughts on what you might like to do today?"

"I know while we're here that Amy wants to take me shopping for some Kiwi designer stuff so I wouldn't look like a total hick and embarrass myself when we first get back. She's going to try and style me into a wife befitting your station," she said, trying to sound unafraid and confident.

"I want you to be you. If people are only going to like you for what you wear, they're not friends," he snapped.

She jumped in her seat at his vehement response. Couldn't he see that she was doing this so he wouldn't be embarrassed by her?

"Actually I must admit I do like the designer clothes, I've just never been able to afford them before."

Gabe felt somewhat placated by Callie's response that she wasn't trying to change herself just for him. He had snapped because he was still feeling guilty at pushing her into marrying him and he didn't want her to change into yet another superficial society princess like Amélie had done all those years ago.

He couldn't bear it if the same thing happened to Callie because it would be his fault. Besides, he liked her the way she was — opinionated, sassy and feisty but also caring and kind, which brought his him around to another puzzling thought.

"Is it weird that we both brought each other gnomes about love?" he said, unsure if he wanted to open this can of worms but it was too late now.

She bit her lip knowing exactly what he meant.

"I guess not, considering we just married for convenience," she said. "I brought mine so that if those gnomes really are magic, you could find that special someone who trusts and loves *you* implicitly. That's why your gnome has her heart and not vice versa."

"Same reason that I gave you the knight swearing his eternal love and devotion to his princess. That's what you deserve, someone who will love and protect you."

A heavy silence fell around them for a moment before Gabe broke it.

"Did I tell you I brought one for Luc?"

"You did?"

Her eyes widened with delighted surprise and he felt a warm tingling shoot through him.

"Yes. It jumped out at me. It's of two gnomes sitting on a park bench. You can tell that they're best friends."

Callie wanted to go over and hug him pleased that he was ready to offer Luc an olive branch but instead she remained firmly in her seat.

"That's fantastic. I'm sure that he'll love it. You know when you said that it 'jumped' out at you, that's exactly what I thought of my choices. They all seemed to just *magically* jump out at me too."

This started a debate over whether they both thought the gnomes really were magic, or perhaps it had been a trick of the light or wishful thinking. Nothing was resolved and in the end they decided that they'd have to let the gnomes settle it.

Now that they had relaxed, they decided to walk around the city remembering all the good times and places they used to go. It was a surprise to see just how much things had changed.

Although they touched and held hands comfortably, neither made a move for more intimate affection and it wasn't until after dinner that Gabe realised that it had to be addressed.

Trying to think up a nice and non-confrontational way to broach the tricky subject without either of them getting mad or annoyed at the other, he ended up just trying to wing it.

"Do you remember how awkward our wedding kiss was?"

Seeing the startled look of panic in Callie's eyes, he mentally kicked himself knowing he should have gently built up to the question.

"Y-yes, why?"

"Because although we're comfortable with each other which is a good thing, we're a little awkward on the intimate stuff."

"B-but you said we weren't —"

Callie's cheeks were fused with heat and to save her from saying the wrong thing, he cut her off.

"We need to be seen kissing or being affectionate in public."

He saw the relief flow through her before she looked thoughtful.

"Doesn't holding hands and hugging count?" she said, even though she knew that kissing would confirm it even more than either of these other things would.

"Of course it does, only the paparazzi or nosy journalists will want to see us kiss, otherwise our marriage will be on the rocks or near divorce. It cements our 'love' and marriage."

Her heart sank that he was right. If she refused to kiss him in public, everyone would just think that they were good friends or not really married even if they protested otherwise.

"So what are we going to do?"

"All we need is to feel comfortable with each other. The kiss doesn't have to be full on."

Again she felt relieved by his words and it made her wonder if there was something wrong with her that she might be the only woman in the world that didn't want a sexual relationship with Gabe or to kiss him like that.

Gabe could see Callie's thoughts flittering through her mind and knew he had just married the only woman in the world that he was going to have to cajole to kiss him and surprisingly it made him want to laugh. He was certain another man's ego would have taken a serious dent by Callie's lack of enthusiasm.

"What I propose is that we practise —"

"Practise?" she squealed in alarm.

"Calm down, Cal. I meant practise just me kissing your forehead, cheek and the occasional quick peck on the mouth until we feel a little more comfortable," he said, trying to put her at ease.

"Okay," she said, still nervous until she saw that Gabe wasn't about to jump on her and just start kissing her willy-nilly.

"Let's pretend we're walking on the street, come on, hold my hand," he said, and she did as he asked. It felt embarrassing to be walking around the room role-playing. "Now, let's look in the jeweller's window."

He moved his arm to around her shoulders and pointed to an imaginary window.

"I think that necklace would look fantastic on you."

She remained silent unable to play make-believe until he looked down at her.

"Come on, pretend," he said, turning back to look at the pretend shop window.

"Ah…I'm beginning to think that you don't know me at all," she pouted, and felt him stiffen as she tried to hide her smile. "That is *way too* cheap for my taste. You can't even see the diamonds. Now that one over there…" She pointed at the imaginary window. "Now that's more like it."

Gabe, happy that Callie was playing along, pretended to be outraged at what she was pointing to.

"That's fifty thousand dollars!"

"Am I not worth it?" she grinned, batting her eyelids furiously at him.

He chuckled and his arm slid from her shoulders up to her neck as he pulled her close with the crook of his elbow and quickly kissed her lips just as any couple would have done.

She froze for a split second and then relaxed as he looked at her grinning.

"See, it doesn't have to be weird or awkward."

She had to agree with what he said and it helped that it had happened so quickly that she didn't have time to even think about it.

"Let's try another scenario. We're walking down the street and paparazzi have us cornered. They refuse to let us go unless we give them a kiss."

He turned her to face him and Callie felt her heart pounding even though it was only pretend but she was ramrod straight and wasn't the least bit relaxed. Feeling her tension, he lightly shook her by the shoulders until he felt her relax.

"There, now you feel a little more relaxed. So the cameras are there," he said, pointing. "And now…" He grabbed her upper arms tighter and pulled her towards him for a smashing of their lips. He then pushed her back slightly and she wobbled.

"See, just like in the movies," he chuckled.

She looked at him as if to say *are you crazy*, but then she thought about it and he was right, kissing him didn't have to be a big deal, they just needed to be more comfortable with each other.

"I guess you're right, only couples trying to prove that they're loved up act so over-the-top. Normal couples don't," she said and he smiled.

"When are you catching up with Amy and spending the day shopping together?" he said, as they both moved away from each other to go back to a comfortable distance.

"Day after tomorrow, okay? We haven't actually planned anything properly."

"That suits. I wanted to know if dad and John wanted to go for a round of golf."

"Great, I'll call Amy and see if she's free," she said, grateful for something to do and relieved that the kissing experiment was over.

Gabe was on the golf course with his father and father-in-law discussing his future with them.

"So what do you think?"

"I'm thinking that you need to leave Europe completely behind, don't even bother trying. Fabien will no doubt make good on his promise and ruin any chance of a career that's not with him," François said in earnest and Gabe silently knew it to be the truth.

"America? Start fresh?" he said.

"Son, if you need money, just ask."

"No, I don't need money but I do know that I have some serious thinking to do about whether to even try working in London or like you say, move somewhere else where grand-père's tentacles can't reach."

"If your grandfather is as difficult and vindictive as all the stories I've heard over the years, then his tentacles will be far reaching, not to mention that he will want to make sure that you don't succeed because then you'll have to come crawling back to him," John said. "Can either of you think of anyone in this world that would hire you that also has the guts to stand up to your grandfather? Hates your grandfather that much that he would not only take you in but also not be bullied or browbeaten by him? Hopefully it's also someone who will treat you well, of course."

They played the back nine and Gabe was in deep thought. He knew no one that hated his grandfather openly. All enemies were usually squashed and crushed into oblivion.

"You're completely off your game," Gabe said to his father as they handed in their score card.

"That's because of you. I've been too busy thinking about what John said about knowing someone who hates Fabien with a passion."

"Then I'll buy the first three rounds, it's the least I can do," Gabe said, appreciating their help and wisdom.

"And that's why I let him marry Callie," John chuckled. "Deep pockets."

They all laughed because it wasn't the truth but it seemed to lighten the mood.

It wasn't until they reached the clubhouse that François had finally thought of someone that could help his son.

"I have a person that might just be able to help. They don't associate with Fabien so his threats wouldn't hold much sway unless he bought them out…"

No one knew how far Fabien would go to get Gabe not only back into the fold but back into line.

"Who is it?" he said, trying hard not to sound too eager or get his hopes up.

"His name is Bryan Mayweather and he's been around for a long time."

"And? What does he do? Or do you think he'll see this as a chance to sell out to grand-père?" Gabe said, wary.

He had been in situations before where people had used him to get his grandfather's money.

As John watched and listened to the two men talk, he knew that if he had any doubts about Callie marrying Gabe because Gabe was just trying to be rebellious and out to spite his grandfather, his opinion had now changed.

The things that father and son were discussing were almost inconceivable to him. He couldn't say only rich families were like this but he knew of no one else who had so much family drama and definitely not to this extreme.

The things that they were accusing Fabien St Croix of possibly doing to bring his own grandson back into line were not only mind-boggling but the seriousness with which they were discussing the problem showed that they weren't being irrational and overreacting.

François had told him over the years what people had done to ingratiate themselves into Fabien's good books or to befriend him. Heck, John had even seen it with his own two eyes but still it saddened him that Gabe too, had seeds of scepticism and distrust ingrained into him.

John had told François years ago that someone had tentatively approached him one day on behalf of Fabien offering more money than he could possibly earn in a lifetime if John and Miranda would just provide a detailed report every now and then on what François and his family were up too.

The thought of spying on his neighbour and friend appalled him and he had turned it down flat. At the time, he only knew that Fabien was François' father but not the truth of who the family were. Not that it would have made any difference to his answer if he had known.

François had thanked him for his honesty and advised John to keep this secret between them only because there was no point in worrying his family but still, John knew that François held a seed of doubt about his neighbour's loyalty.

It hadn't bothered John at all. He kept interacting with his neighbours as if nothing had ever happened and slowly he noticed that François went back to being completely relaxed in his presence again.

Now it seemed that Gabe had the same problems his father had with Fabien. He frowned hoping that Callie would be okay.

"I'm sorry to interrupt Gabe, but is my daughter safe? Callie's not going to be caught up in some sort of family feud, is she?" He had to know that Gabe would protect her.

"I'll protect her as best I can but in all honesty, she hasn't grown up in the way that people who you think are your friends are quick to turn on you," he said, snapping his fingers for emphasis. "I just found out that my best friend, Luc has been one of grand-père's spies for years. He recently confessed this to me otherwise I'd still be none the wiser. The betrayal hurts and Callie has such a tender heart that she'd probably lose her softness and put up a horribly thick wall and that will be my fault."

John appreciated Gabe's honesty even if it wasn't the answer he wanted to hear.

"I can leave her here but honestly, that won't stop grand-père. He'll still be fuming that I married her. That's the crux of the matter and if he wants…he'll crush her to get to me without even blinking an eye and definitely not care if she's an innocent victim. She'll just be his collateral damage — a lesson for me."

"You promised not to hurt her and protect her and yet, how will you live up to that when you yourself have just admitted to being deceived for years. What chance does Callie have?" John said, his anger brewing.

"Because it's only for a year and then we divorce. Grand-père won't make a move that soon because it will make him look bad," he said with conviction

"Does she know just what she's signed up for? That your grandfather could ruin her reputation, her name, make it impossible for her to live any kind of normal life after this, if what you say is true?" John said, feeling out of control.

Although Gabe knew that John was only trying to protect Callie, there wasn't much his father-in-law could do about it.

"Talk to Callie. Like I said, if she's had a change of heart we can always undo our marriage or I can leave her here," he said.

That was the best compromise he could offer. He didn't tell his father-in-law that they hadn't consummated the marriage and didn't intend to.

John had gone home filled with worry and almost roared at his wife before feeling guilty that he was lashing out and taking out his own anxiety on her when his wife had done nothing wrong.

Miranda managed to calm her husband down after he explained what had taken place at the golf course.

"Her reputation will be torn to shreds by that vindictive son of a bitch," he spat, furious and feeling more than helpless.

Miranda had never seen her husband this angry or upset before and part of her was now anxious and concerned for her daughter but she had to believe that Gabe would do the right thing by Callie.

"Callie knew what she was getting into," she said.

"Did she? Did she? Did she really know, truly realise that she could be humiliated in front of the entire world because of *that* man," he raged.

"Perhaps not but it was for the good of Gabe's future."

"He's a big boy. He should have been able to handle this without dragging our daughter into it."

"I know but it made complete sense. I know you don't think so but in a strange way Marielle and I think that they both need each other. They just don't know it yet."

Women, he thought irritably, always wanting the fairy tale happily ever after.

"In the meantime, she'll be torn to shreds."

"I know you're worried. You're meant to be. After all you are her father and you wouldn't be normal if you weren't even the slightest bit anxious for her," she said. "I know I am, but we raised Callie to be the person she is and if she's okay with it then we have to respect her decision and be okay with it, no matter what we think. We'll be here if she needs us."

She was trying to reassure her husband while not wanting to betray Callie's confidence about meeting Fabien and why she made the decision she had. Her daughter had the right to her own privacy.

John pulled his wife close knowing she was right. It was hell knowing that he couldn't protect his own child. Callie was an adult and chose this path. He could only pray that it was the right one.

Amélie dragged Callie around all the stores and gave her great styling tips. By the time they had finished, she was exhausted and tired of changing in and out of clothes.

"This will do until you get back to London and can then buy more designer stuff to suit the occasions you need."

"Thank God, we're finished. I'm exhausted," she puffed, putting down all the bags in their hotel room. "I wish you were coming back to London with us, it would be so much better."

"Me too, but you know grand-père," Amélie said with a tinge of sadness before brightening. "Since you're exhausted, there's only one thing for it…a luxurious massage."

It so sounded heavenly to Callie that she readily agreed.

"Are you sure you only had a massage?" Amélie teased, seeing just how happy and relaxed her sister-in-law now looked. "I don't think I know anyone who's ever come out with that kind of smile on their face."

"I just feel like all the tension has been drained out of me. I feel boneless and wonderful," she giggled.

"Good for you. We'd better get going. Mum said that it's dinner soon."

They turned up at the St Croix home and to Callie it seemed like the men all seemed tense and could use a little massage themselves to relax.

"How was golf?" she said.

"Not bad," Gabe said, leaning in to give her a peck on the cheek, glad that she didn't flinch at the action. "Do you have a moment? I need to talk to you."

She saw the seriousness on the faces of the two fathers and felt her heart begin to pound.

"Sure," she said, trying to sound as breezy as possible but her stomach was beginning to roil.

As she followed her husband outside into the garden, Amélie also went to follow but was stopped by her father.

"What's going on?" she said as Gabe paced.

"I was talking to our dads at golf and your father is rightly concerned that you don't know just what kind of marriage you've really entered into with me," he said, raking a hand through his hair before stuffing both hands into his pockets.

"Of course I do. You've explained it. Dad's just being a loving protective father."

"No, he's right, Cal. To get to me, you'll be collateral damage and grand-père won't even blink twice at ruining your life completely. And when I mean ruining your life, I mean he's going to publicly humiliate you so that everyone on this planet will know your name, and not for good either," he said. "The only compromise I can come up with is that you either decide that you really don't want this marriage and we get it annulled since we haven't consummated it or that you stay here out of the way and I'll forge ahead by myself. I don't mind, Cal."

"No. I told you that I married you to help you. I'm not hiding," she said, emphatic.

"You don't understand, we could be happily living life until one day a person you thought was a friend is suddenly telling the world your most private and intimate secrets. Betrayal like that changes a person, and Callie, you're too nice and tender hearted. Everyone would eat you alive."

"I don't care. One year. That's our deal and I'm willing to stick by you and even if your grandfather could drag up every stupid mistake I've ever made then I'll own it. You need to break away from him. Don't make me regret doing this."

He felt the burden of her faith and loyalty weighing heavily on his shoulders and it felt heavier than being a St Croix. God, he hoped that he was able to carry this off otherwise it would have all been for naught.

They came inside and everyone seemed strained to know what had been decided. She went to her father and gave him a big hug before announcing to the room, "I know you're all worried about me and I thank you but I'm going with Gabe. He's my husband for better or worse. It's a year and if my name and reputation are shredded to pieces that quickly then it just goes to prove how much marrying Gabe was the right thing to do. He'll never be free of his grandfather otherwise."

Her declaration made Gabe's heart burst with pride. No matter what, Callie would always be the wife he wanted and he was willing to do anything to protect her.

Although proud of her, everyone still remained silent on what the future would hold. They could only cross their fingers and hope for the best.

Chapter 12

"One last chance to change your mind."

"For better or worse," she quietly said, gripping his hand tightly to stop the trembling.

"Are you ready?" He gave her hand a little squeeze.

"Yes." She gave a simple nod of her head before taking a deep breath. "Let's do this."

Then it was time to go.

They walked onto the plane knowing that their lovely idyllic vacation was over. This was the first step back to the real world and with that came all the weight and worry of now being Mr and Mrs Gabriel St Croix.

Many hours later when she stepped off the plane, she looked around wondering if they had taken a wrong turn somewhere.

"Are you sure that we're meant to be here?"

Bryan Mayweather, who had agreed to hire Gabe, had wanted to meet him and discuss things in person first. Unfortunately Bryan was currently on his ranch in Wyoming and as they stepped off the plane, all they could see was miles of pasture as far as the eye could see.

"Yes, it'll be fine," he said, taking her hand and as they descended the steps a car pulled up in front of them.

"Mr and Mrs St Croix? I'm Barney. Mr Mayweather asked me to pick you up and take you to the homestead. I hope you had an uneventful flight."

"We did, thank you. Mayweather's spread is not only impressive but beautiful," he said.

"That it is. Let me just grab your luggage and we'll head off."

If Barney was surprised by the amount of luggage he didn't say anything. It was a good ten minute drive to the homestead and Callie was speechless when she saw it. It looked like it had come right out of a magazine it was so beautiful.

As they hopped out of the vehicle, an older gentleman looking happy and welcoming came out to greet them.

To Callie, the man looked like a rancher with his Stetson, moustache, blue jeans and boots. The only thing not quite authentically western in her mind was the fact that he wore a plain white shirt with no embroidery, tassels or pattern on it.

"Welcome to the Double M Ranch," the man's voice boomed.

"Thank you for inviting us here," Gabe said, shaking hands.

"This place is beautiful," Callie said, feeling her tiny little hand almost crushed by the man's warm larger one.

"Thank you. I love this place and spend most of my time here now rather than in the city," their host said. "Come on in and let's get you settled."

The inside of the ranch was just as Callie had imagined it to be and yet she was pretty sure that all the mod-cons had also been installed.

They were in their room freshening up before meeting Bryan on the patio.

"Listen, I'm probably going to be having some long discussions with Bryan. Will you be all right by yourself? I'm not sure what there is to do here," Gabe said, anxious. This would be their first real test as husband and wife.

"I'll ask if he has a library or perhaps I could learn to ride." She smiled brightly to reassure him.

Every time Callie answered his worrying questions, he felt a bit of his burden lighten because she wasn't acting like a spoilt pampered princess who wanted him to entertain her or was dependent on him. Her answers helped reassure him that she was okay with him being busy.

They were discussing polite social issues over a drink and nibbles but Callie could sense Gabe's need to discuss business even though he was acting as relaxed as her.

"Mr Mayweather," she said.

"Bryan, please," he said.

"Bryan, you don't perhaps have someone that could teach me how to ride a horse, do you?"

"You've never been on a horse?" His disbelief made her blush.

"No. I've never had the need but since I'm here on a ranch I thought it might be nice to have a go."

The smile that crossed Bryan Mayweather's was wide.

"Let me just get Barney," he said, rushing off to find his employee.

"Thanks." Gabe looked gratefully at his wife. "I'm dying to know what Bryan can offer me."

"I know. I just hope I don't make too much of an idiot of myself and fall off while the horse is standing still," she laughed, nervous.

"You don't have to do this," he said, wanting to make sure that Callie knew he wasn't expecting her to do things like this.

"I know, but it would be nice to at least give it a try. You saw how excited he was. Besides, I might be back inside in five minutes so talk fast," she said as he chuckled.

Bryan and Barney both came back to the patio.

"Mrs St Croix, Bryan says that you've never ridden a horse before," Barney said.

"That's right but I'm game to try, and please, call me Callie."

Barney actually blushed at Callie's bright smile and Gabe suppressed the urge to laugh at how easily his wife had charmed the older man.

"If you don't mind, one of our more experienced stable lads and I will teach you. It's a good chance for him to learn too," Barney said, asking for permission.

"I don't mind at all. I can't wait to tell people that my very first riding lesson was on a proper ranch. Lead the way," she said, and Gabe could see that she already had the older man wrapped around her finger.

"We'll give them a head start and then join them later," Bryan said to Gabe's agreement.

The discussion over his future employment didn't go the way that Gabe had planned to his surprise and excitement. At first he thought that his father had read this man wrong, that Bryan was in fact being nosy and might want to see Gabe beg and dance to his tune, but he couldn't have been more off base if he tried.

"So François tells me that you've broken ties with your grandfather and true to Fabien's infamous temper he's cut you off and threatened to ensure you remain unemployed so you'll go crawling back to him," Bryan said.

"Something like that," Gabe said, humiliated and silently cursing his father's blabbermouth.

"And now you need to find a job *and* with a company that your grandfather can't simply bully into firing you or buy up just to fire you." Gabe nodded. "Do you know why your father thought of me?" Bryan was curious to know if Gabriel did indeed know the truth.

"No, I don't." He wished his father had told him something other than just sending him off to the wilderness of Wyoming.

"Because I hate Fabien with a passion. That old goat will end up running Hell when he finally croaks. Your father knows this and knows that I'd never sell out to him so you'll be safe with me."

Gabe detected the underlying bitterness and hatred Bryan had for his grandfather. He had just assumed that Bryan Mayweather was just not keen on his grandfather but was stunned by the vehemence.

"Why do you hate him? I mean, a lot of people do, but why do you?" He knew it could be a number of possible things from business enemies to some kind of personal vendetta, to Fabien just being Fabien.

"Let's just say that when I was starting out and needed financing, I asked Fabien for help. I naïvely thought that I was smart enough to see anything underhanded. Your grandfather seemed interested in helping me and then before I could even blink, he had made off with my idea and left me floundering," Bryan said. "Luckily for me, my father warned me of Fabien's reputation for deviousness and trickery and so while Fabien thought that he had gotten one over me, I had the last laugh because I had been withholding the most important piece of the puzzle and without it, what Fabien had taken from me wouldn't work."

Gabe nodded not even the slightest bit surprised at his grandfather's dishonesty. He, himself had seen it time and time again.

"Fabien swore my invention would never get funding or see the light of day and so I continued to do it the hard way until one day a man I had heard of but never met, offered to finance me on the quiet. Be a silent partner, if you will," he said. "Clearly I was now a lot more wary so I had an agreement drawn up down to the most minute detail and everything was in my favour. It all turned out to be unnecessary as the man kept his word and only provided financial aid. He never once asked to be involved. After that I was an overnight success you could say. Try as hard as he could, Fabien could never work out who was financing me and as far as I know, he never has," Bryan chuckled.

That stunned Gabe. His grandfather had the best people money could buy and if they couldn't figure it out, then whoever financed Bryan was definitely a lot sneakier and it would have made Fabien furious.

"That's why when François told me what had happened to you, your father knew that you could work for me in peace and quiet because I'd never give in to your grandfather."

Now feeling relaxed and filled with confident relief that his father had found the one man in the entire world who not only had the gumption to stand up to his grandfather but could also not be bought.

"So tell me about this job offer?" Gabe said.

"I suggest you start work in the middle of the company and that way you can learn the ropes properly about what we do."

"I'm not sure that I have it in me."

Bryan roared with laughter giving Gabe a slap on the shoulder.

"Son, if you're truly your father's son and Fabien's grandson, then I don't expect you'll be there for long."

It made Gabe feel better but still…

"Management don't tend to move on that quick or do you have someone in mind that you want to let go."

It was to Bryan's surprise that Gabe had even thought of that and it showed him that he was bright.

"I'll admit that's true but what I have in mind for you, this would make a great start," Bryan said, rubbing his chin. "Also the man that I'm making you work for, I've had concerns about for a while but don't seem to have any concrete proof. The people in his team seem to leave quicker than others. From what I understand, some have complained of his management style but nothing can be proven."

"So you want *me* to be the spy and confirm just how good or bad he is as a manager?"

How ironic. Now he was being asked to spy instead of being spied upon.

"I'm thinking of killing two birds with one stone as in you," Bryan chuckled, before growing serious again. "There's actually another more serious and important reason why you should start in the middle and work your way up."

Gabe stiffened slightly as an uneasy feeling washed through him. He was already being asked to spy, what else could Bryan Mayweather want with him?

"I want you to take over the company."

Bryan's declaration made Gabe's jaw drop and his eyes widen in shock.

"B-but what about your own children?" he said, trying to comprehend that Bryan was practically giving him the company on a silver platter.

"Neither have ever shown any interest." Bryan waved his hand dismissively. "Ben is a very successful surgeon and Dan started some kind of outdoors company where people zoom through trees or something like that," he said. "Besides even if they were interested, you would still get a stake in the company's ownership."

"Why?" Puzzlement crossed his face.

Seeing Gabe's face made Bryan realise that Gabe truly had no idea about the truth and was elated to be the one to tell him.

"Because your father was the man who financed me all these years."

His brain exploded at the revelation that his father had secretly gone behind his own father's back to support Bryan Mayweather.

"And grand-père *never* knew?" he said, incredulous.

It didn't seem at all possible. Fabien always found out everyone's secrets even through illegal means.

"All I know is that every time I happened to see Fabien, he would scowl and look at me with such animosity. I took much delight in those moments."

"So when do you think you want to retire full-time?" Gabe said, moving the subject back on track.

"I pretty much am now. I only drop into the company once every couple of months but here's where I'd rather be. Robert Jameson runs the company now and is a good sort but perhaps a little soft. So really the question is when can you get up to speed?"

"You've been waiting for me?" The realisation hit like a lightning bolt out of the blue.

"Yes and no." Bryan nodded. "It just so happens that the timing is right for you to start taking the company over since like I said, I'm ready to give it all up. You know your grandfather isn't going to be taking this lightly. He'll start lobbing everything he's got once the news breaks so you're going to have to assert yourself pretty damn quick otherwise the company will go under," he said. "Robert's much too soft to fight someone like Fabien. Go to

New York, start getting into the thick of it, learn as much as you can, clean house, batten down the hatches, and get ready."

Gabe knew everything Bryan had just told him was true. It was a lot to think about and he tried to ponder the next few steps in his mind but was distracted by the thought of Callie's riding lesson as they walked towards the corral. Was she enjoying herself or hating it?

As they approached, they heard her laughing as she tried to scold the horse.

"Wrong way. You're meant to be going left." But the horse paid her no heed and kept going wherever it wanted.

"Shall we try picking up the pace again?" a young man smiled.

Seeing Callie smile back made Gabe's stomach tighten. She wasn't meant to be flirting with other men.

"Yes, let's do it," she said, determination in her voice as the young man clipped a rope to the horse's bridle and began running to make the horse trot.

Gabe could see Callie holding on for dear life as she bounced uncontrollably in the saddle before finally grabbing the pommel and being able to sit better.

"Nope, I still have bad timing, Toby," she said, as the young man slowed his own pace. "I'm still bouncing around like a rag doll."

"At least this time you weren't close to falling off," he laughed, before noticing that Gabe and his employer were in attendance.

Callie saw Toby's eyes dart across the corral and automatically followed them to see Gabe and Bryan Mayweather standing there watching her. She flushed hotly hoping that they hadn't just seen how terrible she was at trotting but knew that they had.

"Hi," she said. "All finished?"

"Yes, we thought we'd come and see how your lesson's going?" Gabe said.

"Not so good," she said.

"Perhaps you should stop for a while otherwise you'll be mighty sore later," Bryan said.

Quickly agreeing, she tried to climb off her horse but Rosita kept moving and not being that confident, Callie ended up with one foot slightly stuck in the stirrup and one hand grappling the pommel for dear life while the other hand was also trying to hold on. Toby finally got Rosita to stand still and she eased to the ground in relief.

"Thanks for the lesson, I'm sure that your next learner will be much better."

"You did great," Toby said.

She walked over to Gabe and realised that Bryan was right. Her legs did feel a little tender and sore just from that little bit of riding and all she had really done was sit on a horse.

"So no bruises? You didn't fall off?" he said, as Callie flushed.

"You missed the part where I got up on the saddle and then almost bounced right off the first time we tried trotting. I think I gave poor Toby a heart attack. I'm obviously the very first absolute beginner he's ever dealt with."

Gabe's jaw tensed. He didn't like hearing her give sympathy to *poor Toby*.

"How did your chat go?" she said, as they entered the bedroom.

Bryan had advised that a long hot soak in the bath would ease any aches and pains in her legs and then dinner would be barbecue steaks and salad, nothing gourmet. Callie had liked the sound of dinner, it reminded her of home but first she really needed a bath.

"Better than I ever imagined. He wants me to take the company over eventually."

"That's fantastic," she said, her face shining as he felt her delight flood through him.

"It means I'll be working extremely long hours and will probably only come home to sleep. Will you be all right by yourself?" he said, concerned.

"Of course," she said, and saw the worry on his face disappear. "Just give me a credit card with an open limit and I'll sort myself out."

She was teasing and crossed her fingers silently hoping that she would find something to amuse herself with since she wasn't meant to work.

"So when do we head back to London?"

"We don't. The company's in New York so we have to go straight there and set ourselves up," he said, hoping she wasn't angry at him.

Her anxiety kicked into high gear. She didn't want to live in New York especially after what had happened the last time she lived there and could only pray that she wouldn't accidentally run into Chantel and Claude.

She pushed all those thoughts aside for now because this was about Gabe, for Gabe, and she was pretty sure that she could avoid her old employers. There was no possible way that they would even move in the same circles, she silently hoped.

Over dinner there was a flurry of decision-making to be done. Bryan admired the young couple and knew that Gabe had struck gold marrying Callie. She was just like his Karen, letting him go off to concentrate on his work while she tended to absolutely everything on the home front from the running of the house to raising their two sons and scheduling their social lives.

He could only hope that Gabe would appreciate and see what he had in Callie. She would be his backbone and strength when things got tough, and they were bound to with Fabien St Croix as his grandfather.

It was Bryan who came up with the idea to end their bickering over living arrangements since Gabe knew that the St Croix apartment wouldn't be open to him.

"Borrow my apartment, I'm hardly ever there these days." He generously offered its use to them.

"It's a lovely offer but we can't possibly accept. You've already done so much for us and who knows how long we'll be there before we find ourselves a place," she said.

"Darlin', I don't mind…honestly. I only go there once a month, if that, or to see my son. If you don't mind me turning up every now and then, you're most welcome to it."

"Of course we wouldn't mind, it's your place. I promise, we'll move as soon as possible."

She was grateful for Bryan's offer, it was one less immediate stress to worry about.

"Well then that's settled. That'll also give you a chance to decide where you'd like to live."

"What are Manhattan prices like?"

She bit her lip to tamper down the flare of panic that had erupted inside her. Could they even afford a place in downtown Manhattan?

"Don't worry about it, Cal. Wherever you want to live will be fine," Gabe said, seeing the flare of panic in her eyes about money.

She tuned out everything else as her mind visualised the kind of home that she and Gabe would live in. It would have to be an address fit for his reputation and hopefully close to not only the business but the big department stores like Bloomingdales and Macys, along with Saks Fifth Ave as well so they wouldn't need a car to get around. She'd make it a lovely tastefully decorated home, not too ostentatious but with enough élan that people would be impressed.

The colours would have to be light and bright as she wasn't partial to dark hues, and the apartment must also get as much sunshine as possible because she loved that feeling of sitting in the sunshine feeling that warmth recharging her.

But what would Gabe like? He'd obviously need some sort of office but other than that, did he have ideas of taste? She almost laughed sadly to herself as she remembered his house in London and how he had never seen the kitchen and an interior decorator had renovated it completely without any real input from him.

She bit her lip wondering if they should get an interior decorator again. She didn't want to make them a laughing stock because people considered the colour scheme or taste in furniture not on trend.

They were getting ready for bed and Callie once again marvelled at how neither of them actually cared that they had to share the same bed. She wanted to laugh that it wasn't like the movies with pillows down the middle or one person sleeping on top of the sheet and the other, under it. There was simply no drama at all.

As always she rolled onto her side to get comfortable, Gabe's voice rang out in the dark.

"Cal?"

"Yes?"

"What were you thinking about at dinner tonight when you zoned out? Are you disappointed that we're not going to be living in London?"

His voice held a thread of concern and she rolled onto her back to look up at the ceiling in the darkness.

"No, I was quietly panicking about where we'd live. You know, what can we afford and do we need an interior decorator or should we do it ourselves? I mean, I don't even know what colours you like or what you might like to have besides an office but even then what colour would you like it to be?" She rattled off all her concerns and thoughts in a rush.

The silence and darkness were a comfort since they couldn't see each other and since he didn't reply she closed her eyes.

"Would you believe that I actually don't know?" His voice sounded almost sad at the admission. "All my life, things have just been done and I've barely had my likes taken into account."

Now that really did sadden her. How could no one have asked him what he liked or disliked?

"Well at least tell me if you have a favourite colour or colours so our new place can have things that you like as well."

She wanted him to feel included in the process. After all, it would be *their* apartment.

"Blue. I like blue, a sky blue or light blue and orange, like a deep yet bright orange," he said with conviction to the darkness and she smiled.

"I like blue too, but a brighter shade and definitely not navy. I can live with orange. Maybe our place should be white and we'll make it colourful with accessories," she said.

"I like that. You can have carte blanch."

She bit her lip wondering if she should bring up the state of their finances. She really did need to be more frugal but she was enjoying dreaming with him. Still, she needed to know.

"Just how much should we be spending on a place? Do you want to be right in the heart of the city or out further? If you're working long hours, I'd prefer to live closer so you don't have to travel so far and can get a good night's sleep."

Gabe smiled into the darkness amused that Callie was mothering him and he felt that loving warmth because of it. It was nice that she wasn't doing everything to her tastes or her wants, that she was considering his needs as well.

"Why don't we see where the office is first? We can always find somewhere to rent if we overstay our welcome at Bryan's place," he said, then whispered into the darkness, "Thank you, Callie."

"What for?" She turned her head in his direction.

"For being you. Don't change," he said, solemn.

"I'll try not to, but all the power of being Mrs Gabriel St Croix might go to my head and I'll lose all control," she giggled. "Goodnight, Gabe."

"Sweet dreams, Callie."

Chapter 13

Gabriel started work the following week so that they could settle into Bryan's place and also do some sightseeing together.

Even though Callie had lived in New York when she was an au pair, she never really saw many of the sights that the city had to offer and since Gabe was being so generous in wanting to show her around, she couldn't refuse.

They discussed which area they would like to live and what kind of place, and both were in agreement — find a place to buy first if possible but if they couldn't find anything then they'd rent.

Callie had been stunned at how much money Gabe was willing to spend on a place and she felt trusted by his honesty with her.

For the first time in his life Gabe was nervous about work. He had been restless all night wondering how his first day was going to go.

Drawing on every bit of his St Croix fortitude he had at his disposal, he knew that he was going to have to rein in his natural inclination to lead until he had been there for a while to get to know just how the company worked.

It was going to be hard to play the meek and diligent employee but if he wanted to take control of the company and learn all the on-goings in an honest way, then playing along was vital.

"How do I look?" he said. "This is one of my old suits, does it make me look like everyone else?"

All Callie could see was a charismatic, handsome man that exuded confidence just by standing there, but knowing Gabe was nervous, she suppressed the urge to giggle and tease him and had to take herself out of the room to laugh.

Only Gabe would think that an older designer suit tailored specifically for him would make him less…*him*.

At work he was relaxed chatting to Robert Jameson. The man, like most, had been in awe of him, and looked nervous especially bringing up the delicate topic of Gabe having to work for Lester Simmons. Someone who was, as Robert diplomatically put it, far less business savvy than Gabe and not a great manager. However, they couldn't seem to prove any of the complaints.

Gabe wondered if Robert knew the truth about just why he was being hired, but knew that Bryan couldn't have told him because it would defeat the purpose of Gabe's undercover employment.

Soon, Robert was leading Gabe down towards Lester's office and after brief introductions Robert left the two men alone.

All his life Gabe had different reactions to his name but Lester's was one of almost glee. The man's derisive, superior, pompous arrogance at having the great Gabriel St Croix working for him was undeniable as he clearly was a man who not only liked the sound of his own voice but wanted to savour the moment. Loving the fact that the famed Gabriel St Croix was nothing more than a mere minion working for him.

Lester was no fool. He, along with everyone else in the world, suspected that Gabriel and his grandfather, Fabien had some sort of falling out and it was almost beyond his wildest dreams to have Fabien St Croix's grandson dropped into his lap, especially since this would be his first job since the split.

Maybe if he played his cards right, he could contrive a way for Gabriel to be in his debt and owe him in the future, especially if the young man regained those lofty heights that Lester could only imagine. He could get Gabriel to give him an even better job with lots more money. But for now, he got to show the younger man who was boss.

"So, since your reputation is so renown, I think I'll have one of the guys teach you our systems otherwise the women will be too easily distracted," Lester joked.

Gabe just sat there bored, not saying anything while silently making a mental note to himself that as soon as he took over from Bryan, Lester would be the first person he dealt to. Just being in the man's presence a short time was enough to know that he had an overinflated sense of self-worth and pomposity, which wasn't a sign of a good manager.

Relieved that Lester had finally stopped talking and showed him to the tiny cubicle that was to be his workspace from now on, Gabe looked at his watch and noted that Lester had talked for well over an hour about pretty much nothing.

Where the time went Gabe didn't know since he had zoned in and out of Lester's sermonising.

Now being in this cubicle was like fresh air.

A young man who had a similarly arrogant air about him approached.

"I'm Corban. Lester asked me to show you the ropes," he said. Wait until he told his girlfriend that he was not only working with the infamous Gabriel St Croix but he was the one to *teach* him, he thought to himself.

"Great. Nice to meet you, Corban. How do you find working here?"

"Fantastic. Lester's a great boss. You're going to love it here."

Although Gabe nodded his agreement, he already had serious doubts about the older man's abilities and hoped that Corban was a lot better.

Unfortunately for Gabe, Corban was a terrible teacher. He knew this because not only did he know more than the younger man, who couldn't answer many of his simple questions, but Corban would keep getting sidetracked to ask Gabe plenty of personal questions that were rather intrusive.

At first when Gabe would make innocent queries about things on the screen, Corban at least had the decency to look embarrassed when he didn't know the answer. But, as the training continued, Corban became pricklier at Gabe's questions and even accused him of trying to be difficult on purpose.

"It's a perfectly logical question for someone who has never used the system to want to know the reasoning behind certain things for better understanding," Gabe said.

Finally Corban gave up and walked away in a huff and Gabe found himself wondering if he was a difficult trainee. Still he felt his questions were justified even more so when Corban and Lester both went to lunch and a woman he hadn't met came over to his desk.

"Do you need some help?" she said.

"Actually I do," he said. "I thought that perhaps I'm just not used to learning new things but I think there may be some holes in my training. I'm Gabe."

"Leanne," she said. "No, its not you…believe me. Being trained by Corban is like being trained by the monkey of the organ grinder. The man can't even do half of the stuff that's required."

Gabe heard the bitterness in her voice and wondered if Leanne's helpfulness was part of some kind of plan in ingratiate herself into his good books. It had happened before.

"How long have you worked here?"

"Five long years. Corban's only been here a year and a half and Ben who's always away 'sick' on Monday has been here five months."

He frowned that two of the employees hadn't been here that long and one seemed to also enjoy taking long weekends.

"What about Lester? What's his deal except that he likes the sound of his own voice?"

That comment made Leanne laugh.

"He's a first-class jerk who only got the job by pushing Carol, the old manager out and greasing up to the HR guy," she said. "Carol was a great manager and everyone liked her but then Lester got the job and everyone began to leave because he hated that they all knew more than him so he began making everyone's working life hell. He'd have HR disciplining them for the smallest things until they couldn't tolerate it anymore."

"But not you."

"No, but I've only hung in here because my husband got laid off at work around the same time and this job pays well so it was better to have a job rather than try and find another one in this climate," she said. "Now, as horrible as it is to say, I get a small kick out of making Lester beg every month when he has to come and ask for my help. I admit I'm petty enough to make him grovel, it humiliates him but he can't fire me because then no one would be able to do all the monthly reports that are needed. But now that you're here…" She shrugged, as if to say that Lester would go to Gabe instead and then fire her.

He felt a sense of dread knotting in his stomach if what Leanne was saying was the truth. True, she was more than a little bitter but who wouldn't be if it was the truth.

"But surely Lester —" he said, before leaving the question unasked. Surely the manager would know how to run the reports?

"Ha! I dare you to innocently ask him to print out a client's report when no one else is around so he can't fob you off. I bet you hear every excuse under the sun about why he can't do it for you."

"Okay but can you show me all the things that I'm missing?" he said, not only to change the subject but to see if she was indeed telling him the truth.

Leanne backed up her words with an efficiency that he thought was missing in the office while also proving just how useless Corban was. In fact she showed him much more than Corban *and* could also answer all his questions with a knowledge that had Gabe impressed.

Before he could thank her she looked at her watch and stated it was her lunchtime, quickly scarpering away as Lester and Corban both returned.

"Still slugging it out? Don't worry, I'm sure you'll be up to speed in no time," Lester mocked.

"I'm sure I will," he said.

"I guess you're just not used to actually *doing* the work. Must be quite degrading but don't worry, I'm sure you'll be our star employee in no time."

Gabe didn't know if Lester's patronising attitude towards him was because Corban was his audience but he made sure to keep looking relaxed and unperturbed at the pot shots so Lester didn't see his irritation, even though his fists were clenched. Behind him, Corban was sniggering at Lester's put downs.

Unbeknownst to Gabe, at lunch both men had discussed him and how they both thought he was overrated and wouldn't it be funny to get rid of him and then the world would see that Gabriel St Croix really couldn't make it without his grandfather's money. But even if he had known, he really didn't rate their opinions anyway.

"I'm just going to get some lunch and fresh air," he said, wanting to get out of their odious presence as soon as possible.

He rang Callie to make sure that she was okay and tried to ease her mind by telling her that his own day was going great.

Callie had decided to look at different property agents with apartments on their books for sale and thus get a feel for the market. The first agency she went into just looked down their snooty nose at her, advising in a tone filled with disdain that none of their properties would be in her price range.

She walked out feeling furious and humiliated but what had she expected, New York was all about appearances and who you were or knew. Still, she didn't want to trade on the St Croix name yet, not until she found something that she liked because she wasn't confident that someone wouldn't try and pull the wool over her eyes and sell her something for way more than it was worth.

Looking at her list of property agents she moved to the next one on her list and got an almost identical response. Crossing them off her list she continued, determined to find one agent who would treat her with the respect a client deserved.

Despondent and about to give up after looking down at her sheet of paper and seeing that she only had three names left from a list of fifteen, and she still hadn't found one person willing to take her seriously. Some agents just asked what price bracket she was in and then declined her patronage.

Deciding that she needed to take a break to fortify herself before visiting the last three names on the list and then having to start using the St Croix surname to get some proper assistance, she was sitting having lunch when her phone rang and she saw it was Gabe.

Putting on her most cheerful voice she answered and prayed that his first day was going well.

"How's your day going?"

Relief flooded through her that he seemed okay, although it didn't sound at all like stimulating work but at least it wasn't as terrible as he had thought it would be.

"How about you?" he said.

"Not bad. It's actually more tiring than I thought have to see all these property agents."

"Is there much out there?"

"Probably the same as every other place on earth, you know, some are great and some are just dumps. I'm trying to concentrate on the location first," she said, not quite lying but she also didn't want him to worry about how resigned she was feeling to having to use his surname to get anyone to take her seriously and show her the properties on their books.

"Just take your time. It's a big investment. I'm sure that what ever you manage to find will be great," he said, hoping that Callie wouldn't just think she needed to buy the first property she saw.

After talking to Gabe her resolve was fortified because she wanted to ease any homelife stress he might have. Feeling stronger, she went to the next name on the list, Brendan Hickman of Hickman Properties and crossed her fingers and prayed to herself the entire way there that this man would be her saviour.

Over the years as a real estate agent, Brendan Hickman had made a lot of contacts and repeat clients. Only when he finally decided to strike out on his own, none of them had lived up to their words and followed him.

All he had received from them was terrible apologies and lip service about their hopes for no hard feelings because they truly would use his services the next time — a complete lie.

Of course, he too had to murmur the correct and proper response that he had understood, but he made a note of every single person who had blatantly lied to his face because the day they came to him, he would make sure that he clipped that ticket a lot more than necessary as payback.

He did have a few loyal and wealthy friends who appreciated his candour and therefore could offer his client's a wide range of property choice.

The door opened and a pretty young lady walked in looking hesitant.

"I'm looking for Mr Hickman. I'm hoping that he might be able to help me find a place to live."

The receptionist was about to call Brendan to the front but he was already out of his office and at the front desk.

"I'm Brendan Hickman. How can I help you?" he said, shaking of her hand.

"I'd like to view the places on your books," Callie said, feeling better that he hadn't turned his nose up at her.

"Wonderful. Come into my office and let me show you what we have. Are you looking to buy or rent?"

He knew that sometimes young people had money and even if they didn't they still felt pleasure at being asked.

"I'd like to look at places to buy first, just to see what's out there," she said, trying to play her cards close to her chest for now.

"Of course, of course. Come and have a seat. Would you like a drink?"

He had been in the game too many years not to get over excited at someone like this woman in his office. Sometimes people wanted to dream, others were spying for the competition and some genuine buyers.

"No, thank you."

Callie looked over all of Brendan Hickman's properties. He had them in location and then purchase amounts but decided that she didn't want to tip her hand too soon and thus she looked at them all including the rentals.

Brendan began to worry that this young woman was just a dreamer. Like most people, she skipped the rundown properties but noted how her eyes dwelled on some of the more expensive properties.

"Are these properties negotiable?" she said, closing the folder.

He felt an instant sense of deflation in him. When people asked for negotiable properties, they wanted to buy the dream for next to nothing because they couldn't even come close to affording it but still he didn't lie, that's not how he did business. He treated everyone as an equal.

"Yes, however, it's still up to the owner to agree to the price."

"Are any of these people desperate?"

Perhaps she wasn't as inexperienced as he had thought given her questions. It was another question designed to give the purchaser the advantage and once more he had to tread a fine line.

"Some are. It depends on the property you like."

He was feeling more comfortable that she was indeed a legitimate client.

"I would like to view number forty six and one hundred and fifty three. Tomorrow if possible."

"Is there any other? I know that some of the others are very reasonably priced for the area and —"

"No thank you, just those two for now," she said.

When she had left, Brendan didn't quite know what to make of Callie Harrison — a waste of time or a savvy property buyer.

That night both Callie and Gabe were too exhausted to go out or cook and so they ordered in and enjoyed catching up on their respective days.

Gabe had decided to tell Callie the truth about his day since husband and wives should share things and found it surprisingly easy and cathartic to do. Because of Gabe's honesty, Callie too told her husband the truth of the attitude of some of the property agents she had seen.

"Lester is definitely going whether I fire him or make a complaint," he said, latent anger brewing inside him just thinking about that pompous jerk.

"So this Leanne woman is the real deal, not pulling the wool over your eyes to make herself look good?" she said, hoping he wasn't being taken in by a pretty face and the fact that he might even find Leanne pretty irked her.

"No, she told me to put Lester to a little test so I did, twice in fact, for two different things and she was right. It wasn't anything hard but as the manager he should know. Let's just say that he had an epic fail both times."

"So how was he even made manager?" she said in disbelief. "If the man is that incompetent, how or why would anyone put him in charge?"

"I asked Robert that same question before I left for the day. He was quite forthcoming that he now suspected Lester had made the previous manager look so incompetent because she had a lot of time off to tend to her sick husband. No one else had minded but the standard of work had gotten so bad that they couldn't let it slide anymore," he said. "She swore that it wasn't her, but she was also too busy juggling home and work and decided that the very generous severance package they offered was too good an opportunity to pass up."

"Lester," she scowled.

"Lester."

Now it was her turn to share her embarrassment at how many property agents had refused to give her the time of day.

"Didn't you tell them who you were?"

He was outraged on her behalf, that people were already treating her terribly.

"Of course not. I wanted to see who was willing to provide the customer service *I* wanted, not be pandered too *and* probably lied to."

She was aghast that he thought she should have dropped her married name but also pleased that he had seemed angry that people had been mean to her.

Gabe didn't know whether to be mad at Callie or just on her behalf but understood why she had done it.

"So did you find *anyone*?" he said, silently hoping that she had and they had something decent or else surname be damned, he'd find an agent for her.

"Yes," she beamed, showing her excited sense of accomplishment. "*And* his properties actually weren't too bad. I've lined up two inspections but there's actually a third, but I don't want him to think that I'm interested just yet, I want him to make me interested in it."

"You're a shark" he laughed. "How much?"

She explained her thought process and even he had to admit to being impressed by her decision making. Even with so much money at her disposal, she was still being careful with it and he had a newfound respect for Callie.

"Sounds like a great plan…and a steal. Make sure you check them out thoroughly when you view them. Do you want me to have a look?" he said, not wanting to crash her party.

"I'll let you know," she said. "Now, if I like the last one, are you happy for me to make an offer? How much?"

She was hesitant in asking because she didn't want Gabe to think that she eager to spend his money willy-nilly.

"How much did you say it was again?"

She told him and he gave her a generous figure to bargain with, one that made her head spin in wonder.

That night, she dreamt of buying her first home. It was going to be an exciting day tomorrow.

The two places that Brendan had shown her on request were perfect if she were a lady to buy to rent out but she wanted to live in it and these wouldn't do and so she played coy.

"Well, I'm just not terribly sure. They just weren't quite right. I wish I had also picked something more high-end so I could really compare and get a good feel that I'm getting bang for my buck, so to speak," she said, indecisive and hesitant.

Brendan took her bait without even blinking.

"There's one close by that we can see. Same neighbourhood and you'll be able to clearly see the difference," he said. "Do you think that the ones we saw were too expensive or cheap?"

He was trying to get a feeling of which way she was leaning but was finding that Callie Harrison was a hard client to read.

"I guess I don't mind paying a bit more if it's really worth it but the price range is right."

A short walk later and Callie stood in the apartment that was about to become her new home, she could feel it. It ticked all the right boxes except for price.

"This is lovely. Now I understand why it's worth so much more than the other two. It's a pity that it's not nearer my price range."

Brendan hesitated. Jewel Ferguson wanted a quick sale but she also wanted top dollar. Would she consider taking less especially when it had been on the market for three months and every prospective buyer had declared it too expensive?

"Well, you said you'd be willing to pay more and the owner might be okay to take a lower offer but not too low, like those other ones. What were you thinking?" he said, praying hard that Callie would at least be in the ballpark that Jewel would at least consider.

Normally as part of a couple, his clients would be looking together and then they would be discussing money within earshot so he knew just how far he could push the sale price but Callie was different, she hadn't mentioned a partner and seemed quite capable of making her own decisions.

She thought about it for a minute and then named a figure praying that Brendan wouldn't laugh her out of the apartment at her ridiculous offer. Seeing him frown, she quickly sought to placate him.

"Oh, I'm too low, aren't I? Look, don't worry about this place. You don't have to tell the owner that some crazy lady offered some ridiculously laughable offer. I'll just have to mull over the other two."

Brendan felt like he should at least try for Callie's sake since this woman was definitely wanting to buy something.

"Let me talk to the owner. If they say yes, I'll get the papers drawn up."

Her bright smile let him know that he was doing the right thing.

"Oh, thank you so much. I'm not in a hurry. If the owner needs time, tell them to take it," she said.

Brendan went back to work with a headache. How was he going to broach such a low price with Jewel Ferguson and get her to agree? Callie's offer wasn't unreasonable, in fact it was the best that he'd had in the three months on the market.

As it happened, it was easier than even he thought. Jewel was over being lumbered with an apartment she didn't want. She wanted to be free and happily accepted Callie's offer immediately after gaining Brendan's assurance that the buyer wouldn't go higher.

By Friday, Callie had brought them an apartment and Gabe had been deliriously proud of his wife at the price she had got for it.

The excitement of the deal had made him spin her around in his arms until she was dizzy and then he kissed her. It was quick like the ones they had practised in the hotel room but the spontaneity had caught them both by surprise and they froze staring at each other.

"Cal, I…I'm sorry. I didn't mean to —" he said, releasing her from his arms.

"No, no, we were both caught up in the moment. It was good practise," she said, mentally kicking herself when she saw his reaction.

"Yes, practise…I have work to do."

He strode off into Bryan's office leaving her alone and the happiness she had just felt disappeared like a puff of smoke.

Once alone, Callie paced and called herself all kinds of stupid for saying such an idiotic thing when Gabe's reaction made it look and feel as if she had slapped him in the face. Gabe was right, if they couldn't even spontaneously kiss and not freak out, how were they going to be able to do this in public? They'd be found out as soon as they stepped out the door.

She was torn between wanting to talk to Gabe about it and leaving it alone. He hadn't come out of the office since he went in and so she decided to go to him. Quietly knocking, she slowly opened the door so just her head could fit through.

"Gabe, I'm sorry to disturb you but I was wondering if we could talk?"

Damn her runaway mouth, she silently cursed, she was supposed to ask if he wanted a drink first to break the awkwardness but it was too late now. Hearing his loud exhale, she knew he was thinking of the inevitable conversation as well and it made her feel slightly better.

"Come on in, Cal."

"I'm sorry I didn't mean to —"

"No, I'm sorry," he said. "For walking out and not talking to you about it. Its just that I guess it caught us both off guard."

His words sounded like reasonable logic to them both.

"Yes," she said. "And you were right. If anyone saw us they'd know that we're not even close to being a couple in love. I'll try to relax more."

"And I'll try to keep all spontaneous kisses to your cheek or somewhere more neutral."

"I'm sure that we'll get more comfortable."

It was then that she realised that they were both being so polite with each other like they were two strangers, not people who had grown up together.

An awkward silence fell over them and to Callie it seemed to be happening more and more, which annoyed her because she had never had this problem with Gabe before and she didn't like the feeling very much.

Then she remembered what she had wanted to ask him before the business of his spontaneous kiss got in the way and made them both awkward with each other.

"I meant to ask you, do you want to see the apartment empty and then help me to decide on colours and stuff or do you just want to be surprised?"

It was nice of Callie to suggest him helping but he wasn't at all confident in that sort of thing because he had never had a say before. All the interior designers knew what was best for him. He shifted uncomfortably because he didn't know how to answer and not hurt her feelings.

"Why don't I come and look at it empty and then we'll go from there. I may have nothing to contribute."

She was elated the he was coming to see it until she saw his face and then kicked herself. She had forgotten about him telling her that he never really had a voice in what he liked but she wanted the apartment to be theirs and if he suggested a bright orange wall, then she would do it because he *mattered* but for now she'd just agree with him.

Baby steps Cal, she told herself and quietly hoped that Gabe might begin to feel differently once he saw it.

Chapter 14

Over the next few weeks the job wasn't getting any better, in fact, Lester and Corban were becoming even more obnoxious and condescending, and it took every ounce of Gabe's willpower to take the high road and ignore them.

Leanne was more than willing to help him when she realised that he not only wasn't going anywhere, but that he had managed some very subtle put-downs of his own.

It also became clear to Gabe that Lester actually had no idea how the reports ran or how to read them. Lester just went along with whatever Leanne gave him after she had made him grovel a certain amount first.

He had to smile at seeing Lester bluster and threaten Leanne as she sweetly refused to do his bidding until he had been sufficiently tormented. As soon as she agreed, he had stormed angrily into his office cursing her all the way to her laughter. She saw Gabe looking amused by actually seeing first-hand what she had told him on his first day and winked.

"She's a total bitch," Corban muttered, passing Gabe's desk.

"Pardon?"

"She's a complete bitch," Corban said, angry. "She works for Lester and thinks its okay to wind him up every month about the reports. I don't know why he hasn't already fired her."

"Probably because then he'd have to do them himself and I'm betting that neither of you know how to."

"You know Lester's been doing some research on you and we know that this is the only job you can get so if I was you, I'd keep my mouth shut before he fires you and believe me, it would be a coup to say that he fired you," Corban sneered.

Gabe put on his bored face and tone before making his reply an ominous warning.

"Or maybe I actually own this company and wanted to get my hands dirty so I could understand the ins and outs of it. If that's the case, maybe you'd *both* better be nicer to me or I'll fire *both* your arses and believe me, it'll be a great feeling."

Corban's face went deathly white unsure if Gabe was winding him up or telling the truth.

"Oh, and Corban, just so we're clear," he said, savouring the moment before twisting the knife in further. "When I mean fired, I mean no reference or acknowledgement that you even worked here."

By the petrified look on Corban's face, Gabe knew his threat worked. A threat that wasn't quite the truth since he would at least give him the barest of references, he wasn't that spiteful.

At least the fear of God had now been put into the younger man and Gabe had to admit to being impressed that Corban hadn't immediately gone running into Lester's office to warn him.

Gabe felt a sense of satisfaction when Corban sat at his desk looking dazed and worried. Maybe some of his grandfather had rubbed off onto him after all.

The next day Lester came in rather cheery and upbeat declaring that since he had such a great team that he'd treat them all to lunch. It was the nervous glance that Lester quickly gave Corban that made Gabe want to laugh, but he suppressed it long enough to agree. Leanne's eyes had almost popped out of her head in shock.

"What did you do?" she whispered in disbelief.

"Hopefully put the fear of God into those two useless wastes of spaces," he said, not fully explaining.

"Thank God. I did feel a bit guilty about bitching and moaning to you on your first day but then I saw how they treated you…so politely yet with a hint of wariness. You gave me the strength to keep coming to work. To be honest, I really was close to resigning, job or no job," she said, relief rolling off her in waves.

Gabe frowned at her confession. Leanne was good at her job and losing her would have been catastrophic.

"Has your husband found a new job?" he said, worried that if she had resigned then they'd have no income at all.

"Oh yes, but it only covers the groceries. It was the best he could get and he's been keeping his eye out ever since, but there's just not much out there for him," she said, trying hard not to cry.

She had felt so stuck in this horrid job for so long that she had become more and more depressed.

"Did you ever complain about Lester?" he said. Leanne didn't look like the kind of person who would put up with a manager like Lester.

"A few times but nothing seemed to come of it. Even some of those leaving tried to complain to no avail. HR kept saying that there was no concrete proof."

"So the HR department…"

"Is a complete joke," she said, bitter. "If you've met Slimy Simon, you can understand why since he and Lester are as thick as thieves."

Gabe frowned. He actually hadn't met anyone from HR yet and was now glad of it. He didn't want anyone knowing that he was staying in Bryan Mayweather's apartment.

"Don't worry, Leanne. Together we'll put Lester in his place," he said, making her feel so much better.

Bryan Mayweather had come for his monthly visit to his company and he and Gabe had been locked in his home office for most of the night. Callie hadn't minded in the least because it was important business for Gabe to deal with and also because she was trying to put together ideas for their new place.

Eventually the two men had emerged from the office looking quite serious but upon seeing Callie's magazines, Bryan asked her what she was doing.

Gabe couldn't resist bursting with pride as he regaled Bryan about how Callie had found them a place to live and the excellent deal she had negotiated. Bryan had been very impressed and Callie beamed at both men's praise.

"So now I'm trying to think of colours we might use and furniture that I like," she said.

"You're not using an interior decorator?" Bryan said, surprised and amused.

"I'm not sure. I wanted to see what we liked first so that if I do end up using one then I have some ideas in mind."

"You remind me so much of my Karen. She was the exact same. Loved those personal touches, I guess that's why the ranch is so special to me because Karen decorated it herself," he said, the love in his voice for his late wife evident. "Do you mind if I take a look at your layout? I might be able to offer another perspective."

The three of them spent another hour discussing the apartment and Bryan was impressed with the location and the layout that Callie was thinking of.

The next day both men went to work. Gabe left at his normal time and Bryan went in later. The discussion both men had last night had given Bryan a lot to think about. His company needed a strong full-time leader. It wasn't Robert's fault that he wasn't the leader that Bryan needed him to be. No, it was time to hand the reins over to Gabe. First he had to visit his lawyers to get the ball rolling.

By the time Bryan walked into the office, he realised just how ready he was to give it all up to Gabe. Gabe would inject a new life into it.

Robert, who was a dear friend and employee greeted him as cheerfully as always but Bryan didn't want to tell his friend just what he had planned until it was a done deal. It was Robert who surprised him after they had discussed all the usual business matters.

"I'm thinking of retiring," Robert said.

"Really? I thought you wanted to work for another five years?" he said, surprised.

"I was but since you've brought Gabriel St Croix on board, I know he'd be more than competent to take over and Bev's been diagnosed with breast cancer," his friend said. "They found it early, thank God. This just made it hit home that I'd like to do more together with her, travel, that kind of thing. I probably would have stuck to my five year plan otherwise."

"I'm sorry. If there's anything I can do for you or Bev. You've both been treasured friends. But actually since you've decided to retire, have you any idea when you'd officially like to do it?"

They discussed matters and also Lester Simmons a little longer before concluding their meeting.

That night Bryan advised Gabe of the truth about signing over the company as soon as the lawyers agreed on terms and that Robert also had expressed wanting to retire.

"It's not because of me, is it?" he said, horrified by the thought that the older man was leaving just because he worked there. Robert didn't seem incompetent and Gabe would have happily kept him on.

"Yes, but only because he thinks that I should put you in charge, take his position and no, it's also a personal decision," Bryan said, pleased that Gabe seemed to be nothing like his grandfather.

"Are you sure that you want to do this now? What happened to testing me out?"

"After talking to you last night I realised that the company has changed and isn't how I left it. It needs new and *strong* leadership — that's you."

"You know my grandfather will persuade all our clients to desert us."

"Here's what we can do. I sign the company over to you. Robert slowly eases himself out of the job and you do all the horrible hatchet jobs on the staff. We keep it as quiet as we can until you've established yourself. Hopefully that will give the clients a chance to adjust to you at the helm."

"I hope this works otherwise your company will cease to exist and believe me, grandfather will enjoy crushing you and me. It'll be his version of a Christmas wish come true," he said.

Both men were thoughtful about the hard road ahead.

Gabe managed to go and see their new empty apartment one night and instantly knew that Callie had purchased well. The place even though empty felt like home to him. They discussed all sorts of colours and ideas including some of Bryan's and for the first time in his life Gabe actually felt like a part of the process and was enjoying bouncing ideas around. Perhaps some of the draw was that Callie never dismissed his opinions like others had in the past, as they were being paid by his grandfather and therefore hadn't wanted to anger Fabien.

Callie listened and offered compromises or her own suggestions. The only room she refused to have anything to do with — that she insisted was totally his own decision — was his office. He did laugh when she screwed up her face at his mention of painting it orange. In the end, he chose a very pale blue.

Callie was elated that Gabe was actually helping her make decisions. She found it easier to picture what their new home should look like although she thought he had lost his mind at painting his office orange. It would be too distracting but if that was the colour he wanted, who was she to argue even if she did feel relief flood through her when he finally decided on blue.

Since Bryan was happy to continue to let them stay at his place, they did until their renovations were done. She took note of all the things that Gabe liked about Bryan's place, like the comfy seat that he always sat in. To Callie it didn't look like much but Gabe swore it was the epitome of luxury and comfort so she tried it but couldn't quite get that same feeling her husband did. He teased her by saying it was because she was too short and petite to appreciate the subtle curves and nuances of the chair. Callie snorted her retort but went out and brought one for him as a surprise.

She was enjoying organising painters and repairmen, and getting cabinetry and shelving made. As more and more things were changed and added, it really began to feel like a home and she could only hope that Gabe thought so too.

The signing of the company ownership papers was not only exciting but also made Gabe anxious about what was to come. As soon as it was done Gabe went back to the office to do three things. Two of them he couldn't wait to do and the third, well, that person would also be a casualty of new management.

Just as he came in feeling great, Leanne was crying in her office. Immediately he went to see her.

"What's wrong?" he said, knowing she would love what was about to happen.

"Lester's fired me because I told him that I refused to print out all our client lists for him."

"What did he need them for?" he said, hoping that there really was a legitimate reason but he couldn't think of any.

"That's what I asked. He's never needed them before and I couldn't think of a logical reason. He wouldn't say and got stroppy and so I refused. There really is no reason that he should need them."

Gabe was furious. Lester was definitely up to something and now he had the power to sort it out.

"Right, stay here. You did the right thing. Has HR spoken to you?"

"Simon was here when it all happened and was the one to encourage Lester to fire me," she sobbed.

Gabe was so irate that he marched straight into Lester's office dying for this showdown.

"So you've fired Leanne for a client list. You do realise that she's the only one who knows how this office runs, right?"

Lester blustered, his cheeks red from embarrassment but there was no way he was backing down.

"Get off your high horse, St Croix. *I'm* the manager here," he said. "In fact, I've had enough of your attitude and you're fired too."

Gabe lazily leant on the chair to help prop him up and smiled in anticipation.

"I bet that felt really good."

Lester blinked stunned. Gabriel didn't look the slightest bit upset at being fired. In fact, he looked *happy*. Instantly Lester's throat was dry and his body started to tremble but he wasn't scared of the younger man, he told himself.

"Since you're in such a firing mood, I did warn Corban weeks ago about threatening me, and I'm sure he passed the message onto you. Now that I'm *vice-president* of the company, I believe I'll see your 'firing of Leanne' and I'll raise you a 'clean out your desk right now and leave the premises immediately or I'll have security throw you out'. *You're* fired, Lester," he said with a cheerful smile.

Lester's jaw dropped speechless.

"You can't do that. HR —"

"Is also fired so start packing," he said, in a tone so cold that it had Lester scrambling for his stuff. Gabe ensured that Lester didn't take anything that didn't belong to him which definitely included no client lists.

"What happened to Lester?" Leanne said, her eyes still red from crying as she saw Lester scurrying off.

"Oh, him. He's left the company."

"*You* fired Lester?" she squawked in disbelief.

"Yes, and it felt damn good," he grinned.

"I wish I could have done it," she said. "How come you fired him, you're only —"

"The new vice-president of the company."

"Really?" Leanne's eyes were wide with shock then she smiled.

"Really," he said, matter of fact. "Oh and by the way, I need to hire a new manager. Want to apply? The salary will be fantastic along with other perks of being a manager."

"Yes," she said with no hesitation and a wide smile. "Thank you so much."

"And guess what your first order of business is?" he grinned.

"Please, tell me I get to give Corban a swift kick up the arse."

"How about out the door?" She squealed in delight making him laugh. "Oh, and by the way, want to touch base with Carol, the old manager? If her husband's better or she's looking for part-time work, tell her we have an opening."

"Yes, boss. I'll get onto it now," she said, unable to contain her excitement.

Next stop was a trip to HR and just as Gabe thought, Simon had been forewarned by Lester and was expecting him with a defiant stance. It took barely five minutes before Simon's bluster collapsed especially when Gabe told him that he'd be going through all of the personnel files and complaints to ensure that HR had been keeping everything thorough and above board.

Once he was happy that the three toxic men had left the building, he ordered IT to change all passwords and to remove any remote access the three might have, and for the first time in what seemed like forever, he went home happy and wanted to celebrate with Callie.

He brought flowers for his wife and was heading home when she called to tell him she was at their new place and that he should stop by after work.

"I'll be there shortly and will bring dinner," he said to Callie's delight.

She couldn't wait to see his face at their finished home.

As he knocked on the door and waited for Callie to open it, an epiphany struck that this was a date. After all, he had flowers and dinner for her and the thought added to his already good mood.

"Close your eyes!" she yelled through the door.

"Cal?"

"Close your eyes or I'm not letting you in."

"Okay, they're closed." He smiled to himself at her bossiness.

The door opened slowly just in case he was lying and Callie — seeing her husband holding a bunch of flowers up for her even though his eyes were closed — was glad he couldn't see her blushing.

Taking the flowers from him and then the dinner, she led him into the apartment and said, "The flowers are lovely, thank you."

"Cal," he growled, still feeling silly as he shuffled inside and heard her giggle as she closed the door behind them.

"Ta-da! Open your eyes!" she said, full of exuberance.

He did as she asked and was amazed by the sight in front of him. Their once empty apartment looked warm and inviting.

"This is wonderful. The best home I've ever had *or* seen," he said in awe.

Splashes of colour were everywhere popping out vividly amongst the neutral walls. He laughed at the cushions on the couch that were bright orange and various shades of blue and to most it might seem tacky but he not only understood that she was giving him a sense of home. He loved it.

"My chair!" he said, delighted. "You got me my chair."

He picked her up and spun her around making them both dizzy before putting her down.

Her face was hot from his compliment and now from his exuberance.

"Well, I had too, otherwise you'd probably steal Bryan's," she teased, loving that he truly liked the apartment and wasn't just pretending for her sake.

"This really is stunning, Cal. You've done a magnificent job," he said, walking through the apartment to look at everything.

Their bedroom looked calm and serene — a room of tranquillity — that she had managed to keep simple by not using too many colours, pillows or frills. It would suit them both. He did however shake his head that even though it was a marriage of convenience neither of them asked to sleep in a separate room.

This was the first time in his life that he had platonically slept with a woman that he wasn't having any kind of sex with and he liked it.

Callie never wanted to cuddle nor was she a restless sleeper. Sometimes he would wake up during the night and realise that she was next to him. He thought that it was because in her sleep she wanted his warmth but when he looked around, she was still on her side of the bed in a deep sleep and in fact, it was he who had gravitated towards her.

Shaking such thoughts from his mind he continued to look around and saw the little shelf she had built for their magic gnomes so that they could both see them every day.

By the time Gabe had finished going through their apartment and being constantly delighted by the results of her hard work, Callie had put her flowers in water and was plating up dinner. What a wonderful first night in their new apartment, she thought happily to herself.

"So what do you think?" she said, eager to hear his thoughts and knowing he at least liked some of the place from his original reaction.

"It's fantastic. Stupendous. Magnificent. Wonderful," he beamed. "You've worked a miracle."

She lapped up his praise, euphoric that he loved it as much as she did.

"And your office?"

"I could happily live in there. You've honestly made it the best office in the world, its perfect. I love the colour."

"You chose it," she said, trying not to take kudos for that.

"Then thank God you screwed up your pretty little nose when I suggested orange. Even I don't think that I could have stood that. I loved how the gnome I picked for myself was there on the shelf in the office. It was a lovely touch. Thank you," he said.

The emotion in his voice made her start to tear up so she quickly changed the topic.

"What brought on the flowers and a fancy dinner?"

"I psychically knew that you were doing the unveiling tonight so I thought I'd surprise my wife," he said, a teasing twinkle in his eye.

"No, you didn't."

"No, I didn't," he chuckled. "It was just good timing that I too wanted to celebrate with you."

"Celebrate? What are we celebrating?"

Her face lit up and for a wondrous moment, Gabe almost saw his entire future with Callie before realising that those thoughts weren't allowed in their agreement so he quickly shooed them away.

"Today I signed the ownership papers. I now own the company so we'll either go onto bigger and better or be poor as church mice once grand-père's done with me," he grinned and she squealed in delight, throwing herself into his arms and impulsively hugging him tightly.

"That's wonderful," she said.

"That's not the best news," he said.

"It's not? How much better can this day already get?" she said, leaning back slightly to look up at him since they hadn't let each other go.

"No, its not," he grinned. "I got to fire Lester and Simon."

"Fantastic. I bet that felt so great." She hugged him tightly again.

"Sure did."

"But what about Corban?" she frowned, wondering why Gabe didn't send the horrible young man packing as well.

"Oh, I let my new manager do that. I couldn't have all the fun," he chuckled.

"Leanne?"

"Leanne."

"This is fantastic. What a fabulously memorable day we're both having. I'm so glad that you brought home such a lovely dinner to celebrate," she said, moving out of his arms to sit down at the table.

He felt an instant disappointment that she had left his arms and knew that with any other woman food would be forgotten until much later after a hearty appetite had been worked up with lots of incredibly mind-blowing celebratory sex but instead he let out a small sigh and sat down to eat.

"I think I've definitely gotten the better end of the deal today," he said, a bright smile still on his face before turning thoughtful. "I think we'd better just enjoy the lull before the storm."

Chapter 15

Gabe's prophecy started to come true not long after when loyal clients were becoming more temperamental to deal with. One even accused him of overcharging all these years and that's when Gabe suspected his grandfather was behind everything. However, it wasn't until a company he was interested in buying shares in to complement his business suddenly announced that they had been bought by one of SCE's companies that he knew for sure.

Robert had kindly agreed to stay on for at least a year as they both battened down the hatches. Gabe was learning to get sneakier, so that the next time he couldn't be out manoeuvred by his grandfather. But even that wasn't enough as things were beginning to look bleaker by the day.

Fabien's money tempted everyone but Gabe knew his clients would regret it in the end but by then it would be much too late for his company.

Gabe was also feeling guilty about the amount of time he was working. He was so swamped that he hardly even saw Callie anymore. She was usually asleep before he came home and he was gone before she woke.

To assuage his guilty conscience, he sometimes sent flowers and called her at least twice a day. But what he was really beginning to hate was her understanding tone of voice. Sometimes after he disconnected the call, he would wish she was like a real wife — feeling neglected and raging at him — instead of simply accepting the situation.

The one thing he did every night was kiss her goodnight and hold her close so he could smell the peach shampoo of her hair as he drifted to sleep.

Somehow having Callie in his arms reenergised him. She was his strength to keep going.

Gabe had just finished a meeting with Leanne when Luc walked unannounced into his office to his shock and surprise, and he almost rubbed his eyes in disbelief. He couldn't hide his happiness at seeing his best friend again. Suddenly the past no longer mattered.

"Luc!" he said, delighted.

"Oh, thank God," Luc said, visibly relaxing. "I thought you might have tossed me out on my ear."

"No. I've been too busy to dwell on the past, and I've also managed to calm down enough to understand why now. However, should you betray me again, you will be dead to me," he said with a serious undertone as both men embraced.

"Promise," Luc said, sincere. "From now on, I'll be straight with you."

"So why are you here?" Gabe said, still in disbelief that his friend was here in front of him. He really had missed the close camaraderie they both shared.

"Two or was it three things? One, I got your remarkable gift so I'm guessing it is magical since you didn't beat me to a pulp."

Gabe had completely forgotten about sending Luc the magic gnome figurine since he had been so busy. It honestly felt like a lifetime ago.

"Two, I heard you were here and Fabien knows," his friend warned.

"Oui, I gathered that," he said. "And three?"

"Chantel's marriage is once more on the rocks. This time she's caught Claude cheating on her on-line, would you believe?" Luc said, angry.

"Again?" He hadn't thought that Claude had slept with the au pair but maybe he had been wrong.

"He denied sleeping with the au pair, remember. Said she came onto him but he declined. This time however, his pants are pretty much down around his ankles."

"How's Chantel taking it?"

"Understandably angry. Feels like everyone is laughing or talking about her behind her back."

"Maybe Callie could meet her and they could go for coffee or something. Both ladies could make a new friend, win-win," he said.

"That would be a great idea but isn't she in London?" Luc said, slightly confused.

Gabe chuckled, he had forgotten that since he had last seen or even talked to Luc that he had married.

"Are you free for dinner? Have I got a surprise for you."

After Luc's happy agreement, they caught up on news especially about Fabien so that Gabe was aware of his grandfather's state of mind which wasn't surprising in the least that the old man wasn't very inclined to let his grandson make his own way in the world.

After Luc left, Gabe rang his wife to advise that he was bringing home a surprise guest for dinner. Callie was torn between the horror and excitement of hosting their first guest. What should she serve? Would their apartment be good enough?

Gabe suppressed the urge to laugh at how Callie had worked herself up into a lather.

"It will be okay. You don't have to cook if you don't want to, you can just order in," he said.

"But what if they don't like our apartment?" she panicked. "What if they think that it's tacky?"

"Then we'll kick them out," he teased, which had the opposite effect of making her laugh to making her even more horrified. He should just tell her that it was only Luc but he wanted them both to be surprised.

"Angel, it'll be fine. Believe me, this guest is pretty easy going."

"Who is it?" she said, not hearing him refer to her with a term of endearment.

Gabe grimaced at the slip and wasn't sure whether to be annoyed that Callie hadn't even seemed to notice but then realised that she was too worked up.

"It's a surprise," he said, as she grumbled some more before finally hanging up because she needed to go and buy some things for dinner.

He couldn't wait to see her face let alone Luc's when his friend realised that he and Callie were now married, but for now he had to think of ways to become a stronger company so his grandfather couldn't win. Luc had offered to help where he could which Gabe had appreciated, just as he was thankful for the news that Luc had brought him of his grandfather.

Callie was miserable and bored. She understood Gabe needing to put in long hours to manoeuvre the company into a position so that nothing his grandfather did could touch him but there were moments when she wished it wasn't so.

Sometimes he would caringly send her flowers, but it didn't make up for the fact that she was bored. They had now been married for five or was it six months? She couldn't even remember as it seemed so long ago but that just meant she was closer to divorcing and having a life again.

On the plus side, they hadn't married for love so she was having no disillusions that he wasn't being what he promised. On the other hand, if they had married for love, she really would feel like an abandoned newlywed wife. She could see how some marriages didn't last after the honeymoon period especially if they were like this.

She did need to start making friends but she wanted them to like her for her, not because she was Gabe's wife. It would hurt so much more when they divorced to know that those people wouldn't even give her another thought.

Now he wanted to bring home a surprise guest for dinner and she was a ball of anxiety hoping and praying that whomever Gabe had invited would like their home.

Dashing to her local butcher, Callie hoped for cooking inspiration otherwise she would have to order takeout, something that she was loathe to do especially for their very first dinner guest.

He put the key into the lock and felt the exhilaration building inside because not only would he be surprising Callie *and* Luc but Luc would officially be their first visitor and he couldn't wait for his friend to see their apartment. Peeking inside just in case Callie wasn't ready, he could hear her in the kitchen and waved Luc inside.

"What do you think of the place?" he said, hoping that Luc would like it or at least tell him the truth before Callie asked him and then he could tell his friend to pretend for her sake.

"Well, it smells delicious and I like it," Luc said, looking around from where he stood. "It seems relaxing."

To Luc who was only used to seeing Gabe's places as highly polished dwellings, this apartment not only didn't look so proper but it looked like a home…relaxing and warm…inviting.

Gabe felt relief at Luc's answer as he shut the front door loudly so that Callie would be forewarned that he was now home with their guest.

Callie was nervous and she jumped a little at hearing the front door knowing that Gabe and their mystery guest were here. She didn't want to embarrass him by not being a good wife and decided that a home-cooked roast was usually a winner…she hoped.

To keep herself busy so that she didn't have time to worry, she made sure that everything in the apartment was in perfect readiness. Peeling vegetables was also a good distraction as she thought about what to wear — casual or dressy. Oh, she wished that Gabe had given her some kind of clue as to their guest. In the end she decided on simple black trousers and a pale yellow blouse and prayed she looked appropriately dressed.

Now hearing the door shut, so she grabbed the counter for support and then took ten very deep breaths trying hard to relax before going to greet their guest.

She heard low voices and then laughter and then got the surprise of her life to find Luc sitting in Gabe's favourite chair.

"Luc," she said, excited to see Gabe's best friend in their home. "I'm so glad that you're our first visitor."

Luc stood, the surprise on his face at seeing Callie was evident.

"You look beautiful as always, Callie," he said, trying hard to suppress his eager curiosity.

"Flatterer," she laughed. "I've been so stressed about Gabe's surprise guest. Can I get you a drink?"

As she left the room, Luc looked inquisitively at Gabe.

"You two got something going? You both look very loved up but then I always felt an undercurrent between you."

Gabe grinned. Now was his surprise and as Callie returned, he happily said, "Actually we're married."

Callie was glad she got to see Luc's face as his jaw dropped open in shock at the news but he managed to pull himself together as she giggled.

Bewilderment still remained on his face as Gabe put his arm around Callie's shoulders and poor Luc tried to find his voice.

"Congratulations. As you can tell, you've definitely caught me by surprise. When did this happen?" The astonishment in his voice was evident.

"Actually, you're officially the first person we've told apart from our families. We married in New Zealand," he said.

"I can't believe I didn't even notice the ring on your finger," Luc said, feeling silly. "So how long have you been married?"

"Not long, a few months."

"I can't believe that no one knows." Luc shook his head still trying to comprehend that his best friend had gotten married.

"I can't say that I've been hiding it but can't also say that I've been shouting it loudly from the rooftops either," he said.

"So was this because you're in love or..." The awkwardness of the question had Luc silently cursing his big mouth as he realised that Callie might not know the truth of it.

"Both," he said. The moment he sort of acknowledged the fact that he loved Callie, he knew he did.

"That's great. I'm happy for you both," Luc said, giving Gabe a bear hug.

Callie went into the kitchen wondering why Gabe had just lied to his best friend. Was he still wary that Luc was spying on him? She didn't know and would ask him later but for now she had a dinner to serve.

She had set the table silently praying that Luc would be okay with her basic meal of roast chicken and vegetables. She knew from cooking for Gabe that he never really cared what she cooked because he was usually too hungry to notice.

She didn't know what was worse, him just eating for fuel or that he never commented.

"This looks lovely, Callie. I haven't had a home-cooked meal in who knows how long," Luc said, making her blush at his kind words.

It seemed silly but it warmed her that he had at least said something nice, she didn't even care if he wasn't being sincere. Gabe, however, bit back irritation at Luc's polite manners making his wife blush.

As they ate, it was Callie who brought up Luc's reason for visiting New York.

"What brings you to New York?" she said, curious, yet still elated that Gabe and Luc seemed to be friends again.

"The most important thing was to see Gabe," he said, as she arched an eyebrow. "He sent me a little gnome figurine and I knew that he had forgiven me."

"It worked. The gnomes *are* magic," she said, delighted.

"Cal, I could have sent him a bottle of cognac and he would have thought the same thing," Gabe said.

"I have to agree with Gabe. Any peace offering he sent would have done it. I did read the little card that came with it but I don't think its magic," Luc said.

"Did you know that Luc has a sister that lives in New York?" he said, subtly changing the subject.

"Oh really? Is she younger or older?" she said with her normal inquisitiveness which Gabe appreciated.

"Younger, probably your age," Luc said. "Actually she lives about fifteen minutes from here. I could introduce you if you like? I know she'd loved to make a new friend especially one that's Gabe's *wife*," he teased, but Callie felt that paralysing fear explode inside her.

It seemed like a good idea since she had finished renovating the apartment and she was now at a loss about what to do next. However, she didn't want to be someone's friend because of who her husband was but since this was Luc she pretended to be interested.

"That would be lovely. Does she work? Married?" she said, wondering if she would have anything at all in common with Luc's sister.

"Yes, she's married with one young child."

"Sounds great," she said, a tad too brightly, making Gabe notice that although Callie's words were positive, he could tell that she wasn't at all comfortable.

Deftly changing the subject for now, it was after Luc had left that Gabe pulled Callie into his arms and kissed her forehead before hugging her tightly, enjoying the feeling of having her in his arms.

"You did wonderfully," he said, as an excuse for the intimacy.

"And you are horrible for making me stress so much when it was only Luc."

"I don't think that Luc would appreciate being called 'only Luc'," he teased. "Besides it wouldn't have been a surprise if I told you."

"I'm glad that you two have made up. Did you see his face when you told him we were married?" She laughed at the memory.

The feeling of Callie's body vibrating with laughter was causing him to become aroused and he subtly moved his hips away from hers so she wouldn't realise just what she was doing to him. The last thing he wanted or needed was for her to feel that he was changing the rules of their agreement by having feelings for her or for her to be uncomfortable around him.

Chapter 16

The most unimaginable thing had happened sending shockwaves around the world. News outlets far and wide recorded the moment.

Fabien St Croix was dead.

This was akin to someone from a royal family dying and every single possible detail was chewed over and over, again and again from who found him and how he had died. But what garnered the most gossip, excitement, attention and column inches was who would attend the funeral.

Speculation was rife over the attendees with some openly declaring that they refused to pay their respects to such a tyrant while others wanted to spit on the dead man's grave. However, knowing that the funeral would be well covered by the world's media, most people would suck up any animosity or hatred to at least attend and put on a good show.

The world's top designers were suddenly inundated with requests for funeral wear because everyone wanted to look their best for the cameras.

Every day articles appeared in the news ranging from Fabien's exploits of success to stories of his tyrannical ways and the things he had done to people and other companies.

When Gabe heard the news before the world, it was from a man who turned up at his office from his grandfather's lawyers expressing their sincerest condolences. Gabe had no doubt that they were trying to curry favour with possibly the next owner of the St Croix empire.

Once the man had gone, Gabe didn't know what to think. He had had a love/hate relationship with his grand-père all his life and now he was gone. While he was saddened that he had lost a grandfather, there was also relief.

Now he could stop constantly looking over his shoulder and it almost seemed like an anti-climax that he never got to throw his own success in his grandfather's face. Neither had his grandfather won by crushing him so destructively that Gabe would never have stepped out of line again.

Knowing that he had to go back to France indefinitely, he called Robert into his office to explain the situation promising that if he couldn't come back, he'd at least find a CEO to take over so Robert could retire or work a little less.

Next he had to find Callie and explain what had happened. He knew she'd be torn between being sympathetic at his loss and relieved that it was all over and she could now go on to live her life.

Callie had just come back from walking aimlessly around the city and had on a whim purchased a few clothes when she heard the door slam shut.

"Callie?" Gabe yelled out to a seemingly empty apartment. He raked a hand through his hair hoping she'd be here but really didn't know what she did with her days since she had finished decorating their apartment.

"Gabe?" she said, surprised and instantly concerned to see him walking towards her looking dishevelled. "What's happened? Why are you home?"

"Thank God you're here," he said, pulling her into a tight bear hug.

He needed her softness and strength right now. Everything was about to change and this moment of peace and quiet was all they had left.

"Gabe, you're scaring me," she whispered, but it was loud enough for him to hear.

"Sorry, come sit," he said, leading her to the bed. "Grand-père's dead."

Gabe noted the shocked look on her face which was the same as his had probably been. It seemed incomprehensible and yet, it was true.

"A-are you sure?" she whispered, her mind spinning in disbelief.

"Yes. His lawyers came to tell me in person this morning." His voice lacked any emotion. He saw her mouth open to speak but reading her mind he answered before she could ask the question. "Heart attack."

"Do your parents know?"

"Probably, if I was told in person then the lawyers would have at least rung my father to advise him. I've pretty much dumped everything in Robert's lap and told him I'd be back when I could or find someone to replace me. Then I came straight home to tell you to pack."

"P-pack?" She looked dazed.

"We have to go to Paris for the funeral."

"Oh right, the funeral. Then we'll come back and…"

"No, Callie. I don't think we will be back for months. There's bound to be a lot to sort out," he said, as gently as possible.

"B-but…" She looked at him with bewilderment. Seeing how terrified she looked, he knelt in front of her and clasped her hands in his. "B-but no one knows. You go and I'll stay and we'll quietly divorce or annul the marriage."

"I know its going to be a huge change but you're my wife. I need you to be there beside me."

It was that almost vulnerable pleading in his eyes and voice that made her heart ache for him. She had no desire to live in France but now she had no choice. She was doing this for Gabe. This would be her last act as his wife before she divorced him.

Silently she nodded, trying to hold down all her fears. He stood looking relieved, honestly not knowing if he could do this without her. He had come to rely on her quiet inner strength that she didn't know she had.

"Okay, you start packing. Don't worry about how much luggage you have, we're taking the company jet. I need to call my father," he said, leaving her still sitting in a daze.

She didn't know what to pack and so she packed as much as she could in three suitcases. Anything that didn't fit she decided she wouldn't need. Then she got out Gabe's clothes and began to sort through them and it made her realise that it was such a wifely thing to do.

He came back into the room and saw her packing for the both of them and just watched her for a minute. Her face looked pensive and terrified but that was only to be expected since he knew she didn't want to go, let alone live in Paris.

As if she sensed his presence, she looked up and saw him watching her.

"How was your father?"

"A bit like me, shellshocked. Grand-père was as tough as old boots. Someone that old and crotchety you never expect to die. The lawyers had gone to see him too."

"Wow, that's a long way just to part such terrible news."

"Yes."

"So, are they all coming to the funeral?" She'd feel much better if she had moral support from them.

"No. Mum's not feeling up to it and Amélie really doesn't want to go so she'll stay with mum."

"Is Marielle all right?"

Gabe appreciated Callie's concern for his mother.

"Yes, it's only a cold but since they don't want to go, we're making it sound worse and therefore a legitimate excuse not to attend. You know everyone will have a field day with their non-attendance, that's another reason I need you by my side."

Callie was instantly jealous of Marielle and Amy and wished she too had a great and legitimate excuse not to have to go to Paris. She hated being put in this position but she knew what she was signing up for when she married Gabe, only she hadn't realised that she had had it so good for so long.

Now she had to jump into the fire pit of Parisian society and swim with the sharks. How ironic. She almost laughed to herself that only a few days ago she was feeling bored and now, boredom sounded like bliss.

They finished packing and left for the airport.

Arriving at the one place that Callie dreaded — the impersonal cold and uninviting fortress — known as the St Croix Palace, Gabe's Aunt Hélène was already there on the doorstep weeping and wailing in a very uncomfortable over-the-top display.

After the appropriate amount of grief had been displayed, Hélène finally noticed Callie standing nearby.

"Who is this?" Hélène said, angry. "Your grand-père has just died and you bring one of your whores here! That is the most disrespectful and hurtful thing —"

Gabe cut his aunt off before she said something that couldn't ever be taken back. She had already gone too far in his books already.

"Tante Hélène, this is *my wife*." His tone was cold.

Hélène's eyes glittered at Callie before narrowing suspiciously at her nephew.

"You lie," she hissed. "You're not married. If you think that this will put you in better stead with papa's will, it won't. He cut you off."

Gabe shrugged and brushed past her holding out his hand for Callie to take and join him.

As she went with her husband, his aunt muttered a very filthy and foul word at her and Callie felt Gabe freeze briefly and then continue inside hoping that Callie didn't understand what his aunt had said.

"Are you okay?" she said, feeling the tension strongly running through him. "Your aunt seemed appalled that I was here."

He gritted his teeth, furious at his aunt for making Callie feel even more self-conscious and wishing she hadn't come.

"Don't be silly, she was just shocked that I was married. Her grief is making her not think straight," he lied.

She knew that wasn't the truth but didn't want to make a fuss, especially since they had only been here all of five minutes.

They went to his apartment which was in the same wing as Amélie's and Callie couldn't help but marvel at how this was about five times bigger than their New York apartment. Suddenly she was homesick for their cheery little place.

A rap on the door announced someone with refreshments for them. She hadn't seen anyone request or even ask them if they would like something but she supposed, after years of living with Fabien, the servants knew exactly what was expected.

She could have kissed the cook as she bit into a delightfully delicious, fluffy and flaky pastry.

"This is delicious." She showed her appreciation, savouring each bite as Gabe shifted uncomfortably in his seat.

Callie looked like a sinfully sweet temptation trying to seduce him as her eyes closed with each bite. Her pink tongue darting out to lick her rosebud mouth and then, when she had finally finished her pain au chocolat, she went to wipe her hands and he wanted nothing more than to grab her fingers and lick them clean for her, but refrained because he didn't want to frighten her with such a blatant overture.

That night Callie was so restless she couldn't sleep. Not knowing if it was because she was back in this place or if it was because Gabe seemed so aloof.

She understood that he had a lot on his mind but he didn't even seem to be able to relax around her. Thankfully, they had dinner in his apartment with Callie relieved not to have to interact with his aunt. She didn't remember meeting her last time, which was a small blessing since she seemed so horrid.

François was due to arrive in the morning and Callie prayed that he could help alleviate some of Gabe's stress and concerns.

Gabe hadn't told his aunt the truth about what time his father was arriving because after picking him up from the airport they went straight to the *Coudert et Vogel* offices as requested. Now they'd know for sure what his grandfather had done and whether he'd been as spiteful as he had threatened or left everything to François or Gabe.

Monsieur Coudert received his two most important clients as if they were royalty and offered his own personal and professional condolences on Fabien's passing.

"Please sit. I know that this must be a very distressing time," Monsieur Coudert said. "But in accordance to Monsieur Fabien St Croix's last wishes this meeting is to take place now before the funeral and public announcement of his death."

The elderly man looked down at his sheet.

"Firstly, you both received word of Monsieur Fabien St Croix's death by a personal representative of this firm, oui?"

As they nodded, Gabe noted that Monsieur Coudert ticked the paper and now everything made sense. Even in death, his grandfather was orchestrating things his way.

"Now we come to all the business matters. Upon Monsieur Fabien St Croix's death, he has instructed that the control of all matters be handed over to his son, François. Now should Monsieur François decline — and Monsieur Fabien sensed that you, Monsieur François would — it would then pass onto his grandson, Monsieur Gabriel St Croix. Should Monsieur Gabriel also refuse then it would be handled by a Trust."

The whoosh of held breath was exhaled but Gabe knew that it was too soon to celebrate. It couldn't possibly be this easy, his grandfather wasn't that kind of man and as soon as Monsieur Coudert opened his mouth, Gabe instantly saw what his grandfather wanted — blind servitude — that even in death he had the last laugh.

"There are however, certain requirements that need to be met. *Anyone* agreeing to take control of all the St Croix business holdings must remain in the position for the next twenty-five years before total ownership becomes theirs. That includes the person who handles the business for the Trust, that would mean the St Croix family would lose *all* control in that case." The emphasis was just in case his current clients misunderstood Fabien's wishes.

"However, should either Monsieur François or Gabriel agree to take control, years already employed will count in their favour. Although there is an additional stipulation that should you, Monsieur François take over, you must remain at the head of the company for an additional ten years since you have already served your twenty five."

Listening the to the lawyer, it saddened Gabe to think that even in death, all his grandfather thought of was business, not once did he think of his family.

"It is also to be noted that Monsieur Fabien was not in agreement with his grandson, Gabriel's choice of wife. Should Monsieur Gabriel immediately divorce Calliope Harrison and never enter into *any* kind of relationship with her again, Monsieur Fabien is willing to immediately sign over all control of the business." He looking pointedly at Gabe. "What say you?"

Now Gabe was outraged. Even dead, his grandfather thought he could run his life and was about to open his mouth and angrily tell Monsieur Coudert what his answer was when his father interjected first.

"Monsieur Coudert, may we please have a moment in private. This is such an unexpected and sudden offer. We must think about it," François said, as the other man agreed but before he left the office, he turned to advise one more thing.

"Gentlemen, I am under strict instructions that you must answer before we can continue. The answer you give, is the binding one, there is no changing of the mind."

"There you go, Gabe," his father said as soon as they were alone. "You finally get it all. Your marriage of convenience worked, so why do you look so angry?"

"Even from his grave he's running everyone's life. I'm tired of it," he said. "I can't believe that I'm just supposed to give up Callie."

"But it's what you wanted." François wondered if his son had finally seen the light.

"I know, but to have *no* kind of relationship with her? That's too harsh even for me. She's my friend and I can't…*won't* just desert her like she never existed. She's done all this for me," he said, frustrated, raking a hand through his hair.

"You have feelings for Callie? Deep feelings?" François guessed, since his son sounded so full of conviction.

This was what both sets of parents had secretly hoped would happen when both children got married.

"Yes," he said, solemn.

"She has feelings for you?"

"No more than a friend would."

"Ah…" his father said, full of paternal concern at seeing his son miserable. "So you haven't tried to court her?"

"No. So much has happened and now grand-père's dead. Callie's not happy being here. How can I expect her to stay married to me and live here?"

He hoped his father would have some miracle answers for him.

"In Paris?" François said, not sure what made his daughter-in-law unhappy.

"Because of what happened with Amélie's sixteenth birthday. This place only has terrible memories for her. I could have left her back in New York and no one even need known I'm married but selfishly I just couldn't. I need her by my side."

"That is a man in love, my son. Believe me, having a multi-billion dollar company is no replacement for love," his father said. "Come, let's finish this and then we'll start operation Courting Callie."

"Operation Courting Callie?" He looked at his father as if he had gone crazy.

"Best I could come up with on the spot," François chuckled.

"Merci, papa." He gave his father a big bear hug.

Monsieur Coudert re-entered his office.

"I'm sorry but I need an answer now as to whether you are willing to immediately divorce your wife and —"

"Non," he said, emphatic.

He could hear Callie in his head telling him he was being stupid but having made the decision and saying it out loud made him feel strong.

"You are sure?" Monsieur Coudert said, his eyes nervously darting from one client to the other.

"Oui."

Nothing more was said and Gabe had a feeling his answer had set off another set of instructions that he wasn't privy to knowing…yet, and a sense of dread shot through him.

"Now, before we release the formal statement of his death, we still need to discuss if either of you wish to take the helm. You get this one chance to make the decision and that is final."

"I do not want it," François said.

"Are you sure?"

"Oui."

"And you, Monsieur Gabriel? Are you of the same mind as your father?"

He was torn. Twenty-five years or less was still such a long time to commit but it was his family's legacy.

"What happens to all the profits?" he said.

"They will go into the family Trust that has been set up for this and then to be apportioned. If you take up your grandfather's offer, you will get a very substantial and generous wage along with shares in the company."

"What happens if I take the job and then decide to leave?"

Monsieur Coudert consulted his notes once more.

"In the event that you voluntarily resign or are voted out before the time is up, you will receive a remuneration package and the company will then revert to the Trust with whomever running it following the same rules as offered to you now."

This made Gabe feel more comfortable and therefore there was only one answer he could give.

"Then I'll do it," he said, before turning to his father to explain. "I need to at least give this a go."

François nodded knowing that his son not only liked a challenge but he wanted to at least try and save their legacy. He just hoped that Callie wouldn't become a casualty in his decision.

"Here is the statement that will go to press tomorrow. The details of his funeral have already been planned. Both of you are expected to make eulogies. The reading of Fabien St Croix's will is scheduled to be read on Monday at ten at the château." Monsieur Coudert-stood to signal the end the meeting.

On the way back to the château both father and son had a lot to discuss about the meeting.

"Callie must never know that I turned down outright ownership of the company because of her. She'll be furious with me," he said, before adding, "and no telling mum or her family either."

As they turned into the driveway they had five more minutes and Gabe used them to warn his father that Tante Hélène was in residence and none too happy especially with the fact that he had a wife.

As predicted Hélène must have been waiting for François to arrive because no sooner had he alighted from the vehicle, she came running out wailing and screeching much like how she had greeted Gabe.

"François, thank goodness you've come," she loudly sobbed, before looking around and noting that it was only him. "Where's Marielle and Amélie?"

"Marielle's very sick and couldn't handle the travel and so Amélie stayed to be with her." He saw the anger in his sister's eyes but didn't care. "Gabe, we'll all have dinner together, oui?"

"Oui, papa," Gabe said, already heading inside not wanting to spend any more time with his unpleasant aunt.

He breathed a sigh of relief, glad that he didn't have to listen to Tante Hélène began her tirade about her brother living in some backwater country and Gabriel turning up with the most unsuitable wife.

Chapter 17

Callie spent the day wandering aimlessly around the suite and then decided to find the kitchen to thank the chef for the beautiful pastries, all the way silently praying that she wouldn't accidentally run into Hélène.

To her surprise and those in the kitchen at having a visitor, the Château actually employed a patisserie chef. She thanked him and praised his delicious delicacies much to his delight and by the time she had left, Armand was under her spell promising to make her whatever her heart's desire. She settled for some lovely pain au chocolat and little lemon meringue tarts and a hot chocolate for afternoon tea.

"Callie?" Gabe called out upon his return, torn between wanting to hold her and not wanting to see the sadness in her face at his news.

"How did it go?" she said, eager for news of her father-in-law.

"We'll see papa at dinner tonight but until then, I need to discuss some things with you."

He sounded so serious that Callie didn't know whether to be worried or not.

"Wait, let me get afternoon tea brought up first and then we can chat," she said, trying to delay the conversation.

"Good idea. I'm going to change so can you also get me something like a panini as well since I missed lunch." He hadn't realised just how hungry he was until she mentioned food. Tugging on his tie, he decided to change into sweats and a tee shirt to feel comfy. By the time he came out, the refreshments had been delivered and Callie once again was drooling over her pastry.

Seeing Gabe enter the room, she looked embarrassed.

"I'm going to be a little tubby if Armand keeps baking like this."

"Who is Armand?" A ripple of jealousy rolled through him. He didn't know any Armand so how did his wife?

"The patisserie chef," she said. "Don't *you* know?"

It was the amazement in her voice that made him chuckle releasing some of the tension in his body. His curiosity was pricked.

"No. How do *you* know Armand?"

"I went to the kitchen today thinking to thank the chef and I got the surprise of my life when I found out that you have your own patisserie chef."

"Of course you went to the kitchen. You do realise that you're the first person *ever* to do that. They must have jumped out of their skin," he laughed, before whispering, "Do we have a dungeon?"

"How would I know?" she giggled.

"Well you're the adventurous one of the two of us. Maybe you've found secret passageways as well?" He arched his eyebrows in curiosity.

"I'll let you know. Now what did you want to talk to me about?" she said, changing the subject.

"After I picked up dad from the airport, we went straight to the lawyers."

Surprise coloured her face. She had assumed that he had just been busy doing work stuff until he got his father from the airport.

"Yes. They requested the meeting as soon as dad landed. We needed to sort out some things before we formally announced grand-père's death," he said, dreading the next part he was about to tell her.

She thought it a little ridiculous since the whole world already knew of Fabien's death.

"Can I ask what was sorted?" There was a nervous tremble in her voice.

"I've agreed to take over the company because otherwise it'll be turned over to someone else to run and own in the future. In essence, grand-père is still trying to call all the shots even in death."

"That's great," she said, trying to sound happy for him. Gabe was finally getting what he wanted.

"Not really. Basically I have to run it for twenty-five years before it becomes my company."

"Twenty-five years!" she gasped. "Th-that's insane."

"It's actually the same deal for anyone who was taking it over. The only bonus is that the years I've already worked count towards it."

"So we're not going back to New York," she said, her voice barely a whisper and looking like she was about to cry.

"No. I'm really sorry, Callie."

He felt like such a jerk. A man trampling all over her and it tore at him.

"I guess we divorce early then," she said, taking off her rings to hand them to him.

"What are you doing?" He looked alarmed.

"I can still attend the funeral…but as a family friend. No one ever needs to know that I'm your wife. We'll divorce quietly and you can continue on without any distractions and I'll go do…whatever," she said.

Her chest felt tight, like she couldn't breathe, wondering why he wasn't happier with her suggestion.

He couldn't believe his ears. Callie was trying to leave him at the first chance she got. Well, he wasn't about to just let her go without a fight.

Before he could tell her that there was no way he was letting her out of their contract, they were interrupted by a knock at the door.

"Callie," François said, giving his daughter-in-law a warm smile as he walked into their apartment. "You look lovely."

"Its good to see you again and I'm sorry about Fabien," she said, appreciating François' fatherly embrace and offering her condolences but he simply waved them away.

"I'm sorry about Hélène. She's quite snobbish, not to mention very bitchy and bitter. If our roles were reversed, she would have been everything my father wanted in a son," he said. "Try not to let her get to you but I'm afraid that she'll never be nice to you. And if she is, watch out."

"Thanks, I will." She appreciated the warning.

"I thought we were meeting at dinner?" Gabe said, silently thanking his father for his timely interruption.

"I wanted to see you both privately first, see how you're both doing."

Much to Gabe's annoyance, Callie proceeded to tell his father everything including her reasoning behind returning her rings to Gabe.

"Oh no, my dear, you are now the gate-keeper or should that be the guard? I don't know, but Gabe needs you now more than ever once it's known that he's the new head of the St Croix empire," François said to her confusion, as Gabe silently thanked his father.

"What do you mean?"

"Gabe being single brings out all kinds of gold-digging, crazy women. If he's married, he can concentrate on work and politely turn away any advances without a second thought."

"Are you saying that women will proposition him, even if he were married?" she said, wide eyed in surprise. She felt so naïve.

"Callie, ma belle, he's Gabriel St Croix — young, mega-rich and handsome as sin. Of course they want him...sometimes its more exciting because he's married, the challenge is much more rewarding."

It hit her like an epiphany. Gabe had told her that there wasn't anyone he could trust enough to marry him to spite his grandfather. Now that it was all becoming clearer and she felt sorry for him.

"No! No, don't you pity me," he growled, seeing the look in her eyes.

"But now I've finally got it. *Why* you chose me. Before I thought I was just handy, even though you said those things, I still didn't truly understand especially since no one in New York seemed to even care that you were there, they must have known surely..."

"I can see the pity in your eyes."

"It's not pity…it's…sadness," she said, somewhat lamely.

"That's pity," he snapped. "You're right, we'll get a quiet divorce. I don't need a pity wife."

The harshness in his voice made her mouth open and close and for a moment Gabe that Callie might cry. She fled the room and Gabe felt terrible.

"Well, that didn't go so well," his father said, dryly.

"I don't want her pity."

"I know son, but then you need to show her what you *do* want but beware, she may not return your feelings. The Callie standing in front of me didn't look like someone in love."

That cut Gabe deeply. Maybe it was just a dream that she would love him like he loved her. He loudly sighed wondering at the fact that he was now worth billions and couldn't get the one person who didn't care, to love him.

How ironic.

Callie let the tears fall as soon as she reached the sanctity of the bedroom. There was no need to be so harsh especially when she was only trying to help. What she said was true, she hadn't truly understood and now it was a big mess. She didn't pity him…she didn't!

"What a jerk!" she muttered.

How she wished they could be back in New York in their apartment. She was beginning to wonder if *anything* good ever happened in Paris because she was yet to see it.

Gabe left her alone until it was time to get dressed for dinner.

"Callie? I'm sorry I was so harsh earlier. I didn't mean to be."

"No, you were right. I just didn't think of it as pitying you. I really don't, you know."

"So what do you want to do?" he said, sitting down beside her on the bed. "If you really want to get divorced, I'll agree. You were right, it's better if we did it before everyone gets wind of it. Being my wife won't be easy, especially now. People will judge you, sometimes harshly, sometimes without provocation or the facts. I don't want you to feel under constant attack but that's the way my life is. You haven't been brought up to have a hard shell that Amy or I have."

She knew he was right. This was what she had feared all along — to be eaten alive by others with their petty gossip and judgemental attitudes. Hadn't she already felt it with Gabe's aunt?

"I don't know. I was getting bored in New York not being able to work and I'm not a big shopper."

"Cal, be yourself…please. Don't do this if you'll be miserable or have to change. I like you just the way you are," he said, knowing that this was as close as he was going to get to admitting that he loved her.

"I hated the long hours you worked, even though I understood, I still hated them." She confessed her terrible secret.

"Why didn't you tell me?" he said, astonished. "I would've made more effort to come home even for an hour."

"That's why." She gave him a wry smile. "You needed to concentrate on the company and not have to worry about a lonely wife. The same thing will happen now but I'm imagining it to be a thousand times worse," she said, the sadness in her voice evident of the reality.

"It will take a while to catch up on what's been happening. There'll also be a lot of dinners and socialising to be done." He nodded his head in agreement.

"If only you weren't who you are. Then maybe we could try it out for a while but you're not," she said, rueful. "I'm just not cut out to be a lady of leisure."

"What would make *you* happy?" He wanted to know how he could help her.

"I really don't know." Her shoulders slumped. In her mind's eye she saw the little gnome she had bought but she didn't want to tell Gabe her heart's desire because he couldn't give her that. "I don't suppose you'd consider living in say London or New York permanently?" She looked at him with such hope in her eyes.

"Not for a long time." He felt like an ogre as he sadly shook his head.

"Thought so."

"Listen, Cal. The funeral's not until Sunday so go out and see the sights and look around. I've got to make a start at work and then tell me your decision."

"That's a good idea."

They changed for dinner and compared to Hélène, Callie looked positively poor and dowdy. Hélène was in a ball gown with jewels dripping on her.

As soon as they had walked in and Hélène had seen Callie she began her verbal assault making sure her disparaging comments were heard loud and clear about Callie not being St Croix material.

Callie could only catch the odd word since Hélène was rapidly speaking French but from Gabe and François' responses, it was not only about her but also not pleasant.

"I'm sorry for embarrassing you," she whispered, as Gabe pulled out a chair for her.

"You haven't."

Dinner was excruciating for Callie as everyone spoke French around her and she knew that this is how she would feel as Gabe's wife anywhere.

Every now and then Gabe and François would speak to her in English but she only mumbled her replies wishing the meal to be over.

Gabe frowned at seeing Callie so unhappy at dinner. He remembered her back in New York so vibrant and happy. Now being back in Paris for a few days she had lost her sparkle and he knew that he wasn't going to woo her.

He was going to let her go.

That night after dinner he told her of his decision.

"I've changed my mind. You can leave whenever you like." He hoped his voice was void of any emotion so not to betray his real feelings.

"B-but why?" Her chest felt tight at his words, shocked that now he was telling her to leave. "I-I thought that you wanted me to take some time to think about it?"

Was he was throwing her out because she couldn't even manage dinner and he didn't want to be made a laughingstock?

"That was before dinner. You looked so miserable and I can't put you through that. You've done more than enough for me, its time for you to go and live your own life," he said, even though part of him wanted her to defy him and stay.

"I'm sorry," she said, tears silently rolling down her cheeks. "I'm sorry that I'm not a stronger person."

He pulled her close and held her in his arms.

"Oh Callie," he whispered into her hair. "You've done marvellously. Don't be sorry for something that I love about you. I'm the one who should be sorry because I can't really help you. You're stronger than you think. You've also been the perfect wife. I can't think of anyone else I'd rather be married to."

It was as close as he could come to saying what was in his heart because even if he did tell her the truth, it would change nothing. His father was right. Callie didn't feel anything close to what he did.

Gabe offered Callie the private jet back to New York and she was grateful for it. When Armand came out to give her some pastries for her trip, that made her smile and cry at the same time at the lovely gesture.

Returning to an empty apartment alone made her miserable as she looked around and all she could see was her and Gabe. She felt a twinge of regret in admitting that she hated his working late but now it was a selfish thought because he had been doing what most husbands do, provide for his family.

Going into their room, she saw the little gnomes they had and picked the one she had chosen for herself up off the shelf and sat down on the bed looking hard at it.

"I need your help magic gnome. I have no idea what to do with my life," she sobbed, disappointment flooding her that it didn't glow or shoot out magical beams of light in answer.

They say that miracles come in all different shapes, sizes and ways, well Callie's miraculous epiphany came out of loneliness.

She had been home in New York a few days before realising as she read the paper and saw Gabe's gaunt solemn face and that of François, how utterly selfish and thoughtless she had been. She should have shown some courage and stayed for the funeral at least but her fears of being laughed at and mocked had been too strong to overcome.

Lightly her fingers ran over Gabe's face as she remembered how she had woken one night to find him holding her in his sleep. She hadn't known if it was a mistake or not so she never said anything.

The next time he did the same thing made her wonder if he was holding onto her like some kind of lifeline or he actually wanted to be near her. She had quietly climbed out of bed and gotten a drink of water to try and make sense in her mind of Gabe holding her in their sleep.

Did he do it every night? Would she have ever known if she hadn't woken the last couple of times? There were so many questions so why didn't she just ask him? Because deep down she felt safe in his arms and he wasn't hurting her in any way. It actually made her feel more lovable that her husband wanted to hold her in his sleep…she didn't want him to stop and knew that if she brought it up he would have.

Wanting to test her theory to see if he was doing it on purpose or not, she climbed back into the bed on his side in which there was now more room and woke with a smile on her face which turned into a frown when she realised that she had slept so deeply that she had no idea whether he had found her again or not because now the bed was empty.

Thoughts of how a good wife should be, even if it was only for convenience, made her miserably note that she was here and her husband on the other side of the Atlantic far away. She could have been a good wife to him if only she was more confident within herself but she never had to play those silly little social games because she always had Amélie and then after they had returned to France, she had thrown herself into her studies.

She gave a loud sigh still staring at the grainy newspaper photo of Gabe. She missed him. She missed his presence. Now that he wasn't around and she had all this time on her hands to think, she could see that he was the kind of man that she could see herself settling down with. They had such an easy rapport and she knew that he trusted her enough to share the important details of his personal and professional life with her. Even seeing his face light up when he saw what she had done to their apartment made her feel warm and fuzzy.

That's when it hit Callie like a bolt of lightning.

She truly wanted to be his wife for real.

She loved Gabe.

The realisation was such a shock that she had to wonder if she was crazy. She hadn't felt any kind of lust for him before so how did she know that she wasn't just imagining that she loved him or if it was real?

This wasn't a movie. This was real life. She guessed the old adage that sometimes you don't even realise what you have until it was gone was true. Leaving Gabe, when he needed her most was a terrible thing to do. She should have been there *for him* and not worried about herself.

Could she summon the required courage to run back to him and beg him to see out the rest of their agreement? Would he laugh in her face if she turned up and declared her love only to find that he didn't feel the same? The cowardice that she had felt in Paris had now returned with a vengeance. It was paralysing her as she felt the strangulation of it taking hold and suddenly it was like her brain exploded.

"No!" she shouted to the empty apartment, standing so abruptly that the chair she was sitting in was knocked over.

She needed fresh air and a plan.

Chapter 18

Gabe was sitting in his apartment at the château having a drink. God, he was tired. Saying farewell to the man you loved and loathed was exhausting as he lurched from feeling guilty about how he had left it with his grand-père and feeling even guiltier for not being sadder that he had died.

Hélène had loudly wailed and shrieked her grief through the entire service and his father had been stoic.

Then there were all the women that had tried to console him on his loss. He didn't want any of them. None appealed. He only wanted Callie and she was a whole continent away being free from the burden that came with being a member of this family.

Tante Hélène had been smug and superior when she found out that Callie had gone back to New York. Her derisive comments made him viciously snap at her and she had remained silent since.

François entered his son's apartment and took one look at Gabe and was concerned.

"How are you holding up?"

If anyone had heard the question they naturally would have assumed it was in reference to his grandfather's funeral but in fact his father was referring to Callie.

"I miss her so much," he said with a heavy heart.

"Then go to her. Who cares who owns the company if you don't have the one you love by your side. Why do you think I chose my family over my father?"

"I can't. The problem actually isn't me."

"Then what is it?"

"It's being a St Croix. All the snobbishness, social niceties, politics and back-stabbing that goes with it. She's not that kind of person. She couldn't handle it when she was sixteen, she sure as hell can't handle it now," he said, bitter.

"How do you know?"

He ignored the question.

"Do you know Armand?" he said out of curiosity, knowing full well that his father wouldn't know the man.

François' brow furrowed as he thought of anyone that he knew by that name.

"Is he one of papa's lackey's? Lawyers?"

"No, I didn't know him either. He's the château's patisserie chef." He gave a hollow laugh.

"How do you know?" his father said, perplexed that Gabe would know his name. Even he didn't know anyone's real name except for the few butlers and maids that he saw regularly.

"Because Callie went into the kitchen to meet him."

"Oh."

The surprised look on his father's face was exactly as expected. No one from his family had ever met anyone in the kitchen. He couldn't even tell you how many people worked in there or even where the kitchen was located.

"Yes, oh. Now do you understand? Women can be vicious but rich society bitches like Tante Hélène are the most vicious of them all and Callie is like a gentle dove who would be chewed up and spat out."

"Then move to New York or London."

"I can't do that."

"Why not? You're running the company now. Just make it subtle enough and before anyone truly guesses the truth, it's done."

After his father had left, Luc had dropped by to make sure that he was okay. At least one thing from all of this was that they were not only friends again but honest as well now.

"I thought this might help you take your mind…off things," his friend said, as they sat quietly and had a drink together.

"What will?"

"Chantel thinks she knows the name of the woman that Claude is supposedly cheating on her with."

"I thought she separated from him?"

"So did I, but I guess my sister would rather have money and be miserable. She probably won't leave unless she finds another rich man to take care of her since she's never done anything in her life that resembles work so…"

Lightning stuck as Gabe suddenly understood with clarity that he had wanted Callie to do the same thing…be another bored housewife. No wonder she hadn't been happy. He had been an idiot.

"Who is it? Someone we know? Is it serious?" he said.

Normally he wouldn't have cared about whom Chantel's husband was sleeping with but he needed the distraction and something made him curious.

"Natalia or as we know her, Leticia," Luc said, grim.

"Letty?" He almost choked on his drink. "She's still using that website?"

"Sounds like it unless Claude is her only conquest now."

"Did you tell Chantel?"

"God no. That would have been one truth that she couldn't deny no matter how much she wanted to. Her good friend and her husband cheating around on her. *And* if it's been Letty more than once, it only makes it worse."

Gabe understood the implication. Sure, he had dumped Leticia but it still sickened him to think that Claude Mercier had been one of her conquests even then.

"What are you going to do?"

"I'm going to pretend for now that I can't find 'Natalia' and am going to have a little chat with Claude," Luc said, then changed the subject. "When's the reading of the will?"

"Tomorrow at ten."

"I leave tomorrow night so if you need to catch up…"

"Thanks, I can only hope that there won't be too many strings attached."

Monsieur Coudert arrived promptly at ten as promised and Hélène was beside herself with excitement. Before her father's death she had to jump with his every command and hated the fact that he thought her useless just because she was female. That was one of the reasons she had hastily married Guy Dupré because he was wealthy and had catered to her every little whim.

After Marcel was born, Guy stopped even attempting to be romantic saying that he now had a St Croix heir and there was no need for all that nonsense. Her bitterness slowly began swallowing her whole until she became so out of control in her attempts to exact some kind of revenge on Guy for his ignoring of her.

After Marcel's disastrous scandal celebrating being the new heir, he had been taken to a rehabilitation centre and from there would be conscripted into the French Army, Fabien explained to her horror.

Now she was no longer at her father's mercy.

Now she would have her inheritance and could leave her horrible life behind and start anew.

She had hardly heard a word of what Monsieur Coudert was even saying as she imagined herself on an island being worshipped like a goddess and treated as such. Never again would she have to grovel and dance to someone else's tune for money. Finally, she'd be rich *and* free.

Monsieur Coudert's voice broke into her daydream.

"As you know, Monsieur Fabien St Croix's business empire has already been sorted before his funeral just as he had wished.

So typical of her father, Hélène bitterly thought, business always came first.

"First I shall read out all things pertaining to Hélène Dupré, Fabien's only daughter."

She tried hard not to show her excitement at what was to come.

"Hélène Dupré will inherit five pieces of art..." I'll pick the most priceless and sell them off, she thought, mentally rubbing her hands in glee. "Situated only from the dining and guest bedrooms."

I hope you're rotting in hell papa, she furiously thought knowing that there were only two reasonably priced ones in those rooms.

"You will also receive an annual allowance of two million euros a year. After ten years, it will increase to three million. You shall not be entitled to receive a euro more."

She wanted to scream and shout contemptible things but her upbringing forbade such an outburst especially in the company of others that weren't family.

"However, when your divorce becomes final, you will also be allowed a monthly allowance of fifty thousand euros and not a euro more."

She was livid. Absolutely furious. Her own father expected her to become nothing more than a beggar on the street. If he wasn't already dead, she would have happily killed him with her bare hands.

Monsieur Coudert continued without caring about Hélène's reactions and emotions.

"My underachieving and spoilt grandson, Marcel Dupré, will upon completing rehabilitation and serving in the French Army, receive a sum of one hundred thousand euros a year and not a euro more. He will also undertake random drug testing at any stage and should he decline or test positive, the inheritance will be immediately revoked."

Hélène was once again fuming that Gabriel received more than Marcel since her nephew was now running the St Croix business empire and that salary alone was at least a hundred times more than the annual pittance Marcel would be receiving.

"I'll sue!" she screeched, not caring about appearances. She had had enough of this farce.

Monsieur Coudert remained calm obviously having seen this kind of reaction before.

"Oui, madame, you may sue but there's strict instructions to immediately cut off all money for the remainder of both of you and your son's lives unless of course you win."

Hélène knew she couldn't afford to sue unless she was guaranteed a win and instead she inwardly raged.

The elderly man waited a moment to see if Hélène Dupré wanted to carry on with her protest but as the room remained silent, he continued as if her outburst had never happened.

"Now as to the rest of the estate…Madame Dupré, you are free to leave," he said.

Once again Hélène felt slighted and belligerently said, "I will stay and hear how unjust papa's will is."

"Actually there are strict instructions for you to leave now," Monsieur Coudert said, his tone stern. They all waited for Hélène to leave the room but she wasn't about to budge.

Suddenly the door opened and a man entered.

"Please show Madame Dupré out," Monsieur Coudert said.

Gabe was impressed by the timing before realising that the wily old man must have given the man some kind of signal.

After Monsieur Coudert had finished the reading of Fabien's will and departed, both François and Gabe were solemn. As predicted everything was left to both of them but only because there was no way that Fabien would give the family heirlooms to anyone else. It would have created a scandal and Fabien was all about appearances and protecting the family name at all costs.

"So now what will you do?" his father said.

He shrugged not knowing what to say. He felt alone and missed Callie's quiet strength that gave him his strength.

"Do you think that we should give Tante Hélène some more money?" he said, concerned that she had been treated badly.

"If it makes you feel better," his father shrugged. "You heard papa's reason. He still died with the regret that she wasn't his son, that I was, but he was still chauvinistic enough to leave the majority of it to us."

They decided that they would offer to buy Hélène a house anywhere she wanted, and a generous lump sum, nothing more.

Hélène after having a few hours to digest that she wasn't going to be flush with funds agreed. She was going to find a house somewhere as far removed from Paris as possible, then she wouldn't be able to hear anyone laughing at her.

"Take care, son. I hope that you and Callie can work out your differences. I'll tell everyone what happened. I know that they'll all be crossing their fingers for you both."

"Yes, well…I guess we'll just have to wait and see. I've asked so much of her already so I'm not holding my breath that she miraculously changes her mind."

Gabe was feted and offered condolences wherever he went. Some of the people he knew had come to the funeral and others paid lip service which didn't bother him in the slightest.

He was working like a demon and no amount of invitations to soirees and dinners managed to stop him. Of course with true St Croix politeness he managed to fend off most invites with the feeble excuse that he needed to catch up on business. Most understood but some tried to persuade him that a break would be nice.

He knew that meant that women wanted a chance to pursue him but he wasn't even close to being enticed. Even the gossip magazines and websites were all having a field day speculating over his romantic future. Still he ignored it all as best he could.

He also talked to his father daily, needing the reassurance and gentle guiding advice of a parent, and the more they discussed the idea that François had brought up after the funeral, the more he liked it.

Paris had no real meaning for him. Like Callie, none of his memories of the château or the city were truly happy and so he began to slowly spend more time in the London office. As his father had advised, there was no reason why he couldn't move the head office to another city and London to Gabe was where he had actually felt free from his grandfather.

It was also that close to Paris that he could catch a flight or train if he was needed over there.

Now all he needed was to get everything sorted and then he was going to go after his wife and bring her home. He only had a short time left on their marriage agreement and he hoped that she would welcome his gesture of moving the office — which was as much for him as for her — and that she might allow him to court her.

While Gabe was slowly changing the offices around, Callie walked around the more expensive shops of New York observing how the wealthier women looked and acted — they all seemed to look so stylish and chic. She went back to the apartment depressed that she wasn't at all like them. She knew that she needed help and there was only one person she could trust enough to do this for her…Amélie.

Her sister-in-law was so excited about the turn of events that she readily offered to come to New York and help Callie out.

Nervous about Amélie's arrival, Callie hoped that her sister-in-law would like their apartment and when Amélie saw it and was genuinely delighted, she relaxed.

The two weeks that the women spent together was almost like going back to their childhood and it was one long slumber party. Together they transformed Callie into a wife suitable to the St Croix name in appearance.

To work on her lack of confidence, Amélie dragged Callie around to meet with people that she wanted to help with her newly formed St Croix Foundation, making Callie talk to all the people to help woo them into pledging money or their support.

Slowly Callie felt more and more confident in socialising with these people and when she had told Amélie that some of them were so normal, Amélie had giggled saying that yes, not everyone was a snob like she had been.

It was a few nights later that Callie had her meltdown as they talked about Callie and Gabe's relationship.

"How could I have done this to him?" she said, her voice full of anguish and guilt.

"You haven't done anything. Gabe understands."

Amélie's words just heaped more guilt on Callie's shoulders that her *husband* was so understanding.

"Look at this picture of him. I should have been by his side, supporting him like he asked when we married. Instead, I ran away like a scared little girl and left him to deal with everything by himself."

The photo in question that she thrust at her sister-in-law, showed a very solemn looking Gabe taken at the funeral.

Amélie noting how upset Callie was, didn't have the heart to kick her friend when she was already having a personal crisis, but there was one more piece of news that Callie didn't know.

"Take a few deep breaths, Cal and calm down," Amélie said. She felt her own inner self relax when Callie took one deep breath and then another, but she was also wringing her hands, filled with dread that the moment's calm would shortly be shattered as soon as she announced the latest news.

"Cal? There's something that I think you should know."

"What? What is it?"

"Apparently there are some very quiet whispers that Gabe's rumoured to have married." Seeing Callie's eyes widen and her mouth open, Amélie hurriedly continued. "But it's just a rumour since Gabe hasn't commented and won't as its no one's business."

"B-but no one knew," Callie whispered, looking somewhat pale.

"We think Tante Hélène leaked it because she's angry at grand-père's will."

"Oh God, poor Gabe. Not only does he have to run Fabien's empire with people wondering if he can do it, but now he's also humiliated by having a wife too cowardly to stand by his side. He must be wishing he never married me."

"Gabe understands, Cal…*truly*," Amélie said, but saw the sceptical look on Callie's face.

It was the last night that the two women would be together for a while and both Callie and Amélie felt almost depressed.

"Maybe I should stay and help you with the Foundation," she said.

"You know you can't, as much as I want you too. You need to be with Gabe."

"But what if I can't do it?" She felt tears well up. "What if he doesn't want me? He might have found another…" She couldn't finish the sentence because just the thought terrified her.

"I've been talking to him and he really truly sounds miserable. I'm also pretty sure he hasn't found another bedwarmer because I can guarantee that he misses *you*."

When Amélie told her parents about going to New York to help Callie, her father had cryptically said that he hoped that Callie's eyes had opened.

At the time, she had thought that her father had meant that Callie was moving on with her life, but now after spending time with her best friend and sister-in-law she was beginning to wonder if Gabe loved Callie.

Lord knew after all the heart to heart talks both women had over the past few weeks it was clear that Callie had just worked out that she loved Gabe, enough to get help for her lack of confidence.

"I'm absolutely petrified," she whispered, the tears falling.

Amélie wasn't sure if Callie was talking about Gabe or just in general but it was her job to bolster Callie's confidence.

"Just do what I did when I first returned back to Paris…act like a St Croix. They don't have to explain themselves and if people don't like what you're wearing or whatever, then you just act fine with it because you're a St Croix and you beat to your own drum, you don't *ever* follow the masses."

"*You* had a tough time assimilating back into Parisian Society?" It was a profound accusation that rolled off Callie's tongue.

"Oui, I truly hated it. I wasn't allowed to be me, I had to be this *princess*." Amélie said the word with disdain, tears in her eyes. "Soon it became second nature to be a complete bitch because then no one would know that I lacked confidence and was scared. *I'm so sorry for the way I treated you at my sixteenth birthday.*" They hugged each other tightly. "I'd forgotten how to be me and I also didn't want anyone to think that I enjoyed a poor person's company since I had constantly looked down on them."

"I understand. Back then I didn't, but now I do. I guess we're all just insecure at some stage in our lives, mine just happens to be now."

"You can do it and if you need any help, you call me and I'll be on the next plane. I'm sure I can still find that haughtiness again to squash anyone who dares to be mean to you," Amélie said, and Callie was grateful for such a loyal and loving friend.

Chapter 19

Disembarking from the plane Callie felt a jumbled mess of nerves. Creating the plan with Amélie to surprise Gabe was the easy part. Putting it into action was the part she was dreading.

Amélie had found out that Gabe was in London and that had Callie breathing easier because she knew Nigel would at least let her into the house.

They had discussed the pros and cons of going to Gabe's house at length before deciding to get a room at Claridge's to make Callie feel more comfortable.

Amélie, of course, organised it before Callie could chicken out and put the room under Gabe's name.

A car from the hotel was sent to the airport to pick up their esteemed guest. This was Callie's first chance to test out and use her newfound confidence. The poor driver had been about to argue when she had advised that she was the passenger he was to chauffeur.

Brooking no further argument, she firmly said that she was indeed the passenger and should that not be true, she would take all the blame upon arrival at the hotel. The driver still looked uncertain but reluctantly agreed, and she wanted to shout that she had done it, asserted herself and it felt great.

Upon her arrival at the hotel, they hadn't even blinked an eye when she checked into the suite under Gabe's name making her wonder if this sort of thing happened all the time.

Thanks to Amélie's wily schemes she knew that Luc was in town and felt better having his support to surprise her husband.

Luc, being the helpful partner in crime came up to the suite so that they could have some privacy to discuss ideas.

"Luc, thanks for agreeing to help me," she said, still wondering if she was doing the right thing.

"Anything for Gabe and his happiness," he beamed, delighted that Callie had asked him to help.

"Yes, well, we'll have to wait and see about that," she said, her confidence wavering.

"Callie, it will work out, you'll see," he said. "But you will have to wait for a few days because he's in Paris at the moment."

Her face fell as neither she nor Amélie had thought that Gabe wouldn't be here to surprise. Taking a deep breath she wasn't going to panic or be upset, she would use the next few days to bolster her courage and practise what she planned on saying to her husband.

"My sister and her husband are in town and I'm supposed to meet them for dinner tomorrow night, would you like to come?" he said, not sure if Callie would be up for socialising since the look on her face was one of anxiety and fear.

"Oh, I don't want to impose," she said, feeling that knot in her stomach get tighter.

"It's no bother. It'll just be us. You can help make us a happy even foursome."

This was her moment to know if she truly had found some sort of confidence within herself or not. Luc was Gabe's best friend so surely his sister must be lovely as well, she thought.

"That sounds lovely but only if I'm not intruding," she said, praying that she was doing the right thing.

"Don't be silly, besides I was supposed to introduce you both in New York, remember?"

Luc's smile reassured her. It seemed like so long ago that he had come to dinner.

"That's right, you said she lived in New York," she said, feeling better that at least they could talk about New York if nothing else.

"Great. Why don't we have dinner downstairs since you're both staying here?"

"Wonderful and…thank you," she said, and they both knew that it was for his understanding and kindness.

The next night Callie was once again a mass of nerves deciding what to wear. Taking Amélie's advice to just wear something classic that suited her, she went with a black dress she had found earlier in New York.

Checking herself a dozen times in the mirror to make sure that she truly did look presentable and that Luc wouldn't be embarrassed to introduce her to his sister, she heard a knock at the door. Finding Luc on the other side wasn't a surprise and she found herself glad that he had come up for her.

"Ready?" he said, admiring the woman standing in front of him and silently thinking that Gabe was truly a lucky man.

"Ready." She took a deep breath and exhaled.

The dining room was very ornate and opulent and it actually pleased her to see that some of the diners looked like people who to them this was a treat and it made her feel less nervous.

When Luc had reserved the table, he had asked for one of their more discreet ones hoping that it would make Callie feel more comfortable than being out in the middle where everyone could see them. As they approached, he could see his sister and brother-in-law were already seated and there was a flicker of disdain in Chantel's eyes and fear in Claude's.

Luc wasn't sure if it was because his brother-in-law was worried about seeing him after knowing that he and Chantel were having marriage difficulties or not, but he ignored it because Chantel's reaction was more worrisome.

Callie almost stumbled as they approached the table and she recognised the two people already sitting at it. Her heart began to race. Luc's sister was Chantel Mercier of all people. Oh, why hadn't she asked who his sister was before all of this, now it was going to be very uncomfortable and awkward.

"Chantel, Claude, I'd like you to meet —"

"How dare you bring this, this whore to dinner, Luc," Chantel viciously hissed.

Luc was taken aback by her vehemence.

"What are you talking about? This isn't, this is —"

"Oh, we know *who* she is, don't we?" Chantel spat, as Claude just silently sat there looking as uncomfortable as Callie felt. "This is the whore who slept with *my* husband."

"What? Are you saying that Callie is the woman from —" Luc looked confused.

"*This* slut is our old au pair."

Luc turned to look at Callie who was pale.

"Is this true? Are you my sister's old au pair? The one who slept with Claude?"

Callie voice was lost. She didn't know what to think or say and she was trapped in a nightmare.

"Y-yes, b-but I didn't sleep with him."

Luc's head swirled at the confirmation.

"Liar!" Chantel hissed.

"Tell them the truth," she pleaded to Claude.

Before anything more could be said and she could run away back to the sanctity of her room, the maître 'd came up behind her.

"Is everything all right here?"

Sensing that they were making a small scene, they had no option but to sit at the table.

"Yes, we're fine, thank you," Luc said, but anyone with two eyes could see that there was an awkwardness involving all the people at the table.

"Right," he said, wanting to get to the bottom of this for everyone's sake including Gabe, who wasn't here but Luc knew his best friend would be upset to find out that Callie was the au pair Chantel was accusing of sleeping with her husband. He raked a hand through his hair. God, what a mess.

"Claude, I think it's about time we hear *the truth*, don't you?" His cold tone had Chantel opening her mouth to snap at her brother, but the look he shot her just made her close it and sit there shooting daggers at Callie who was wringing her hands in nervousness.

If Claude maintained his innocence and kept claiming her as his lover, then Callie knew without a doubt that Luc would tell Gabe and there would be no marriage reunion. She tried to stare at a blank spot on the wall but couldn't help but glance at Claude to see if he was going to own up to the truth or throw her once more under the bus. She saw beads of perspiration on his forehead and he looked almost afraid.

"Well, Claude, did you sleep with Callie or not? I thought that you *alleged* that she had just hit on you but you turned her down? Now it's that she slept with you?" Luc said.

No one but Callie noticed that Luc's hands had repeatedly clenched and unclenched such was his anger.

"N-no," Claude said, and Callie felt all the tension release from her body.

"What do you mean 'no'? You told me that she hit on you, that you slept with her? Don't you dare try to protect her just because she's here with my brother," Chantel said, irate.

"It's the truth. I made it up," he said, ashamed.

"Why?" Luc said, instantly relieved that Callie hadn't slept with Claude.

Claude was too much of a coward to admit the truth and was quickly trying to think of a plausible excuse. He had already been caught out with his wife about Natalia but she didn't know that Natalia was her good friend

Letty. He also didn't know if Callie knew the truth either but knew that she must have overheard something of his infidelity.

So like the coward he was, he simply mumbled, "I don't know."

Chantel was stunned that her husband had made up a lie to rid her of the best au pair she had ever had. She also knew that his answer right now wasn't the truth either and if they weren't in public she would have been giving him a tongue-lashing that would leave his ears ringing for weeks.

"Under the circumstances I believe that you both owe Callie an apology," Luc said to Callie's shock.

"Why on earth should *I* apologise to the help?" Chantel looked absolutely furious at her brother.

"Because you accused her of something she didn't do."

Chantel just remained silent glaring at Callie. Claude, however, mumbled, "Sorry, Callie."

To Callie it was severely lacking in every way but she wasn't about to complain because she simply didn't care. Her name and reputation had been cleared and in front of Luc, someone she could trust so she didn't care, not even about Chantel. It was all water under the bridge as far as she was concerned.

"I think I'd like to go now. I'd say it was nice to see you again, but it wasn't," she said.

"How dare you…" Chantel's eyes narrow at the slight.

"Let it go," Luc growled. "You need to sort out whatever this…" He waved his hand at the couple. "Is and then move forward. Chantel, I'm tired of your moaning so if you continue to stay with Claude then that's your lot, I'm done."

The look of shock on Chantel's face at her brother's words turned to rage.

"You did this, you've turned my own brother against me," she hissed at Callie who simply shrugged.

"Luc is his own person," she said.

"She's right, Chantel," Luc said.

"But what about Suzette?"

"What about her? She'll always be my niece."

"She can't come from a broken home," Chantel whined, and for the first time tonight, Callie realised that Amélie had been right. She didn't feel terrible for stating her own thoughts and beliefs and truly didn't care what Chantel or Claude thought about her. They were a blip on her radar. The thought was quite empowering.

"Then sort it." Luc looked hard at Claude, who looked like he wanted to crawl under the table or at least anywhere but here.

"I'm sorry about tonight," he said, escorting Callie back up to her suite.

"Don't be," she said. "It actually taught me something important that I needed to learn. Thank you for standing up for me."

"I can't guarantee that Chantel believes that you didn't sleep with Claude. And, I can't believe that you were their au pair and I never knew," he said, incredulous.

"Well, it wasn't hard. They lived in Mexico and she didn't want any family to visit and then in New York, well we were hardly there long enough before I was fired."

"Do you know why Claude made those accusations against you?"

"I do but I don't think that it's my place to say," she said. "What's done is done."

Luc admired Callie's discreet nature and told her that he was going to call tomorrow to confirm the plan. Callie was relieved that Luc didn't pester her for the truth because she didn't want to cause even more trouble between the obviously unhappy married couple. Although the thought did cross her mind to wonder if Claude was still cheating on Chantel.

Chapter 20

Gabe had just landed from his quick visit to Paris and was about to call Luc when a man looked at him with a bright smile.

"Mr St Croix it's an absolute pleasure to be driving you. Don't worry, I know exactly where you want to go."

Instead of calling Luc like he had planned, he took the silence of the ride as a chance to think of how he was going to get Callie and then bring her back to London and tell her that he had moved the office for them. That he really wanted to continue their marriage.

He didn't want her to feel pressured if she thought he had done all this for her. He needed Luc's help to brainstorm just how to surprise his wife.

Soon they were stopping and the driver jumped out and rushed around to open the door for him.

"Here you are Mr St Croix," the driver smiled.

Gabe looked out the door and realised that he was outside Claridge's Hotel. Nonplussed by why the driver would bring him here of all places, he hopped out while the driver helped retrieve his one bag waving the porter over to help.

"Why am I here?" he said.

"You've booked a suite here. I brought your guest a few days ago," the driver said, but seeing Gabe's confused look on his face wondered if he had done the right thing as nervousness erupted in his stomach.

"Sorry, of course. I'm just a bit tired that's all," he said, hoping to cover up his bewilderment as the driver look relieved.

Gabe wondered if someone was using his name as some sort of scam and it had just been a total coincidence that the driver was the same one who had picked up 'his guest' the other day and assumed that he would want to be driven here as well.

Now he was about to go in and get a key to his suite and catch the person out. If they were lucky, he'd let them go with only the clothes on their back.

The porter went to follow him with his bag but he didn't need witnesses to what might be about to happen and took it from the man and proceeded with an anger that was rapidly brewing.

Entering the room, nothing looked any different until he went into the bedroom and noted the woman's clothing hanging in the closet and make-up in the bathroom. So that was why the driver was so cheery, he thought that Gabe had a woman here to welcome him.

There was no indication to the woman's identity and so he did what any curiously annoyed person would do, he made himself comfortable and waited.

What Gabe didn't know was that his ex-girlfriend, Leticia had seen him enter the very same hotel that she was staying in for the week. Gabriel wasn't known for his midday assignations and it had her intrigued.

She knew that if she had married Gabriel St Croix then she would rightfully have just become one of the richest women in the world since Fabien had died. But alas, he wanted faithful monogamy and she just wasn't that way inclined.

"Letty!" A female screech of excitement sounded in the lobby as a well-dressed woman came rushing towards her, her arms wide and her face full of happiness. "I'm so glad that you're here."

"When you told me that you were planning on a visit to London, how could I not come and see my good friend," Leticia said, hugging her friend then looking around for Chantel's little girl. "Where's Suzette?"

"At home." Chantel just waved her hand away dismissively. "I wanted to have a romantic trip with Claude but it seems that my marriage might truly be over," she said, miserable.

Leticia put her arm around her friend and they went to the dining room to have some lunch. Chantel told her everything from finding out that Claude was cheating on her with some woman on the internet named Natalia, to Luc having the nerve to bring her old au pair to dinner and then to find out that Claude had lied about sleeping with her, although Chantel was still doubtful whether he spoke the truth or not about that.

"So there really is no hope?" Leticia said.

"I don't think so. But I can't leave him, I have no money," she whined. "I'm not cut out to be *poor*."

"You know who I saw come into the hotel earlier and go up to a room?" Leticia said, a great idea entering her devious mind.

"Who?" Chantel's eyes widened in interest at the juicy gossip her friend was about to impart.

"Gabriel St Croix."

"Really?" she squealed, excited. "Do you think that he was meeting someone?"

"Gabe?" Leticia said, his name now invoking disdain. "I doubt it. He wasn't into midday assignations — believe me I know. He's a workaholic."

"Then why is he here?"

"Why don't we go to the reception desk and ask, just to confirm and if he happens to have a room, why don't we pay him a visit," Leticia said, curious to know what her ex was doing here as well.

"But don't you and he…you know, not like each other," Chantel said, nervous about doing something so rash and yet excited at the thought. If she could get Gabriel into bed then she could happily ditch Claude especially since everyone knew that Gabriel was now the owner of the entire St Croix empire thus making him richer than Croesus.

"Chérie, please, its all water under the bridge. Come on, let's go see."

The two women, managing to find out what room Gabriel was in by lying, giggled all the way to knock on his door.

Gabe, who had become tired of waiting, opened the door surprised to find his ex-girlfriend and Luc's sister on the other side. He frowned at how they would know that he was here.

"Ladies, what can I do for you?" he said, not inviting them in. This was the last thing that he needed. He was waiting for his mysterious guest and knew it couldn't be either of these two because they would have had a key but he didn't need them hanging around because he didn't want to scare off his prey.

"We heard that you were here and wanted to come and say hello," Leticia said as Chantel just excitedly nodded her agreement.

"Hello and goodbye," he said, starting to close the door.

"Wait!" Leticia quickly said. "Come on Gabe, be a good sport and let us in. After all, we haven't seen each other in years."

"There's a reason for that," he coldly said, and once again went to shut the door.

"Gabe, *please*," Chantel begged. "My marriage is breaking down right before my eyes and I can't seem to get hold of Luc. Please can we come in?"

He relented at Chantel's pleading but only because Luc was his friend but he had to find a way to get rid of both women quickly.

"Hmm, nice suite. I'd love to say that I'm sorry about Fabien but let's face it, he was a horrible bastard and I'm glad he's dead," Leticia said, full of bitterness, remembering what he had done to her to destroy her reputation.

He simply shrugged.

"Yes, Gabe. I'm very sorry about Fabien, too," Chantel said, placing her hand on his arm. "If you need to talk about it, I'm always here to listen."

Gabe looked down at Chantel's hand on his arm and politely removed it.

"So what's wrong with your marriage this time?" he abruptly said, hoping that Chantel would tell him and then leave.

"Claude's cheating on me with some internet woman named Natalia," Chantel said.

Gabe shot Leticia a filthy look but she was unapologetic.

"You're sure?" he said, his jaw clenching and wondering if he should out Chantel's friend himself.

Leticia's lack of conscience and concern for what he might say was almost gleeful. Did she want to be found out? He wasn't sure and remained silent.

"Yes, I confronted him and he said it was only a couple of times."

He didn't know if that was the truth or not and Leticia didn't seem to be at all bothered by the conversation.

Suddenly he heard the key card in the door and it slowly opened. Now he was about to find out just who the woman was that had used his name to get this room.

"Callie?" he said, incredulous upon seeing his wife standing in front of him. He almost rubbed his eyes as if he might be hallucinating.

"Gabe!" she shrieked, shocked at seeing her husband standing in the room in front of her before realising that there were two other women in the room as well. "Chantel?"

Different pairs of eyes darted from left to right to everywhere. The only person who was drinking in the moment was Leticia.

"Callie? What are *you* doing in Gabe's suite?" Chantel said, once her shock at seeing her ex-au pair once again was over.

Callie felt that dreaded panic roll through her and it took a few very deep breaths to resist the very real urge to run out of the room and cry.

Remembering what Amélie had said, knowing and hoping that Gabe would support her, she looked at her ex-employer and noted that Chantel for all intents and purposes may look polished but in truth, she had dark circles under her eyes and looked tired.

Perhaps it was thanks to last night but she wasn't afraid of Chantel anymore and so she simply said, "It's actually none of your business."

"How dare you speak to me like that," Chantel hissed, before turning to Gabe and lowering her voice a little but not enough that they all couldn't hear. "This woman was the au pair who slept with Claude." She tried to sound completely devastated.

Gabe looked hard at Callie. Her initial response to Chantel had surprised him and he liked that she wasn't running out the door but Chantel's titbit of information had him shocked.

"*You* were the Mercier's au pair?"

The astonishment in Gabe's voice made her sigh as Chantel gave her a gloating look of victory.

"Yes, but as Luc cleared it up last night, Claude admitted he made it up."

She prayed Gabe would believe her but he said nothing and simply looked at Chantel for her response.

"He was scared that Luc might do something rash so Claude told Luc what he wanted to hear." Chantel defended her husband while shooting daggers at Callie.

"Well, let's get Claude here to clear it up once and for all," he said to Chantel's horror.

"He's out," she hastily said.

"So call him or better yet, why don't I call Luc? He's a good judge of people and can tell me for certain if he thought Claude was lying," he said, refraining from saying *again*. It seemed to Gabe that all Claude did was lie.

"Luc will say anything you want to hear," Chantel said, knowing it sounded weak as Gabe studied his best friend's sister.

"In that case, I'll take Callie's word," he said, as she beamed at him.

"What? Why?" Chantel cried, shooting her old au pair daggers and then waspishly saying, "You still haven't explained what you're doing here. The hired help have no place in this room."

Chantel had said that Callie had been with Luc last night and that stab of jealousy sliced through him before twisting. He hated the feeling that his wife had come here on some kind of romantic assignation to be with his best friend or to demand her divorce so she could be with Luc.

He decided to once again remain silent waiting to see what Callie would do and arched an eyebrow letting her know that he wanted her to answer.

"As I said before, Chantel, it's simply none of your business."

The cool tone with which she delivered her answer made Gabe burst with pride.

Before anyone could say or do anything a cellphone rang and all eyes turned to the other person in the room that had all but been forgotten. A quick conversation and Leticia was smiling.

"Well, this has been extremely interesting but I'm off to see my boyfriend."

"But what about shopping?" Chantel wailed that her friend was deserting her.

"Tomorrow. Now I have a very *hot* date." Leticia looked at Gabe and saw no signs at all of jealousy to her regret. "Pierre doesn't like to be kept waiting."

"She's so lucky," Chantel said, envious as they watched the door close. "Her boyfriend loves to just drop everything on a whim for her. Claude's never been like that for me. And Pierre's rich. You should see some of the presents he's given her."

Both Gabe and Callie noted Chantel's envy of her friend but decided it was better to remain silent than to encourage her to wallow.

"Yes, Letty's managed to come up trumps, that's for sure. Pierre Bouchier is a real romantic and a catch."

Callie's eyes widened in shock as she silently gasped. Gabe caught his wife's reaction but said nothing. Callie would tell him the cause later. Chantel didn't notice Callie's reaction at all but continued to look miserable as Gabe gently managed to usher her to the door.

"Look, go find Claude and sort it out once and for all, otherwise you'll never be happy. You know that whatever you decide, Luc will support you. Now, I have to talk to Callie so if you don't mind, we really need some privacy."

Chantel opened and closed her mouth, bewildered but did as Gabe asked and left.

As soon as the door was shut, Gabe turned to Callie, his eyes were a mixture of confusion, desire and questions as he searched her face and she shifted uncomfortably.

"Okay, before we start on what this is all about, tell me what you know about Pierre Bouchier and then we can talk without any distractions," he said.

She happily agreed, grateful not only for the distraction but hoping she could manage to relax a little before they launched into the difficult conversation they were about to have.

They sat down and got comfortable and Gabe waited patiently for Callie's explanation.

"It's true. I was Chantel's au pair — the job I was fired from in New York. I lived with them in Mexico and then New York. It was the day Chantel called me home from the park distraught that her friend was coming to visit and that Claude didn't like her. That night Claude had been working late and Chantel had gone out to dinner with her friend so I was still up when Claude came home," she said. "I made him a coffee and was taking it to his office when I overheard him on the phone. He was arranging an assignation with someone. I pretended that I hadn't overheard but he must have suspected and accused me of hitting on him to Chantel. There was never any mention of me sleeping with him. Anyway the next morning Chantel fired me on the spot which was when I came to London."

Gabe had already guessed where this was going but still wanted to hear it from Callie's lips.

"I never told Chantel what I had overheard because she wouldn't have believed me anyway. Claude had been booking a hotel room under the name Pierre Bouchier. I don't know if he still uses that name or it was a one-off, but it was a shock to hear the name again especially since Chantel's friend is supposed to be his girlfriend. Do you think that Chantel's friend knows that Pierre Bouchier is Claude and a married man or do you think that there really is another Pierre Bouchier?" she said, concerned for Leticia, a woman she didn't even know and that just reminded Gabe of Callie's tender heart.

Thanks to Callie's story, all the missing pieces of the puzzle had now been found. Leticia had clearly been cheating with Claude for months, years even. That was Leticia all over, enjoying screwing her best friend's husband and then listening all about Chantel's marriage difficulties knowing that she was the reason.

He needed to let Luc know what Callie had just told him and then his friend could decide on the best course of action.

"Can you excuse me for five minutes? I think Luc needs to know that his brother-in-law and his sister's friend are definitely having a long-term affair."

"You mean…the woman that was here earlier…*she's* truly sleeping with Claude?" Callie gasped.

Gabe wanted to laugh at the shocked look on Callie's face. She had more than hinted at that conclusion only moments earlier but it seemed she hadn't paid attention to her own logic.

He nodded and then left her to sort out her jumbled thoughts while he called Luc. As expected his best friend swore down the line at the revelation.

"You're sure that Callie's sure?" Luc said, with a hopeful hint of hesitation that perhaps she was wrong.

"If you had seen her reaction to Claude's alias then you wouldn't even have to ask."

"What do I do?" Luc said.

"If I'm correct in guessing, the lovebirds are either in Letty's room right now or in another under his pseudonym."

"You want me to get Chantel to catch them both in the act," Luc said, miserable at the prospect of having to do the dirty deed.

"Look, I don't know Chantel that well but I have a feeling that she needs to see it with her own two eyes to believe it."

Gabe felt terrible for his best friend and Luc could only reluctantly and miserably agree.

"Good luck," he said.

Now he had to get down to the business of Callie's sudden appearance. His gut twisted. She was like an angelic assassin and until he heard the words to the contrary, he couldn't stop thinking that she had come for a divorce.

She was still sitting exactly where he had left her and as soon as he returned she looked over at him with concern.

"How's Luc?"

"Fine but unfortunately he's going to have to do the ugly deed by getting Chantel to catch Claude and Letty in flagrante."

"Surely he could just tell his sister?" Callie gasped in horror. Seeing Gabe's head shaking no, she then ruefully said, "There's no other way?"

"No. Chantel isn't the type of person to believe something like this. I mean, your best friend and your husband, especially since they supposedly didn't like each other. It's hard to get your head around something like that. She needs to see it with her own two eyes," he said, and this time it was Callie who nodded, knowing that what Gabe said was probably true.

"Anyway, back to the original question, why are you here and staying in a room under my name?" he said, trying to sound calm when his heart was rapidly pounding. He could only hope that when Callie asked for her divorce that she did it quickly, like ripping a plaster off.

"Why are you here?" she said, not wanting to start an argument but Gabe should never have been here.

She had been going to get Luc to bring him here and she was pretty sure he hadn't done it early.

He looked over at his wife and saw nervousness in her eyes making him decide that it was easier to answer her question than play ask and answer questions with questions. He might not be that eager to learn the truth and then thought back to the way that Callie had talked to Chantel, so confident and it made that flicker of hope flare inside him.

"Would you believe that the car I asked to pick me up from the airport brought me here," he said to the astonished look on her face.

Luc, the weasel, had double-crossed her.

"The driver said he knew exactly where I wanted to go because he had already brought someone a few days ago under my name. I decided to check-in to *my* suite and wait for the person who was using my name to return."

She exhaled a breath and then silently apologised to Luc for her earlier disparagement of him.

This was it.

Her chance to tell Gabe the truth.

To tell her husband that she wanted a real marriage.

To tell him that she loved him.

That old feeling of panic started to well up inside her again and she slowed her breathing to try and break its momentum or to somehow try and squash it.

Gabe could see the anxiety rise within Callie and sensed her warring with it. She had never been like this with him and that in turn made him feel panicked so he took her hand to reassure her.

"It's okay, Cal. Take your time. You know you can tell me anything," he said. His thumb gently rubbed her hand but that feeling of dread just wouldn't go away.

She looked down at their hands for a minute to compose herself and then looked straight into his beautiful blue eyes. The green flecks seemed hypnotising as she felt herself calming.

"I...I came to say I'm sorry for running out on you at Fabien's funeral. A wife doesn't do things like that. I should have been there to support you and not selfishly worried about myself." It seemed like every word was stuck in her throat.

He breathed a sigh of relief. Callie was here to apologise, not ask for a divorce. He called himself an idiot for even thinking it.

"I told you I understood and I still do. But why didn't you just go to the house? Why come here?" he said, his heart had a tight squeezing sensation.

His words made it easier for her to continue, knowing he wasn't mad.

"I wanted to surprise you, only you surprised me," she said, before her voice quietened. "When I was in New York I had a lot of time to think…about us."

There was that twisting in his gut again. He had counted his chickens too soon. Callie did want a divorce after all. Defeat flooded through him and his heart was now aching. He wasn't going to beg her to stay because she had sacrificed so much for him already. He couldn't ask her for more. He would let her go.

He didn't speak.

Couldn't speak.

He could only listen.

Her heart was pounding loudly as she looked down at their hands. What she had to say next, she couldn't look at him, didn't want to see the rejection on his face.

"I missed you."

Her words were so quiet that it was like a little puff of air and Gabe froze unable to believe that she had said three words that had now started a bonfire blazing inside him. Taking his other hand, he gently cupped her face to tilt it up so he could see into her beautiful yet misty eyes.

She looked uncertain, scared and he knew that it was his turn to say something, to wash away all doubts.

"I missed you, too."

Her eyes blinked at him. Was she hearing correctly? Did Gabe say he missed her? Hope burst forth until she realised that they were friends, of course he would have missed her but not in the way she had missed him. Dare she take another step into the unknown?

"I-I meant that I missed you, your presence, sharing things. I…I…" This was the moment that she had to declare her feelings. "I want to be your wife for real — not convenience. I've fallen in love with you," she blurted out and then cringed when he remained impassive.

Suddenly he was on his knees in front of her cupping her face, pulling her gently towards him so that they were a mere breathe apart.

"I want you too. I want to be your husband for real. I'm in love with you," he said, his voice thick with emotion that she barely had time to register his words when his soft lips touched hers.

Her world exploded into bright lights and colours and it was as if she could see the rest of her life flash before her eyes. Years of love and happiness.

He stood and scooped her up, taking her to the bed.

"I wish we were in our little apartment in New York," she sighed. Unable to believe she was about to sleep with the boy next door — her husband.

"The place doesn't matter," he said, wishing the very same thing. "As long as it's you and me. That's all we need."

His words were profound and she couldn't agree more as they kissed each other with all the passion that they felt knowing that they loved each other.

She twisted to look at the man who was now her husband in all ways, the love shining in her eyes.

"I love being held in your arms. You make me feel so loved and safe."

"And I love holding you. You seem to give me the strength I need to get through the day."

She smiled brightly, liking that she could support him in some small way.

"I moved the head office to London so I only have to go back to Paris when I need to," he said to her delight, earning him another passionate kiss. "Wow, if you like that, then what do I get when I say you can have carte blanche to redecorate the house," he chuckled.

Her hand moved down his body to the one place that was like a velvet glove on the outside and hard as steel on the inside. Her hand worked him gently as he closed his eyes enjoying her touch.

"You get to help make us even more of a family," she whispered. "Make me pregnant, Gabe. I want your children."

His eyes flew open as he stared into hers and realised that more than anything he wanted to be the father to her children, to see her stomach swollen with new life. It was a heady thought.

About the Author

Serena Black's love of reading romance novels, watching soap operas and rom-com TV shows and movies, opened her eyes to a world of romance that could be funny, adventurous, dramatic and sweet.

Now nothing makes her happier than to give readers the same bit of romantic escapism that culminates in happily ever after. No matter where her readers are, whether the day is wet and wintry or one for lazing on the beach, she hopes they pick up a book so that they might laugh, cry or even enjoy the arguments and always close the book with a loud romantic sigh.

Contact Serena at www.serenablackauthor.com.